Come
Rob

A cult with suspected Iranian connections – what could be more frightening for average American parents when their son abandons their cosy college plans for him and vanishes into another world. Challenged by the problems of understanding a very different mind set, they draw on every resource they have. Action-driven father, brooding mother – both are somehow untrained for this difficult situation. The American way has not prepared them. Is their son being schooled for active service in some religious war, or is he merely hooked on an ideal foreign to them?

A timely novel, bringing the problems of the world into the lives of ordinary people.

Michael G. Casey

To my clans . . .

and Robbie, whoever you are

Come home, Robbie

Michael G. Casey

THE O'BRIEN PRESS
DUBLIN

First published 1990 by The O'Brien Press Ltd.,
20 Victoria Road, Rathgar, Dublin 6, Ireland.

British Library Cataloguing in Publication Data
Casey, Michael
Come home, Robbie.
I. Title
823.914 [F]
ISBN 0-86278-214-7
Typeset at The O'Brien Press
Printed by The Guernsey Press Co. Ltd.

The O'Brien Press receives assistance from
The Arts Council/An Chomhairle Ealaíon

Part 1

Chapter 1

Awkwardly, Sal shoe-horned her long frame out of the Honda, went round to the back and opened the tail-gate. She gathered up the books first, the remaindered fruits of a sale in Georgetown. One of them, on career guidance, might help Robbie, whose indifference about his future was beginning to worry her. Was he saying to Bob and herself: If you can't sort out your own lives, don't attempt to sort out mine?

Maybe, because of the coming divorce, they had lost the right.

A relatively new neighbor greeted her with a wave and a facial flourish, not quite a smile. 'Summer's here at last.'

'Yes, indeed,' Sal agreed. She hadn't sized up this rather mousey newcomer yet and wanted to keep a certain reserve. Sal liked to choose her friends rather than have them thrust upon her by an accident of location or a realtor's whim. At least she liked to think this; actually she didn't have many friends.

'But the AQI. Oh Lord, the pollen count ...' The woman tried harder, shaking her head in disbelief at elements so conspiring.

'Yes I know. I know. It's so ... draining.' In a flurry of sympathetic sounds and nods Sal made good her escape, balancing the books in the crook of one arm while reaching for her keys with the other. Air Quality Index, what next? A happiness quotient? Where would she rate on a scale of nought to ten?

She went in through the garage which gave some protection from the deadening heat and suspect air. Bob had put up the screen doors that morning, one of which, spring-loaded, slammed behind her as she went into the house, barely missing her heels. She stooped to pick up one of the books which had fallen.

'Robbie! Give me a hand with this lot.' No answer. Nothing new about that. He could be deaf at times. Sighing, she dumped the books in the den for re-arranging later in the bedroom which, since Bob had vacated it, doubled as her study.

She went back out to the car for the groceries, convenience items mainly, ready to be bombarded in the microwave. Fast eats for people with deadlines and divorces pending. She had also bought some Fruit of the Loom shorts and socks for Robbie who seemed to devour – or metabolise? – such items.

It took two trips to get it all in. She plonked the last A&P bag on the table and sorted the contents, some dripping slightly, into presses and fridge. Soon she would not need so many groceries. The strange, quirky thought was not yet dismaying. She would still have her own interests after all.

'Come on, Robbie! Pizza time. Mozzarella topping. And I've got you a book.' Where the hell was he? Since school broke up he'd done nothing but lie around the house all day, all arms and legs, fidgeting with his downy beard, changing TV channels with a speed that matched his mood swings, spending hours locked in the bathroom. In other words all the lumpish awkwardness of an eighteen-year-old about to see his parents go their separate ways. Well, he'd survive. What were the stats? One in three marriages went rocky, or was it closer now to a half?

A good omen: he had done well in his finals. On the other hand that's what made his indecision about college so galling.

Despite everything, of course, she loved having him around the house. One of his spontaneous smiles was reward enough for a week's hassle. She was on a hiding to nothing.

'Robbie, where are you? Come and get it.' She was leaning across the kitchen table to turn on the air conditioning when she saw the note. Robbie's small careful script. She remembered when he'd affected a wild, formless scrawl to prove something or other. Always working on his image; the bane of adolescence. She read it through, disbelieving.

Dear Mom and Dad,
I need time out. There is much to think about and to think through i.e. to some sort of conclusion.

I've gone to do a two-week course with the Chaikha Rani. The theme is Communications. You know that old chestnut everyone talks about but no one actually does?

The cash situation is OK so don't worry. I'm not leaving the address because they don't encourage it and because I really do want to be alone for a while.

I think the course is going to help us all. You'll see. I'm not giving up on you guys.

Will write as often as I can.

Love,
Robbie.

Sal carried the note into the lounge and read it again, standing. Then she sat down slowly, still scanning for hidden meanings or evidence of a hoax. None came. Robbie had upped and gone. At first she was annoyed; the nerve of him cutting out like that without any warning and deliberately not leaving an address. A taciturn lump around the house for months. Now this.

Knowing that he wasn't given to rash acts, she turned to the motive behind it and swallowed hard. However ill-advised, he had done it for them; that much filtered through. But who on earth were the Chaikha Rani? Some quasi-religious outfit, she thought. Instinct or vestigial memory, of a color supplement perhaps, put her on tilt. With growing unease she called her mentor, Father Molloy.

He didn't beat around the bush. 'It's a very sinister organisation, Sal. Much more dangerous than a cult. And it may be tied into the Iranian thing. I'll explain later. But you've got to get Robbie out of there. And fast ...'

'Father, you're scaring me.' The priest's bluntness had the force of an assault. Her voice trembled on a plea for time to absorb the shock. He didn't relent.

'I mean to, Sal. This is bad. Believe me.' As if he didn't trust her ability to act, he added, 'Let me talk to Bob.'

'He's not here.' He was with Linda, the woman he would marry after the divorce. The sun that sliced through the venetian blinds suddenly seemed doom-laden. A dead heat from a bleached sky. The floor gave way under her feet.

When the dizzy spell passed she knew that she would have to call Bob even though she had vowed to herself never to contact him in that apartment. There was no choice now. With an effort of will she dialled the number. No answer. Another try just in case. Nothing. Her heart lurched at the prospect of waiting this out alone; there was everything to do and nothing to go on. She sat down and clutched her moist hands to keep them steady. Her anxiety mounted with the inevitability of a fruit ripening and it fed on a sense of betrayal. With rare clarity she knew that something dire had set its seal on the family.

Chapter 2

Although she badly needed a drink Sal knew she couldn't handle it, not in this situation. There was no point either in trying to work on the parish magazine that she edited with Father Molloy. Her mind swam with questions. What had her well-meaning son walked himself into? Had they brought it on themselves in some way? They had had no option but to tell him about the divorce. At the very least he deserved an explanation of the long silences and maimed conversations that had enveloped him in the house for the past year or so.

It was last fall, just after the evening meal, when they told him. All through the meal the silence had been denser than usual, congealing around the odd piece of forced trivia. They had eyed him across the table, covertly, trying to pick the right moment. He must have sensed there was something in the air.

Finally, Bob put down his coffee cup and told him straight out, man to man. He knew no other way.

Robbie's eyes were wide but otherwise there was little visible reaction. In a way he wasn't all that surprised. For months he had had the uncanny feeling of walking in on guilty silences, the smell of brimstone in the sullen air. Quietly, and with no peripheral movement, indeed with a stillness that became unnerving, he heard them out, as the points were notched off. 'Irreconcilable differences ... these things happen' – this one accompanied by sad shrugs –

'We'll always be there for you ... even better rapport ... We've our own lives to lead, too.' Yes, he absorbed it all like a heavy-duty punch bag, hardly wincing as the blows rained in. It was a sour litany of platitudes. What else could rationalise such a monumentally crass decision? His silence, that of a spectator at a freak show, seemed to spur them on to greater rhetoric. It was a parody that went cruelly wrong; it wasn't real. Then came the inevitable solicitation to which he replied with another question – Was there any other way?

'How do you *think* I feel about it?' He kept his head well but he was churning inside. They waited for more. He obliged. 'Twenty years down the toilet. Well, it's your decision.' And it was theirs. That's what was so maddening. They were completely wrong-headed, more off the wall than he had ever been in his eighteen years on the planet. And yet he did not have the right or the clout to make them see it.

'It's not as dramatic as it sounds,' Bob said. 'We'll still be ... close.' He leant over the table, his face shadowed by the ceiling light, trying to drive home his point.

'Good. Glad to hear it. I'm relieved.'

'Robbie, this is serious,' Sal said quietly.

'Oh? I thought Dad said it wasn't very dramatic. Maybe it's just a farce?'

'Come on now,' Bob said heavily. 'This isn't easy for us either.'

'All right then. Cards on the table.' Robbie's veneer was wearing thin and his voice went to a higher register. 'I think you're crazy. I know you've had your differences. Christ, who hasn't? Have you ever tried to work them out? Have you ever spoken in the last year without shouting? Nothing good comes easy. How many times have you told me that? Don't ask me to understand because I can't.' He looked from one to the other. His parents. And turned away, forcing back the dumb tears that had started to well up behind his eyes but mercifully receded.

'It's like this,' Bob tried to explain. 'It's taken us a while to realise that we're ... different personalities. And as we get older the differences, you know, sort of widen ...'

'Who are you telling?' Robbie recovered his composure. 'I know you're like chalk and cheese. So what?' He thought of all the times he had been bewildered by their different reactions. When he was twelve he had done a geology project that none of his classmates managed to complete. Because of that he didn't hand the project in. His Dad was delighted. 'Way to go, Rob. You didn't show up your pals.' But Sal was horrified. 'You owed it to yourself. Who are you trying to impress, your classmates or the teacher?' So one parent thought he'd acted well, one of the boys; the other felt he had failed himself and succumbed to peer pressure.

Other instances flooded through his mind. They had their differences, indeed. Who knew it better than he? But it shouldn't matter. How could they not love each other when he loved them both? It was a simple equation but he couldn't make them see it. He looked from one to the other in confusion as he had so often done before.

'I know it's difficult to accept,' Sal said. 'But you'll see in time that it's right. For everybody.' Did she sound less convinced? He wasn't sure.

'I won't accept it ever,' he said woodenly. 'And I know that you're not consulting me. It's already been decided. As you say, it's your lives.' He shrugged delicately, hiding behind a forced indifference that was immediately betrayed by his next question. 'When is this ... split going to happen?'

This was an easier one which Bob fielded. 'Oh, not until you're well settled in college. Don't worry about that.'

'Fine.' He sipped his coffee but his hand shook. A broken home. Christ, he thought it only happened to other kids like Geoff and Jenny. And look at them.

'And, of course, it will all be ... amicable,' Sal added.

'Glad to hear it.' His face was burning. 'I guess you'll be competing to win me over. Isn't that one of the spin-offs?'

'Well, you never know ...' Bob forced a smile, missing the sarcasm. He had dreaded telling him and was relieved that the worst seemed to be over.

'Give it time, Robbie,' Sal suggested quietly. 'I'm sorry we had to spring it on you like this but there was no other way.' The silence that followed was a necessary circuit-breaker.

At length Robbie looked up from the contemplation of his hands. 'By the way,' he spoke directly to Bob. 'Being a Catholic, Mom won't be free to marry again but you will be. So you'll be gaining the most.' He wasn't sure why he said it; maybe it was nothing more than an observation.

Bob leant forward earnestly. 'That'll be taken into the reckoning. It'll be a fair settlement.'

'A fair shake for one and all,' Robbie said half-aloud. He suddenly had a vision of himself as a kid on the Boardwalk at Virginia Beach, running between them, each holding one of his hands, every now and again on the count of three being swept up into the air which resounded with laughter. What was that Zen thing about clapping with one hand? He excused himself and went to his room.

He lay on the bed looking at the ceiling. When Jenny had left him for Geoff he thought that nothing would ever hurt like that again. He was wrong.

'Well, we've told him,' Bob said, stroking his mustache with a cupped hand. 'He didn't seem to take it too badly.' A single-issue man, he assumed that what was said was what was meant; that's how deals were done, his deals at least. But Sal was more tuned to hidden agendas, to the gravity of silence, especially where Robbie was concerned; he had her layering after all. The subtext was all-important.

'I'm not so sure.'

'Oh, he's all grown up now. He can handle it.' He was surprised by her reaction and by her clouded face. Since he knew she would never use Robbie as a weapon in the hustings – she was much too straight for that – he had to infer that her doubts were real. But he also knew from the distant glaze in her gray eyes that she was not ready to put her doubts into words. So he blustered on. 'Anyway it's not as if we're going to disappear into the wild blue yonder.'

'No,' she said half to herself. 'Just a comfortable distance.'

The next few months had passed in relative calm, if not peace. Bob was away a lot and Sal buried herself in her work, often visiting Father Molloy at the presbytery with bundles of manuscripts to be refereed and edited. She gave more and more of her time to the magazine as if building up credits which she could draw on later to fill the vacuum after the divorce.

When she and Bob were together in the house there seemed to be a tacit covenant to avoid arguments, since, with separation looming up, there was no need to raise any of the issues which had plagued them in the past. In this modest truce they stayed quietly in their respective bunkers, simply ignoring the no-man's-land between. Robbie was working hard for his finals and spent hours in his room.

The house held a monkish silence except for the purring of the heat system and the occasional rattle of windows, brought on by the last gusts of winter. It was a strange interregnum, as if they were all on retreat, incubating their own hopes, making their own assumptions without any mutual reference point. In truth they were drifting towards rapids.

After Robbie's finals the pressure began to build again. Sal had always assumed he would go to college because that had been the happiest experience of her own life. She had tasted real freedom at Barnard which had given such relief from the dirigism of convent school and home. And there had been a sense of privilege, too, that made one use the time well. College had helped her forget the dreads of her childhood and let her natural strengths filter through, at least for a time. There was no question about it; Robbie had to have the same opportunity.

Bob had the same presumption, though for different reasons. He simply wanted to do better for his son than his old man had done for him; it was a natural progression of generations, the American way. He had worked hard to bring this about and, on Sal's advice, had taken out an endowment policy to cover tuition fees. The policy was ready to pay off. Everything was set.

Robbie had met with career counsellors and taken aptitude tests. Example: When looking out a train window do you tend to count the telegraph poles or admire the scenery? Answer: Mainly the latter. Thus Robbie was streamed for the humanities rather than the sciences. Bob, however, was uneasy about this verdict and the war of the two cultures was frequently waged in the over-stuffed lounge of their home in Langley, Virginia, not a stone's throw from the headquarters of the CIA.

But on one thing there was agreement. They wanted to get Robbie settled before the divorce. He was their first and last joint endeavor.

Shortly before he had left home for the Chaikha Rani, Robbie announced that he'd changed his mind about college. They were on the deck at the back of the house preparing a barbecue. Bob straightened up from the hibachi grill, sauce brush in hand. The smoke from the steaks and charcoal added to the ethereal summer haze which had about as much substance as the scene of domestic peace.

'It's just not for me,' Robbie tried to explain away the bombshell. 'I want to get off the treadmill at least for a while. To get my bearings.' He noticed their startled reactions and was well aware of the threat he posed to the fragile peace. 'So there's no point in arguing about what I should take ...' They made him feel like a project. He knew they meant well but that just made it all the more difficult. He shifted uncomfortably on the redwood bench, his long brown legs tucked awkwardly under him.

Sal was the first to recover. She pushed her sunglasses up her pale forehead until they nested in her rather lank fair hair. 'Robbie, I don't know what the problem is. But you must have a chance to make a choice, an educated choice, about what you want to do with your life. University gives you that opportunity. It's the only ...'

'You're going,' Bob interrupted, throwing off his striped chef's apron. 'And that's that. What do you think we've worked for all these years? How far do you think you can get nowadays without a good education?' He took a long pull at his beer and bit a stick of celery with his strong teeth which showed in a kind of snarl.

Sal felt uneasy at his lack of subtlety. He was a good salesman by all accounts but he couldn't sway Robbie with such blunt admonitions. Besides, she felt there was more to Robbie's recalcitrance than met the eye.

'An education is important, for Chrissake.' Bob added another unhelpful truism. His eyebrows were knitted together, forming a strong ridge at the base of his forehead, a legacy of scar tissue built up during his boxing days. It was an expression of frustration, nothing more, but it came across as menacing and intolerant.

Robbie sat at the patio table looking from one to the other, hoping they'd get off his case. He was fair and smooth-skinned like Sal but with his father's stronger features, a handsome, sturdy kid, the product of a bounteous country and well-meaning parents. His clean-cut appearance, however, belied his state of mind. News of the divorce had set him back; he couldn't deny it. He had those same amorphous feelings that had swirled around him when he was about fourteen, as if something deep inside hadn't quite gelled. He felt slight again, unprepossessing, not able to judge the effects of his thoughts or actions, because, conceivably, there weren't any. His confidence was going. He had even taken up that old habit of aping the mannerisms of people he admired, as if he had no personality of his own. Despite his good exam results he reverted to an earlier assessment that he was just a slogger, having to work like mad just to keep his head above water. And he had worked hard. The problem was that for most of his study time his head swam with all those squirming possibilities of who he was or should try to become. Sometimes, in the past few months, he'd had to escape from all that mindfucking, as Geoff called it, by popping pills. But they only gave a temporary calm.

'Architecture. Now that'd be good,' Bob said trying to be more constructive. 'Buildings, monuments ... Something that lasts ... It's artistic too,' he added by way of compromise. He peered skywards as if looking for the top of some monument reaching into the hereafter.

'You don't have to program him,' Sal demurred, wondering, not for the first time, how Bob could be so dogmatic with such little thought behind his pronouncements. 'He'll find his own way once he goes to college and meets his peers.' She tapped her wedding ring against the table. The ring was embedded in the fold behind her knuckle as if grafted into her flesh.

'He could waste a lot of time looking around.' Bob couldn't help it. In his book, education had to be useful, lead to something positive. The idea of a son of his swanning around campus, going to Frat parties and discussing the mating habits of the Hottentots, did not appeal to him. That, presumably, was what Sal had in mind. If she had her way Robbie would end up as a wishy-washy liberal who didn't know his ass from page eight.

'Don't you understand?' Robbie sighed, shaking his head so that his longish hair swished about his face until he stroked it back. 'I just don't have the commitment right now.' That was too vague an objection, he thought, but then his own motives were none too clear. The vagueness made him more forthright. 'The whole idea sucks.' He laid his head on his bare forearms which were crossed on the table. He knew how ornery he must seem, how he was disappointing them. But for some reason, which was as strong as it was unclear, he just couldn't oblige.

Bob moved towards him. 'It sucks, does it? We used to say "stinks". That's progress? Listen, don't study English literature, will you.' He looked at Sal as if he'd proved a point. Relenting, he put a hand on Robbie's shoulder. 'Now come on, Rob. See it from our side. We're just trying to help you get on. Jesus, if my old man had given me a break like this ...!'

Robbie hung his head stubbornly, shredding a cardboard coaster on the redwood table. The sun had come round the edge of the striped awning and forced him to move further down the bench into the shade.

Sal watched his distracted movements which contained all the self-blame and punishing innocence of his early years. It was disconcerting to see herself so clearly in him; she wanted to hold him, put her arms about his neck, her face next to his, to prove how good he was, how that really was all that mattered, ultimately. But in the meantime there were practical things to be worked out, preparations for a full life ...

'It's not what you think it is.' She tried to reach him, her eyes wide. 'It's a blank check. You do your own thing.' She used his own idiom rather uncomfortably. God it was all so trite, the whole scene. Why couldn't he see sense? The adolescent conceiving himself. Maybe it was a process that had to be gone through, however turgidly. But where was the spark of originality? Was it conceivable that Robbie didn't have it?

'I know what you're saying. But it's just not on.' Robbie watched a cardinal bird break cover like a spurt of blood from a pine tree and snatch some bird seed from the little plastic house mounted on a pole. He remembered the time they'd put up the bird house. Squirrels appeared from nowhere and darted up the pole to raid the bird seed. Bob greased the pole but the squirrels didn't give up. They kept on trying to climb the greasy pole, slipping and sliding in a frenzy of frustration. Bob and he watched from the kitchen window, helpless with laughter. It seemed years ago.

More recently, he and Geoff had sifted through the same bird seed looking for cannabis.

'You just can't throw away those good grades,' Bob said sternly. God, how he hated waste. What on earth had gotten into his boy?

'I ... I worked too hard to get them.' Robbie hated admitting it but he owed them some explanation. The problem was satisfying both of them with the one answer.

'Oh come on,' Bob said dismissively. 'You've got the smarts. You don't have to work so hard. Anyway what's wrong with a little work? It's good for you.' He put some bread rolls on the grill to use up the lingering heat of the charcoal and hickory. No, he didn't like waste of any kind.

But it wasn't just the hard work, Robbie thought. It was the uncertainty and the loss of faith in himself. Why had all this doubt descended on him in the last few months? And how could he explain these fears to his parents who had never to his knowledge run from anything? The family folklore was impressive. His mother had always been top of her class and his Dad had courage to spare. He had once taken part in a rodeo with a fractured pelvis. It wasn't their fault that they wouldn't be able to understand; it was just that inadequacy was outside their realm of experience. Achievement was the coin of the household.

He just couldn't argue any more or risk a recurrence of the wrangling that always lay dangerously close to the surface these days, so he excused himself and escaped indoors.

Bob made to follow, but Sal restrained him. 'Let him go.' She watched Robbie go through from the deck to the kitchen. The screen door slammed behind him with a finality that struck at the heart.

'Maybe he does need some time by himself to mull it over,' Bob conceded. 'It's probably just eleventh-hour nerves.'

She wasn't listening. Let him go – the phrase repeated itself in her mind. There was a strange unity between the words and the slamming of the door that reflected the cold efficiency of a steel blade. The feeling that surged through her had the resonance of *déjà vu* although the meaning, whatever it was, seemed to lie in the future.

Robbie sat at his desk, his chin resting on a fist. Even his room depressed him now; it was like a library. Over the years Bob had put shelves everywhere and Sal had quickly filled them up with well-chosen books and records. Maybe he'd always been a project. There had been some concessions to childhood, however – a smooth floor for running toy cars on, Redskin pennants on the closet door, a few track ribbons (they awarded them even if you came last) and a Little League baseball cap.

The room reflected the ambiguity. To be a credit to both parents he would have to be a deep thinker *and* a wide-end receiver, a do-gooder *and* a left-handed pitcher. Because of the dying communication between his folks the conflict could not be resolved; indeed it left a void which was filled by cruel burlesques of each other's viewpoint. So he vacillated, caught in a wasteland, staring helplessly from left to right, wanting to move but not knowing which path to follow.

He unlocked a drawer in the desk. There was no aspirin left so he took, after some hesitation, half a quaalude and started to leaf through the Chaikha Rani material Geoff had passed him in class some time ago.

'... Communications or how to reach people through the Science of Creative Intelligence ... How to be at peace with yourself and in harmony with the life force ...' There was the remarkable promise of learning how to be aware of being aware. In that enlightened state everything would become possible. The course went beyond TM and Scientology and offered nothing less than the pure energy of the superconscious.

Much of the literature was hype, he knew, but he was drawn to the central idea of harmony and the peace that would flow from that. What were the alternatives? Conventional religion hadn't done much for his folks or for him; in fact, it was probably one of the elements in the rift.

He read on avidly. Yes, in answer to the questionnaire, he did want to get in touch with himself and those close to him. He did want to clear his mind and have the spirit of creative intelligence enter his being. Maybe after the course he could consider college in a more positive way; enlightenment and apperception seemed consistent with straight A's. Math wouldn't intimidate him any more and make him scratch his pimples and sometimes jerk off just to ease the frustration. Peace ...

He could vaguely see himself after the course, content and secure, with an easy relaxed smile on his face as he dealt confidently with every problem that cropped up. Jenny would be impressed by his self assurance; she might even leave Geoff and come back to him.

Already he began to see more clearly what had been bothering him about college. He didn't want to be packed off and 'settled' while they went ahead with the divorce with an easy conscience. By refusing to be a pawn in the separation game he would make them re-examine the choice they were making.

But why stop there? The thought was seductive and powerful. Surely if he mastered the art of communicating he would be able to pass it on to them? And that had been their problem all along; they had lost the ability or the will to reach each other. It was just a matter of re-learning the technique. He could help to bring them together and he would certainly try. They would be his project now. The inversion was brilliant. This was precisely the kind of insight the Chaikha Rani offered. The damn thing was working already and he hadn't even got past the brochure. He felt better than he had all year.

He would call Geoff who had a contact in the Rani, someone called Paajit, and make the arrangements. His skin began to tingle as the decision took hold.

For a while Bob and Sal remained on the deck. The kids in the neighboring yard grew tired of frisbee and jumped into the small pool shouting, 'Can-opener.' They were finally whisked indoors by their Mom who signalled vigorously with a gravy-stained oven glove.

The silence was broken only by reference to Robbie.

'Is he going to spend the rest of the vac locked in his room?' Bob mused aloud, exaggerated wonder on his strong, impacted face. 'He's got to decide soon.' He rolled the corners of his mustache one way then the other, leaving unkempt sprigs of dark hair at both ends.

'I'll talk to him later.' Sal wound down the striped awning and folded the scalloped frills as the sun declined behind the sycamore trees at the back of the yard. A merciful breeze ruffled her linen surplice-like smock.

'So will I.' Bob wiped his hands on his denim shorts cut from old jeans. He still reeked of charcoal-lighter fuel.

'Will you?' The question was barbed.

'Yes.' He was conscious of the rebuke. 'When I get the chance. I'm pressed for time, you know.'

'Yes, I do know,' Sal replied. 'You've got a lot on your plate.' This was a reference to his affair with Linda Tognetti. 'When are you moving out?' she inquired coolly, her delicate eyebrows arching over cowled gray eyes.

'In a couple of weeks. Or,' he changed tack, 'as soon as Robbie's made up his mind about college.'

'Whichever is the earlier,' Sal prompted as if anticipating the legalities of the divorce. She stacked the dishes and assembled the silverware with deft practiced movements.

'I guess so.' Bob put away the barbecue equipment in a corner of the deck. It occurred to him that he might never be using it again.

'What if Robbie doesn't change his mind?' she pressed, leading the way indoors.

'Oh, he'll come round.' It was inconceivable to Bob that anyone could refuse such an opportunity.

'You're always so certain ...,' she began but decided to hold her peace. She picked up a book, which usually signalled her withdrawal from conversation, and moved into the lounge.

'Look, Sal,' he said, 'let's not fight. Or brood,' he added, noticing the book. He sensed that the reference point was shifting from Robbie to them; these days it felt uncomfortable when that happened. But this time he wanted to clear the air. 'You can have whatever you want,' he said solemnly. 'It's better than greasing the palms of those goddamn divorce lawyers.'

'Good,' she said, turning a page of her book.

'Or an annulment ... whatever ... We need a clean break. No recriminations.'

'Fine.' She lit a cigarette which indicated that she was concentrating on her book. He looked at her, locked within the confines of her own mind, and realised with a start just how much Robbie took after her.

Estrangement had been a subtle process, culminating in a feeling on both sides that there never had been any initial attraction. This was not true; it was just that memory could not surmount fresh wounds. Once there had been a sort of synergy that allowed them to laugh at their differences, but slowly over the years they'd reverted to form; their separate perspectives became more noticeable. Sal imbued Robbie with high-minded values, backed up by as much affection as her own natural reserve would allow. Bob tried to toughen him up – when he wasn't out scratching for the almighty buck.

A self-confessed chauvinist, he was determined to be the main breadwinner. Since Sal had come from a fairly well-heeled family – mainline Philly still had a certain cachet in his mind – he put himself under the gun to provide and, in a way, to make up for his own lack of credentials.

The pressures told; fissures appeared and turned into fault lines. Discussions became arguments, facts became issues. There were times when she thought of his salesman's gimmicks and bar-room humor with a sinking feeling. He sometimes wondered if she knew anything about simple living, getting by.

It had taken a long time to drift out to the poles where they now sat, fixed and uncompromising, playing out the maiming game of stereotypes: she was frigid, he was crude and over-sexed; she was a staid intellectual, he a fun-loving moron. Thus, the wedge was driven home. They were two heavy-weights who stayed in neutral corners, brooding. Her dismay was matched by his disillusionment. Neither could any longer fathom the strength that was once there, that was constant as still water, that had become deformed and used up foolishly in blind alleys of captious argument and resentment.

Most of Bob's colleagues had extra-marital affairs. Bob had not lacked opportunities, but he was not a cheat and had a strong sense of loyalty towards Sal. But then Linda Tognetti came along.

Chapter 3

After the fraught barbecue and Robbie's strange reaction to college, Bob felt guilty about disappearing for the weekend, but he tried to console himself with the thought that Sal, as she herself would claim, could straighten out Robbie without any assistance from him.

The Gattopardo was a plush club in the North West section of DC, favored by businessmen and politicians out on the town. The liveried doorman touched his cap in recognition as Bob paid off the cab and walked across the strip of red sisal towards the canopied entrance. Once inside he paused for his eyes to become accustomed to the mellow, Tiffany-lit gloom, then worked his way down the brass-railed bar until he found a stool that gave a good view of the stage. The bartender made him his usual vodka martini with a twist.

It was always exciting waiting for Linda to appear. He could have gone backstage but somehow he preferred to wait out front, savoring the anticipation. As the star, she didn't come on until later and there would be other acts before she appeared.

While he sipped his drink an odd recollection came to him. When he was a kid in Browning, Montana, his old man won a bull-riding event in the local rodeo against tough competition. Bob was so excited that he rushed up to his father afterwards and hugged him. His father removed his chaps, stowed his gear and led him out of the locker room. Then he grabbed him by the wrist and grated, 'Don't ever do that again!' When Bob finally left the loneliness of those big skies, for there was nothing for him on that dusty ranch, his old man probably wrote him off completely as a dude or a snake-oil salesman. He had gone back once only, for the funeral.

There was a slight commotion at the front of the club. Bob looked round and saw his friend, Art Guetta, involved in a minor skirmish with a couple of drunks at the door. Art, an ex cop, was a sort of club supervisor cum bouncer.

'Now be reasonable, guys,' Art was saying. 'This isn't that kind of joint. Go on home and sleep it off.' After the drunks moved off in a flurry of face-saving invective, Art joined Bob at the bar.

'That laid-back approach of yours is sure effective,' Bob said. 'You handled it well.'

'Why get hyper?' Art asked. 'When I was on the force I reckoned that all GBH's were due to guys losing their cool. There's no percentage in it.' Even in his tuxedo Art managed to look sloppy, and his big middle-aged face was as expressive and mobile as a three-ring circus; something was always going on in it.

'You've never lost your temper with any of those schmuks?'

Art thought for a while, his shaggy head sideways, thumbs hooked through his suspenders which even at full stretch left his pants billowing around his rump.

'Well, if you have to think about it, I guess you haven't.'

'I guess you're right at that,' Art said.

'You're a pussy cat,' Bob observed. 'Compared to you St Francis of Assisi was a hood.'

Bob grinned. He always got a kick out of Art and was glad they were neighbors in Virginia, even if Sal tended to keep him at a distance. Art did other jobs for Aldo Tognetti, the owner of the club, who despite his family connections, was not mainline Mafia and, according to Art, was no more 'creative' than the average entrepreneur. Still, it had crossed Bob's mind once or twice that Aldo, whom he'd met only once, might not take a very positive view of a forty-year-old encumbered salesman dating his kid sister.

'I'm just used-up,' Art said. They both laughed. 'Anyway,' Art went on, 'there's nothing much going down. It's all pretty legit these days.' He made a see-sawing motion with a large hand mottled with liver spots.

They watched the strippers for a while. One girl had a superb figure and enjoyed giving the works to every guy in the house with her pelvic thrusts and hip rotations. The drummer in the combo was sometimes out of synch with her extemporaneous bumps and grinds and they would grin ruefully at each other when the gears failed to mesh.

What they lacked in art they made up in pizazz. Every now and then a man would approach her from the audience and slip a folded bill into her garter; she was soon bristling with greenbacks.

'She's Barbara,' Art said. 'Hasn't she the cutest little butt?' He smiled fondly. 'But she's so skinny. Look at those shoulder blades. They're like fins.'

'I'm not looking at her shoulder blades.' Bob was amused at Art's clinical descriptions. Maybe the man was used-up. But he was the same when they'd first met fifteen-odd years ago, a sort of favorite uncle, woolly and well-meaning.

'She should eat more,' Art insisted. 'I'm going to hafta talk to her.'

The whole tenor of the club changed when Linda came on to sing. The burlesque was over; here was simple style. She wore a calf-length black chiffon dress without any accessories. A hush followed the initial burst of applause. She freed the microphone from its stand, shook out the lead and looked at the audience through green eyes that seemed phosphorescent in the spotlight. Bob went hot and cold, drinking in those orbs, the retroussé nose which was often pink-tipped in cold weather, her slightly everted mouth. It was amazing to think that she loved him and, with those child-like features, could be so inventive in bed.

She went into her first number, 'You Don't Send Me Flowers Anymore', putting just enough wronged innocence into it. Bob's rapture continued; he couldn't be objective about Linda. But he had been associated with other singers and had in fact emceed some small shows at one point in his career – just another kind of selling. Although Linda had her limitations she was superb with certain kinds of material that suited her image and vocal range.

Her next number was, 'Send in the Clowns'. Again there was the same bittersweet quality that held the audience spellbound. Rapt by the husky intimacy of her voice and with the nervous expectancy that waits on an echo, Bob's breathing grew shallow.

She announced the final number of the set as being for someone special in the audience. It was 'Man with the Slow Hands', specially arranged for her, moodier and more sexy than the other songs. But she didn't ham it; instead she let the lyrics carry the mood, eulogising the qualities of her lover. The counterpoint to the innocence of the other numbers was striking; no one felt it more than Bob and he could only nod when Art whispered, 'Some guys have all the luck.'

There was that pent-up disbelieving second of silence when she finished, then a burst of spontaneous applause.

'Thank you,' Linda smiled, replacing the mike. 'I'll be back later.' She walked off to renewed applause and joined Bob at the bar.

'Unbelievable.' He kissed her, then shook his head, lost for words.

'That good, huh?' She sipped the campari and soda he had waiting and held his earnest stare over the rim of the glass.

'You really torched that last one,' Art remarked.

'Was it too much?' she asked. 'It was the first time I tried it out.'

'Of course it was too much.' Art said, misinterpreting.

'It was just fine,' Bob reassured her. 'And thanks for the dedication.' His voice sounded unnatural, as if someone else was speaking over his shoulder. Everything about her moved him and threw him off balance. She sat on the barstool next to him, fluffing out her dress to avoid creases.

'And I thought it was dedicated to me.' Art put down his beer and sighed.

'Better go and bounce a few drunks. See you folks later.' He ambled off dolefully.

Bob took Linda's face in his hands and kissed her on the mouth. She gave a rueful grin and a wink that touched an imp's regret; the glance also whispered, 'later'.

'When I see you on stage … well, it's sort of magic …' His hands descended limply on the counter like caught prey giving up the ghost.

'It's real, Bob.' She reached for his hand as if to return it to the living. Having a sense of the artificial glamor surrounding her job, she was keen to defuse his talk of magic.

He looked away from her and said, 'I want to hold you so much it hurts.' His voice had the tone of a child's confession. If Art had overheard he would never live it down. His salesman colleagues would have taken up a collection to get him into treatment fast.

'I love you, too.' Her smile touched him and nudged its promise along.

At times like this when she was in the limelight he felt insecure. 'Why?' he demanded. 'You could have your pick of a million guys. I just don't get it …' At a respectful distance the bartender polished glasses with infinite patience, raising them up for final inspection in the mellow air, each one a winner.

'Are you fishing?' She smiled at him, noticing the furrowed perplexity in his face.

'But …' Older, encumbered, dumb, he was ready to spill it all, his demerits, of which a legion. Really dumb.

'No "buts". It's happened. You are the one in a million. *Come sono fortunato*!' She laughed suddenly. 'You really find it hard to accept a compliment, don't you?'

'Do I?' It hadn't occurred to him before.

'Yes. But you'd better get used to it.' She held his hand more firmly. 'Don't put yourself down. You have a strength I'll never have.' Her eyes close to him gave up the rich depths of the iris, flecks of coral beneath the translucent green.

'Like what?' He was intrigued. It was nice when she analysed his character, a new experience. He was no longer the stereotype that Sal saw in him.

In fact it was passing strange that Linda seemed to think he had substance, whatever that was, whereas Sal, well, only God really knew what she thought, but he could reasonably infer that she put him close to the flaky end of the spectrum.

'It's hard to describe. A sort of energy I get from you.' She sipped the campari reflectively. 'If you decide on something important you go after it and a ten-ton truck won't stop you.'

'I'm stubborn, you mean.'

'That too.' She laughed. 'But it's more than that …' Her pensive mood was suddenly broken by a signal from backstage.

He watched her weave her way back through the tables towards the stage, her walk slightly boyish, returning the glances and smiles of people as she passed. I am a lucky bastard, he thought. His confidence returned. In less than two hours he would be with her in her apartment.

Chapter 4

He loved the disarray of her apartment, the casual chaos of everyday things. The bedroom was draped with lingerie, closets bulged with frilled and feathered paraphernalia, necklaces dangled out of drawers like Dali's drooping clocks, and pantyhose mingled with peacock feathers in a Chinese vase by the dressing table.

The lounge was good, too, with its loud abstract paintings – one was almost definitely upside down but who cared? – stacks of music sheets, open purses spilling their contents on glass-topped tables.

The bathroom was best. There was perfume and powder in the air, and uncapped lotions and liniments graced the porcelain shelves and towels of all shapes and colors were draped over the shower rails.

And there was cross-fertilisation between the rooms. A bath robe could wind up hanging from a spice rack in the kitchen or a satin pillow slip might appear, to pose as an antimacassar, in the lounge.

The flowsy confusion somehow made the apartment seem too old for Linda, who was twenty-eight, as if she were some theatrical doyenne or even the Madame of a geisha house. Bob sometimes called her apartment, 'the sweetest little whorehouse in the district,' and Linda would peal with laughter, fling something somewhere and announce that she liked the loved-in look.

Linda came originally from a large Neapolitan family, and was life-loving and spontaneous; these qualities enabled her to stand on a stage and knock 'em dead. She had little time for people's reactions to her; they could take her as they found her. She knew she would never be a great star but that didn't cost her a thought. Marriage and kids were sometimes in her thoughts but she wasn't in a hurry.

She sat on the floor, cross-legged, playing her guitar, dressed in a big floppy quarter-back's T-shirt. Bob sat behind, his arms around her. Time was also in glorious disarray; it had been midday before they woke.

'It's very difficult to get A minor in this position,' she complained wryly.

'Should I stop holding you?' Bob asked.

'Let me think about it.' She turned around and looked at his craggy unshaven face. She bared her teeth and snarled, 'Animal.'

'Thanks.' He tried to look offended.

'Would you like a song to soothe the savage beast?'

'Breast,' he corrected. Lively cadences of week-end Georgetown drifted up from M street, young singles cruising this brisk bagatelle of bistros and boutiques.

'Don't be rude,' She brushed his face with a preppy pony-tail tied in a rubber band.

'It's savage breast,' he explained.

'I know.' She laughed. 'But you see how my mind works? Word association. Animal, beast. Get it?'

'I like how your mind works.' He kissed the nape of her neck through wisps of youthful down, a legacy of being sent with her brothers to the barber.

'No chauvinism, dollink. Now would you like a song or not?'

'Yes, please.' They were young together. She offered him a song and he accepted; fun had never seemed so easy before.

And yet when he took her in his arms her eyes would become filmed and grave. Her changes of mood fascinated him. They were unpredictable but without artifice; she had simply no fears about showing her true feelings. It was all new to him, invigorating ...

'What would you like?' she asked tuning the guitar.

'"Give Me Five Minutes More in Your Arms".' He pressed his face into that casual frayed knot of pony-tail and breathed in her several-layered scents, lanolin and musk and sun-dried linen.

'I don't know it. It must be a golden oldie.' She turned round and gave him an impish look that saved itself for his reaction.

'It is,' he said ruefully. 'OK, let's see.' He rubbed his chin, rasping his beard. 'Nothing nightclubby. No Cole Porter or Rogers and ...'

'Cole Porter?' She laughed. 'Who's he?'

'All right, I'm ancient.' He grinned. 'Don't rub it in. Something folksy then ... I've got it, "The Wichita Lineman". You know the one where the guy goes nuts listening to the hum of the power lines, the singing in the wires?'

'He doesn't go nuts,' she chortled. She crashed out an open E chord, adding a Flamenco flourish. 'Where did you get that from?'

'He does,' Bob insisted. 'That's why he needs a short vacation. But even then he can't get the job off his mind because "that stretch down south will never stand the strain". Sure, he goes nuts.' He nodded confirmation to himself.

Linda looked at him closely, noticing his calm eyes and the way he chewed his mustache. She suddenly felt sad.

'I don't really know that one,' she said slowly. 'Here's one you'll like, "Vincent".' She moved the capo up a few frets on the finger-board, tightened it, then picked up the tortoiseshell plectrum.

She sang in a hushed voice that haunting modern classic that brought the painter and his works so vividly to life. There was in the song the sad wisdom of a life spent recklessly in trying to prove its own impossible vision.

His head on one side, listening keenly, Bob could feel her breath ebb and flow as she was drawn into the song, its lilt and rhythms and chastening writ. She carried it and surrendered to it at the same time, giving a sense of discipline and indulgence in equal measure. To Bob it was remarkable how she allowed her feelings to be so apparent as they entered the music and came back enhanced and somehow purified. The music slowed, the chords turned to minors. '"But I could have told you, Vincent, this world was never meant for one as beautiful as you".' Waiting on the earlier refrains to come together, as driftwood finally beached by small waves, Bob absorbed the brunt of the song.

'Poor bastard,' he said at length. 'They really shafted him. And the same pseuds would now kill for one of his paintings. I guess some things never change.' Linda felt down, the song had taken something from her and opened a view of trampled dreams.

'He went mad too,' Bob observed, not noticing how quiet she'd become. A bowl of fruit on the coffee table offered red and green curves to the sunlight in the room, shadow tapered inwards filling space; everything seemed miraculously as it should be, proper and defined, offering an intuition about the nature of objects.

'His paintings are so ... *meravigliosi.* He gave of himself,' she said haltingly. 'You ... have the same gift.'

'No, I don't.' He laughed outright, missing the point. 'I can't paint a barn door. I'm a goddamn salesman. What are you talking about?' Seeing she didn't share his amusement he stopped chuckling and scrambled round to sit beside her. The guitar made a hollow chime as she put it down to make room for him. 'It's only a song. What's the matter?' His arm round her shoulders felt the dejected shrug, a frail attempt to square up to superior odds.

'It's so unfair ...' She struggled for expression ... 'to victimise people who give everything they have. It is so cruel. *Non mi da pace*!'

'It's called free enterprise.' Mistakenly, he thought this might cheer her.

'Be serious.' Her face clouded over, stung by his glibness. 'You don't have to humor me.'

He tightened the bracket of his hand round her shoulder. 'You Europeans ... You've had too many wars. No one has to die for glory any more or suffer to make it.' It occurred to him that this was something he could just as easily have said to Sal. 'America,' he added, 'is living proof that you can have your cake and eat it.' As if further proof were necessary he went to the fridge and opened a bottle of Asti. Padding back in his bare feet – he hadn't yet moved in his slippers – he pressed a glass of the lively wine to her lips. 'To life, and damn the begrudgers.'

'Salut.' She looked at him over the rim of the fluted glass. 'Maybe the fates will be kind.' Her spirit renewed itself on this thought.

'Sure,' he agreed. 'But you can't stand pat. You have to go for it.' Holding his glass aloft he sat down cross-legged on the cushions without spilling a drop.

'You don't believe in ... *come si dice*? ... predestination?' Her smile, triumphing over the found word, lingered on for his answer.

'A mover and shaker like me? Of course not.' He thought of a Don Rickles quip. 'Thank God I'm an atheist.'

'I'm not so sure.' She leant against him. 'But what I am sure of is that I need this atheist.'

'We'll soon be together, Linda. It's only a matter of weeks. The lawyers have taken the depositions ...' Silencing him with a kiss she forced him back, her hand at the nape of his neck. 'I'm going to convert you,' she said, drawing back to see his eyes.

'Anything,' he mumbled, 'Hinduism, Jehovah ... whatever ...'

He frowned in disbelief of pleasure so unbridled yet tinged somehow by sadness – was there after all an inexorable rule that sought payment for a gift? He felt so drawn to her that tenderness came easy. There was in the beginning the older man's urge to impress, to beat the competition. But she had taught him to relax; there was no young Turk breathing down his neck. So there was no performance anxiety, no need to orchestrate, and yet he felt more potent than ever simply because it was of no consequence. She had given and taught him so much that somehow she seemed wiser beyond her years.

Starved of compliments for most of his life, her release freed him and made him soar when she called out his name in warning and invitation.

'Honey, it's all right.' He held her close, feeling the slick of perspiration which gathered in the long cleft of her curving spine, still seized by residual echoes. Propping herself up on an elbow she gazed at him as if to confirm his existence. 'I don't know why I cried. Did it bother you?'

'Of course not. It's natural.'

'Are you speaking from wide experience?' Her gaze, still unwavering, grew kittenish.

'The widest. You know me.' He started to stroke the hair back from her face when the phone rang.

'Damn!' She reached over to an end-table and picked up the receiver, shaking it free of some unidentifiable lingerie. 'Oh hi, Barbara.' Her face brightened instantly in recognition. She removed the remaining tears with flicks of her index finger as she got into a kneeling position to talk on the phone.

'But that costume's had it,' Linda insisted. 'We've got to get you some new ones.' She covered the mouthpiece with her hand and said to Bob, 'It's Barbara from the club.'

'The one with the thin shoulder blades?' he asked. She nodded and went back to her conversation.

'Yes, there's a place in Springfield Mall ... I'll go with you. Sure ... They have some marvellous stuff. Aldo will spring for it ... Of course ...' As she spoke she absent-mindedly caressed Bob with her free hand. An idea grew mutely between them; glances, at first questioning, became conspiring, then locked on the logistics of the modest fantasy. Linda's eyes closed and she blindly replaced the receiver on its cradle or in the vicinity thereof... The room took on a roseate glow from the declining sun, soft and filtered like the patina behind eyelids, an inner amber light.

'That was mean,' she accused him afterwards.

'You could have quit anytime,' he pointed out, the soul of reason.

'No, I couldn't. That was the problem.' Her self-deprecating laughter came giddily in short bursts like payouts from a bank of fruit machines, and continued, muffled, as she pulled the T-shirt over her head.

'What is Barbara going to think?' She smiled pensively; it would be fun telling her. Tying up her hair she went through the swing door into the kitchen to fix dinner.

Bob transferred himself to a couch and lay there, listening to the kitchen sounds, dimly aware of the glorious disarray of things, of time and of moods, in this bower of the senses.

The phone rang as they sat down to eat. Linda answered it and handed it to him in silence. Sal spoke too rapidly for him to catch more than the barest outline. But that was enough.

'I'm on my way,' he said, struggling into his jacket.

Chapter 5

With her shoulders hunched so that the sternum seemed to have collapsed inwards, Sal looked beaten. She sat in lamp-light, toying nervously with the tassles of an embossed cushion that lay in her lap. Having arrived home breathlessly, Bob stood reading the note from Robbie, a sharp focus narrowing his eyes.

'What do you make of it?' It didn't seem quite as bad as the phone call had suggested.

'The Chaikha Rani is more fundamentalist than Krishna or Scientology or any of the other cults. I don't buy that bit about a "course". I think he's been inducted.' All day Saturday and on and off during the night she had cursed Bob for being away. To her chagrin, the anger had turned to relief when he came through the door – even though there was nothing he could do.

'Well, it only lasts two weeks, whatever it is. And he's OK for money. Who knows? Maybe it will straighten him out.' He spread his hands, offering that possibility.

'Don't be ridiculous,' she snapped. 'The Chaikha Rani is the most sinister organisation there is. It was formed by radicals who broke away from other cults and went underground. It even has connections with the religious revolution in Iran. I've checked it out with Father Molloy ...'

'He doesn't know everything ...' Bob began. But the point had struck home. The memory of the hostages in Iran came flooding back, the entire US held to ransom for a whole year by a bunch of looneytunes, Carter broken and mocked by that feeble rescue mission that blew up in his hollow-eyed face. Then Irangate, and Reagan pleading 'plausible deniability' ... this was the stuff of global politics. How could it reach into his home?

'I've read about them myself,' she said sharply. This was an exaggeration, but justified in the circumstances.

He looked at the note again as if for inspiration. 'We'll just have to get him back.'

'How?' she demanded. 'Just tell me how.'

'Get the number of this ... Chaikha Rani outfit ...'

'My God, don't you think I've tried that? They're not listed.' His habit of stating the obvious grated on her nerves. She had gone through all the options alone; now he would drag her through them again. She could see it coming. She even guessed what his next question would be.

'His friends,' Bob said right on cue. 'They'd know something. Their parents ...' He paced the parquet flooring, biting his mustache. 'That kid, Geoff ...' Absentmindedly, he rattled loose change and keys in his pants pocket.

'I've tried them all while you were ... away.' Weary beyond words, she lit a cigarette and drew the smoke right down into her lungs. He noticed the pain in her face, that headache tension that turned her skin to parchment.

'Sorry,' he mumbled. 'I know what you've been through.' He stopped pacing as a thought came to him. 'His room. Robbie may have left something there. A clue.'

'I've already looked.' She passed a hand across her throbbing forehead. Filaments in her left eye clouded her vision and warned of a migraine.

'Let me double-check.' He took the stairs two at a time, still bewildered, not knowing how worried he ought to be.

He went straight to the desk, which was littered with text books and notepads – evidence of the last weeks' cramming before the finals. He went through the hutch and shelves, examining and rejecting books, record sleeves, old report cards, photographs. But not even the contents of the waste basket, which he sifted through on his knees, revealed a clue.

One of the desk drawers was locked. After searching through the other drawers in the pedestal, he came back to that one and forced it open with a screwdriver.

There was still no information about Robbie's whereabouts, but the contents of the drawer were a revelation of a different kind. There was an empty gin bottle and several plastic pill containers, most of which had been bought on prescription. He identified valium and tofranil; others he could only guess at. There was also a half-finished letter to a girl called Jenny. Much of it had been crossed out but he managed to make out some phrases. '... I don't remember too much about the party after you left with Geoff ... Why did you? I guess it doesn't matter anyway ... going to flunk the finals probably ... Bad news on the home front. You've been through it ...? Nothing to look forward to, and all that crap ...'

Bob sat on the edge of the bed unaware that he was trembling; he had looked for a scratch and found a gaping wound. All he could think of was Robbie trying to cope on his own as if he had no one to turn to. How could he have felt so isolated, living under the same roof with parents who loved him? Mixed-up kids came from other homes. It was crazy. He tried to banish the evidence of his own eyes.

His next instinct was to blame the system, those undisciplined kids, especially Geoff. But gradually he began to examine his own conscience, his priorities over the last few years, his job, his business dinners and, yes, Linda too. It was a harrowing inventory. He hadn't put out enough to Robbie, told him where he stood with him. But surely he knew! He must have known ...

Having followed him into the room, Sal looked at the same exhibits and thought for a long time.

'I knew he was ... under pressure.' That much was true but she had somehow assumed that pressure, as in her own case, was constructive, like a deadline that had to be met. God, how could she have been so wrong?

'Why didn't he tell us?' His voice broke on the question. He raised his arms and let them fall helplessly to his sides, oblivious to the sight of Art's teenage sons doing basketball dunks in the asphalt drive across the road.

'Maybe he was afraid we wouldn't understand,' Sal said. 'He role-played a bit. I sensed that much. Tried to pretend his good grades came easy. I didn't know he had such ... a poor image of himself.' She fought for control; it was important to keep a clear head.

'This so-called course,' he began. 'It's something about communications? Oh, Christ ... It's his way of ...' He couldn't finish the sentence.

'Reaching us? Yes.' It was all becoming clear, too clear.

He stood up abruptly and drew a deep breath. 'We must do something.'

'What can we do, except wait for his next letter? And hope.' The hum of lawn-mowers reached into the house. There was also the rasp of a distant chainsaw as some neighbor pruned fruit-laden branches that threatened joggers on the sidewalk. Business as usual in suburbia. The real mid-summer heat was beginning. Soon the house-tending activities would be deferred until the sun went down, for people would stay indoors during the draining heat of daylight hours.

The next letter arrived three days later. Bob and Sal read it together at the breakfast table.

Dear Mom and Dad,
This course is exactly what I need. It has a spiritual side which is fantastic. It would really appeal to you, Mom, in particular.

You used to tell me how wonderful it was to have real commitment. Remember? How, when you really loved doing something, it required no effort, no conscious effort. Well, that's exactly how I feel. I'm 'zoning', as the tennis pros say, absorbing everything about the course without even trying. It is just flowing into me. When I think of how I used to knock myself out in school! This is so liberating by comparison.

I've also had my first key factors. These are insights about the nature of reality which most acolytes don't experience for months. The most powerful one is about, you guessed it, love. For the first time in my life I understand what that much abused concept means. Needless to say, I feel it very powerfully for both of you and pray that you will feel it for each other before it's too late. Because I know it's there. You just have to clear your minds, lose the clutter of conditioning and let it flow through you. There are techniques for doing this which I can explain to you later.

The organisers say I'm ideally suited and have asked me to stay longer than the two weeks. No extra fee is required. It's a sort of scholarship. Of course, I accepted immediately. It's a great opportunity and the people are wonderful and loving. When I really get in touch with myself I'll decide about college, maybe even architecture! Who knows?

I'll write again soon.
Love,
Robbie.

There was a New York postmark on the envelope but no address or phone number on the letter.

Sal left the table, her face sodden with dismay, and stood with her back to Bob. From there she moved into the shade between the two windows facing east. Her heart went out to Robbie. Why in God's name had they told him about the divorce? They had meant well, so had he, but there was some presence out there on the road to hell beckoning for a sacrificial victim ...

'They're getting to him,' she said grimly. 'Pretending he's found himself, pretending they need him.' Taking a tissue from the sleeve of her blouse she dabbed at the perspiration that gathered in the hollow of her throat. Apart from the fear of losing Robbie there was an added hurt. After years of nurturing him she felt usurped by strangers who purported to teach him about love. It was as if her advice to him during his formative years had been designed solely to prepare him for the Chaikha Rani. She brought the tissue to her mouth to quell the nausea that reminded her of morning sickness eighteen years ago.

Seeing the angular lift of her shoulders, Bob tried to take a more positive view. 'But he does mention college. Who knows? Maybe a few weeks with those strangeos will help him get his act together. I mean they're not into drugs or anything and there's no mention of Iran or any of that Islamic stuff. And he sounds quite excited about it all.' The tone of the letter was indeed in stark contrast to that despairing half-finished note to Jenny. There was, however, more hope than certainty in his voice.

'Don't be naive,' Sal said curtly, unaware that he was trying to help. 'Can't you see what's happening? For God's sake can you not see it? I spoke to Father Molloy again yesterday ...'

'Oh, him?' he snorted. 'What does he know? He's the one who made me sign away my rights ...' He wondered why he brought that up. Promising Father Molloy that he wouldn't interfere in the spiritual formation of his children hadn't cost him a thought at the time.

'What are you implying?' Sal demanded, stubbing out a freshly lit cigarette. 'That I'm responsible? Is that it? Oh, my God ...'

'I'm not implying anything,' he said wearily. It was his turn to head for a safe anchorage as the storm clouds gathered. 'I'm just keeping an open mind for the time being.' He left the table and collected his briefcase from the hallstand. The car which had been sitting in the sun was like a blast furnace and the air conditioner didn't bring him any relief until he was half-way to work, by which time his shirt clung to him like a wet rag.

Sal chain-smoked for the rest of the day – the only outlet permitted for her anger – and by evening her lips were raw. She had not been able to do much work and this added to her frustration.

The next letter, which arrived the following week, made it difficult to keep an open mind.

> Dear Mom and Dad
> Wonderful news. Now that the course is coming to an end, Paajit, our temple leader, has personally asked me to join the fellowship of Rani. Can you believe it?
>
> I accepted immediately and have already taken my vows. The transformation is extraordinary. I sometimes feel the presence of Rani in my soul and see a golden light surrounding my brothers and sisters. I'm blown away by it. All guilt vanishes. When Paajit touches my eyelids the traitor within disappears.
>
> We have moved our temple to continue our work in more peaceful

surroundings. There is so much to be done to fight the evil of the world, to confront the Adversary, the enemy of peace and inner harmony. When I was a kid you told me about Satan but I never really believed he existed as a person. Now I know. We call him Lakhryon, mortal enemy of Rani. But he is the Beast who must be fought over and over again. As Paajit says, the field of battle is man's heart.

Now at last I know where my place is.

I also know you will understand some day.

Robbie.

Sal didn't even try to control herself. She collapsed in tears, covering her face with her hands. Bob touched her lightly on the shoulder.

'We can fight too, Sal,' he said grimly. 'It's just beginning.'

'You don't know what you're up against,' she sobbed. 'I never told him Satan was ... Dear God ...' She became incoherent. 'And he just said Robbie, not "love" Robbie ... They're taking him away from us.' She gripped the arms of the chair to stop shaking. 'And it was Dostoevsky who said that ... They're lying to him in every way, brainwashing him ...'

'Take it easy,' he said gently. 'There must be a way.' He looked again at the letter and couldn't believe his eyes. 'Christ Almighty! The postmark says, London, England!'

She didn't even have to look. 'And all he says is that they moved. He doesn't even know where he is.'

'We don't have to take this.' His voice rose as the adrenalin surged through him. 'I'm not standing for it. It's against the law!' He grabbed his car keys, rushed to the door, then hesitated. He looked back. 'Will you be OK?'

She nodded slowly and said in a barely audible voice, 'It's not against the law.'

She was right as usual. His lawyer explained how religious freedom was protected under the constitution, how thousands of other families were similarly affected, without any hope of redress. He mentioned something about individual cases making bad law but Bob wasn't listening.

He then tried the Iranian angle. He spent two days researching names in the State Department and another three trying to get an appointment with an official on the Middle East desk. The official said there was nothing the State Department could do. The link between the Chaikha Rani and Iran was tenuous at best and in no way raised sovereign issues. Besides, the Ayatollah's teeth were drawn and detente was the new game in town. Bob played his Vietnam Vet card, but to no avail. He got sympathy which he didn't need, but no offer of help, not even an idea to go on.

Leaving the State Department he walked for a while along the Mall trying to clear his head. He was surrounded by monuments to freedom and justice, each granite stone, every bronze plaque engraved with brave rhetoric. There had been a time when a visit to the Mall filled him with pride. He went back to his car which was double-parked and had accumulated a number of tickets.

After that he spent several days in a trance, which turned with time into a helpless rage.

Sal rallied fairly well during the following weeks. Her composure was even stronger than usual, a reaction to her emotional outburst over Robbie's last letter. Father Molloy was a frequent visitor to the house and she relied heavily on him. They spoke a language which Bob found hard to understand, the language of Job, of acceptance, expiation of guilt.

In fact Father Molloy's pious visitations, as Bob called them, bothered him more than he cared to admit. It wasn't that he had anything against the rather well-meaning priest. But he didn't agree with his views about resignation and surrendering to a higher power. It was difficult to argue with him, however, and in any case Sal would have been offended. There was some grim humor in being cuckolded by a celibate, but the fact remained that Bob's role was undermined and he felt more and more helpless.

Worse, he knew that every day that passed was a threat to Robbie's mind. There were no more letters.

Chapter 6

Linda lay with her head in the crook of Bob's arm. She had hardly moved for the last hour, letting him sleep. It was interesting to study his face in sleep; it was calm, icon-like, in contrast to its normal vitality. She noticed some deeper creases in his face, especially above the bridge of his nose where the dark bushy eyebrows curved upwards. Robbie's disappearance was clearly taking its toll.

He would do anything to get Robbie back. She was struck by the strength of his paternal instinct, though not really surprised by it. It was pure instinct, as unthinking as it was profound, and it sometimes made her feel inconsequential. The energy she'd always felt in him was no longer diffused, but condensing like the eye of a storm.

She had an urge to get a scissors and trim his eyebrows while he slept but, no, it would have been too wifely an act, outside her domain. Instead, she traced his eyebrows with her forefinger as a prelude to waking him. Maybe she should let him sleep and suffer the consequences?

He stirred slightly but didn't wake. Linda drew her fingertips through the hair on his chest in a circular pattern.

'Holy shit. What time is it?' He sat up abruptly. 'How long have I been asleep?'

'About an hour. It's OK' She stroked his cheek, smiling at his bewilderment.

'I'd better make tracks.' He ran his hand through his dishevelled hair and blinked several times to get the sleep out of his eyes.

She helped him dress, her fingers still touching him. She smiled as she watched him hopping from foot to foot, putting on his pants and socks.

'What time is your wife expecting you?' She knew the answer; it was a question in more ways than one.

'Sixish.' He looked at her ruefully. 'You know how it is, Linda. I can't ... walk away now. Not just now ... not until Robbie ...'

'I know, ' she said quietly. 'Don't worry about it. First things first. Right?'

Her smile faded when he left. She didn't have to be at the club for another three hours and she tried to occupy the time by cataloging her tapes and compact discs. But it all seemed so thankless and unimportant. The apartment was bleak and empty without Bob, whose presence filled it like a boulder. When he left she had a sense of departure; she wished the time would pass more quickly. Performing on stage would help get her through the night. But for now ... she left the cassettes strewn on the floor and went for another shower.

As soon as he crossed Roosevelt Bridge and merged on to the Parkway he loosened the tie he'd just put on. The air conditioner in the Buick still wasn't working well; he was being turned on a slow spit in more ways than one.

It was late summer but most trees were still in bloom; white and pink dogwood, tulip trees, junipers, yellow poplar, hawthorn and opaca. He had sold landscaping once and knew the names of most flowering trees. It was important for salesmen to know the names of things.

He had a talent for selling; he had the drive and was good with people. Maybe he could have gone into the more lucrative arcane fields of marketing or advertising, as Sal would have liked, but he wasn't a back-room type, a hidden persuader. He preferred to be out front in the scrimmage of the market place.

His job involved liquid lunches and dinners with clients. He could handle liquor but he knew that it scared Sal who had painful memories of her father's alcoholic drinking. It was one of the things that had come between them. Breath fresheners hadn't helped, touching became rare, intercourse rarer still. The myriad events that led to separate bedrooms were, in hindsight, trivial compared to the effect of separation.

Robbie was constantly in his thoughts. Understanding a little of brain-washing techniques from his tour of duty in Vietnam, he knew that time was not on his side. His own helplessness unnerved him. Even as he drove through this placid countryside that gave silver glimpses of the Potomac through the rich foliage of a tumescent summer, his heart pounded for action so that his chest felt like bursting. But there was nothing he could do. He had met the smooth-faced bureaucrats and lawyers, he had lain awake at night wrestling with shadows until the dawn came up with nothing but the promise of another wasted day. Rage alternated with sickening worry; they had somehow, all of them, lost the deeds on their own lives.

He parked in the driveway, gathered up his briefcase and commission book and walked towards the Cape Cod style house.

'Hiya, Bob.' The greeting came from Art who was in his own front yard sprinkling the lawn.

'What's new, Art?'

'Damn crab grass has me licked.' Art's crinkly face was screwed up in the sun's glare. 'If it's not one thing it's another.' He voiced the age-old complaint of settlers involved in an endless struggle to prevent nature from restoring the wilderness that was once there.

'I'll get you something for the crab grass,' Bob offered. 'At trade.'

'I'd sure appreciate it.' Art mopped his forehead under the peak of a baseball cap. 'Going bowling later?'

'Naw.' Bob nodded toward the house as if to suggest domestic commitments. Art nodded gravely; he understood.

Passing the sycamore tree in his own front yard Bob noticed something as if for the first time: the rope burn on the branch from which Robbie's tire used to hang. His mind filled with memories of fifteen years ago; how Robbie watched in eager anticipation as Bob fixed up the swing, how Robbie curled up along the inside rim of the tire, hesitant at first then growing in confidence, beginning to swing back and forth, a slow smile of delight appearing on his face, pleased with his new toy and even more pleased because he wasn't afraid. Dear God, was it conceivable that even then he had to prove himself?

Bob recalled the jaunty walk he developed later on, the puns he learned so he could get laughs in school, his painful attempts to be smart. Why didn't he know he didn't have to work at being accepted?

Bob's breath caught in his chest. What had they done to him? He leant against the tree, his nails digging into the bark. Blood and sap. And a silent nightmare roar of loss.

Chapter 7

He recovered slowly with a pitcher of martinis and sat in his recliner, trying to read the *Post*. He felt like a lodger; it wasn't a household any more. There was a time he'd have gone with Robbie to watch 'Star Trek' in the den, his arm around the narrow shoulders, trying to answer questions about time warps, intergalactic travel, the winking reaches of space. It seemed a very long time ago. And it was strange how his thoughts seemed to focus on Robbie's pre-teens as if he hadn't really known him in the recent past. Maybe not so strange.

The lounge was over-furnished and a little old-fashioned with its Colonial-style settees and lamp standards, Persian rugs and tapestries and Sal's collection of porcelain figurines which sat on the mantelpiece of the brick fireplace. Neither of them cared much about decor. Stuff just accumulated over the years, usually at trade discounts. At least the walls were unpapered, which gave some sense of space.

Through the kitchen hatch he could see Sal prepare, or rather unwrap, dinner. As usual her glasses were pushed up visor-like into her hair which was tied in a bun with a rubber band. She'd obviously been reading most of the day. A copy of *The Errors of Rigorism* lay on an end table in the lounge. The bookmark had shifted about a hundred pages since morning and the neighboring ashtray was full of half-finished cigarettes.

'Did Father Molloy call today?' Bob inquired.

'No,' she called back from the kitchen. 'He's giving a retreat in McLean.' She didn't elaborate, knowing how Bob felt about him.

He went back to his paper, she to her chicken-in-a-bucket. The silence was the sound of Robbie's absence. It was almost three months since they'd last heard from him.

'There's a story here,' Bob remarked to make conversation, 'about a guy, a card counter. He's so good the casinos have barred him. There's no justice. Imagine having a system that works, and not being let use it.' This brought no response.

'Blackjack,' he added, giving it one more shot. Through the bow window he could see one of Art's grown sons painting a boat on blocks at the side of the house. The boat was named *Artcraft*; last year Bob had helped to launch it in the tidal basin.

'Dinner's ready,' she announced. He put the paper aside and sat at the walnut table in the dining area of the open-plan lounge.

'Why doesn't he wear a disguise?' she inquired, serving the chicken and saffron rice.

'Who?' He vacantly watched the Neighborhood Watch patrol car cruise by outside. It would be his turn to lead the local vigilantes in two weeks, if he remembered the roster correctly.

'This gambler. To get into the casinos.' She sat down at the other end of the table, flopping open her napkin.

'I guess he could at that. That's a good idea.' He watched her pick at her food, his wife of twenty years, and wondered who she was.

Yet there had been a time when he didn't have to wonder, when he had been bowled over by her quiet charm and delicate looks, so that he was untypically restrained in her presence and flattered that she would even deign to go out with him, a guy who'd left school at fifteen, a rube from Montana. His pals used to kid him about falling for a broad with class.

But behind all of this there had been a deep appreciation of her quiet strength and her constancy that made everything seem to revolve around her. Exactly why it hadn't lasted would always be a mystery, as inexplicable as a natural disaster or the collapse of a cantilevered bridge. He sensed that over the years she had changed more than he had. She had come through the sixties trying to save the world, only to discover that the world didn't want to be saved. Maybe she'd never forgiven him for Vietnam. Before that she used to rib him about his right-wing views, but afterwards all was silence. He had caught her once leafing through her Barnard Year Book with tears in her eyes. She said something about 'a lost generation' and that was all.

He looked at her now and wondered how she would cope with the present crisis, which was real. Her eyes were more hooded than ever, cowled by tired eyelids. As she bent slightly over the table her graceful neck seemed vulnerable, waiting for an axe to fall.

'How's the chicken?' she asked without looking at him.

'Fine, thanks.' He was a guest, with a guest's politeness.

'And the rice?' She smoothed back a loose strand of hair and dabbed the corner of her mouth with her napkin.

'Good. Fluffy,' he added. That's what one said about rice.

The ritual continued. He wondered why he felt obliged to come home. Was his physical presence of any value to her? He doubted it. He felt like an outsider looking in on the scene. They were cardboard profiles or the shadow images in Victorian cameos. A grandfather clock calibrated the silences with resonant tocks as the weights swung glumly in the teak casing. He tried again.

'I had a reasonable day today.' Why was he telling her this?

'Good,' she answered. 'You sold a site?'

'Yes.' They weren't sites exactly; they were multiple destination deed warranties based on a time-sharing concept. It would take too long to explain the difference to her. But it was passing strange that she didn't know what he sold for a living.

'Not bad going,' he continued bravely. 'There's not much money around. We haven't seen Reagan's trickle-down yet.' In fact his own sales record had been slipping and he couldn't really blame it on the recession.

Sal made no response and that was it for him; he clammed up. He was miffed that she wouldn't even try to initiate any conversation and she had a habit of looking past him as if he didn't exist. But he didn't have her stoicism and it was hard for him to keep quiet. After a while he blurted out, 'They're not sites; they're MDDWs. Oh, what's the point,' he ended lamely. Let it lie, he thought; get back into the bunker and keep your head down.

'Is this an issue for you?' she inquired clinically, making a direct hit.

'Don't patronise me,' he grated. 'Christ Almighty!' He slammed down his silverware.

'Please don't take the Holy Name in vain.' She put on her long-suffering face. Her defences were in place; she had sanctuary. He was the infidel at the gate of the cathedral. She sat erect, still picking at the chicken, her glasses now in place, glazing her eyes. He looked despairingly for help at walls and ceiling.

'You blame me, don't you? Yes that's it.' He flung his napkin on the table knocking over a glass of water. 'It's my fault. I should have known.' He slapped the heel of his palm against his forehead.

'Your sarcasm lacks subtlety,' she remarked, mopping up the water, as if she'd always had to clean up after him.

'What the hell are we playing at here?' he demanded helplessly. She could be so infuriating; it was like wrestling with a shadow. 'Do you blame me or not?' He chipped the nails of one hand with the thumbnail of the other.

'Why should I blame you?' She refused to be drawn.

'Because infidelity is a mortal sin,' he blurted out, 'in your book.'

'You mean your ... affair?' Her lips were slightly pursed in a semblance of distaste, putting his adultery on a par with poor table manners.

'Yes. That's exactly what I mean. Your loving God doesn't like that, so he zaps our kid.'

'What do you think?' She maintained her demeanor though he had touched a raw nerve.

'I don't believe any of that religious stuff. And,' he pointed a finger at her, 'you're crazy to even think about it.'

'We're both to blame,' she said at length, prepared to accept her own responsibility. 'But maybe not in the way you think ...'

'Look, get off that guilt trip. Your father made you a Puritan. Forget about guilt. Robbie disappeared. It happened. It's not a punishment visited upon us. It just happened.' He drummed his fingers on the table-top, leaving sweat marks that vanished quickly.

'Things don't just happen.' Sal shook her head slowly. 'There's always a reason. We may not understand it, but there's always a reason.' His reference to her father startled her; it was as if he had an intuition ...

She began to clear away the dinner things, her movements slow and deliberate. Everything about her was calibrated to pre-selected rhythms which failed to slow her racing pulse.

'Then why did he join that crazy cult ... or whatever the hell it is?' he asked in exasperation. 'Tell me.' Behind the challenging tone of the question was a deep desire to know her mind.

'Maybe we spoiled him.' She shrugged to indicate that she was just speculating. In fact she was being evasive. There was a part of her life that she had never revealed to him and it had a bearing on this which she couldn't deny.

'You mean you spoiled him,' Bob said less heatedly. At least they were talking.

'All right,' she conceded although she wasn't convinced. 'But only because you cut him down to size often enough.'

'And what about you?' He followed her out to the kitchen. 'Doing everything for him. Homework, brushing his teeth, dressing him until he was seven or eight. He couldn't even tie his own shoelaces until he was almost in his teens.'

'At least he knew I cared. With you he always had to compete just to feel accepted.' She knew she was exaggerating, but it was his fault; he had forced her to respond. The silence proved that she had wounded him.

'Yes, but when was he supposed to grow up? Stand on his own two feet?' Bob was defensive, trying to account for himself. 'You tied him to your apron strings. And then he was so nervous with girls ...' He recalled painfully the fragment of a letter to Jenny. But there had been other instances too.

'Don't give me all that phoney macho stuff,' she said curtly. 'You never understood him as a person. You just wanted him to behave, to perform, like a robot. Your love was conditional, doled out like Brownie points. He was hurt so many times ...'

'When did I ever hurt him?' he demanded. He was shocked by her version of things. Had she always believed this?

'What about the time you found him with that boy? He was only eleven, just experimenting. It was all so harmless. And that time he was hit by a baseball and cried. You gave him hell for weeks. All he wanted was stability. He's got it now, mindless stability.' She knew she had gone too far. It wasn't that Bob had been deliberately tough; it was more the example he set. She knew how perceptive Robbie was, how he sensed his father's competitiveness every time he shouted at a fumbling quarter-back on TV or went jogging in winter without a track suit or bragged about some deal he'd pulled off.

'You're so wise after the event, aren't you?' He was smarting. 'Whatever I did was for his own good. For him. But this is typical of you. Always advising behind the scenes when it's too late. Intellectuals don't have to do anything, just reflect and ponder. You see all sides of everything and do nothing. I'm the front man. You've always left me out front ... to make decisions. Then you carp and complain ...'

She turned from the dishwasher and faced him. 'At least I don't go off half-cocked and then wonder why everything's gone wrong. How many times have I saved you from your knee-jerk reactions?'

'Hold it right there ...'

'Go on. Tell me that any decision under fire is better than none. That's your usual cop-out. Enlisting for Vietnam. Volunteering. On a whim. With no thought or discussion ...'

'Now we're getting to it. What if I had discussed it? You'd have roped in Father Molloy and all your conchie friends and spent the next ten years debating it over tea. Just tell me one thing. What have you ever done? Done. As in action?'

'Who's been writing to congressmen and senators?' There was a tremor in her voice.

'That was my idea.' He hammered a finger against his chest. 'You just drafted the letters.'

She closed the dishwasher and leant weakly against it. 'What good did it do?'

'That's it, isn't it? Nothing can work in your book. Because it's God's will. Come off it ...'

'I don't want to discuss it any more.' They faced each other across a fraught space, charged with grief and blame and visions of what might have been. They needed to shelter from that explosive air. She picked up her book from the kitchen table and began to read. The subject was closed, sanity preserved to live another day. He looked at her, bent over the book, fumbling to find her page.

'The Errors of fucking Rigorism,' he fumed, leaving the room.

She felt sick and helpless, vaguely aware that she was working her own guilt off on him even though he had forced the confrontation. Her guilt feelings ran deep, derived from memories that she could never share with him.

When Robbie was born she was terrified at first because he had to spend some time in an incubator to help his breathing. Then she was so grateful and relieved when he was pronounced normal and healthy. But that had just been a reprieve. Now came the reckoning.

She sat under a standard lamp that threw two parabolas of light on the white flock wall, one above and one below the plain cylindrical shade. Around the shaft of the lamp was a little brass-railed tray like a crow's nest that held her note pads, cigarettes and lighter. This was her part of the house and she was territorial about it. She could sit reading under the canopy of light for hours on end with the lost look of a woman under an old-fashioned hair dryer. From that position too she could see her porcelain figurines in the glass cabinet across the room. This time it was different; the habit and trappings of concentration no longer worked for her.

Bob went upstairs, his blood pounding. He looked into Robbie's room and sat for a while on the neatly made bed. He knew that Sal tidied the room every day. It was like a shrine, he thought. The image terrified him. Whatever it takes, he swore. He would not seek to give any quarter. As he hung up his jacket in the closet of his own room his eyes were drawn again to the lock box on the upper shelf, in which he kept a .22 Remington hunting rifle.

Chapter 8

At the resort next morning Bob finished his coffee in the main facilities building and went out to greet his clients in the reception area. He wore his fawn suit with the European waist and satin lining, designed, the label said loudly, by Bill Blass who did for the First Lady too – his selling suit, the pants of which he pressed himself in that electric gismo like a vertical hot plate, which he had had to acquire five years before when Sal withdrew her services. She had always hated ironing.

'Glad you could make it, Mr and Mrs Williams,' he greeted them. 'And how are you, young man?' He tousled the head of their little boy, Rosco. 'Let me show you what we're all so proud of here.'

He drove them in his Buick to a secluded spot by the lower lake and went into his introductory spiel, explaining how the advantages of a multiple destination time-sharing arrangement were far superior to the traditional holiday home. He believed in what he was selling. There had been legal problems with time-sharing arrangements before he became involved in the business, but these had been resolved.

Although there was three hundred dollars commission riding on the Williams family decision, Bob somehow could not psych himself up for the job in hand. He worried about whether he was losing his touch. His presentation was much less slick than it used to be.

'... So you see,' he concluded, 'the main advantage is mobility. You can use similar facilities at any of our resorts around the world. The accommodation units are of the same high standard, even down to the jacuzzi. Basically, what we have here is a new concept of space and mobility.' The words were tried and true, but he had to dig deep for them and they came out caked with debris.

'Sounds like Einstein's theory of relativity,' Mr Williams remarked drily.

'Yes, you could say that.' Bob tried to laugh but he could no longer crack that reassuring smile that revealed plausibly uneven teeth and helped the deal go down. He wondered if the Williams were serious prospects or whether they had come just for the prizes which were offered in the promo fliers to lure people to look over the resort. He tried to read Mr Williams's eyes through his owlish glasses, wondering why the computer that selected these people came up with so many Federal employees. Still, you never could tell. After years of selling he had learnt how different people could be. The diversity had always fascinated him and he respected it. That's what helped to keep him reasonably honest.

A modest sun glanced on the lake water. In a clearing, two squirrels played and suddenly darted up a tree, chasing each other through a labyrinth of branches. Bob put the car in gear and started the next leg of the tour. Mr

Williams fastened his seat belt even though the speed limit was only ten miles per hour.

Bob pointed out the attractions by rote, the different areas set aside for hunting, picnicking, hiking and skiing. His own appreciation of these scenes seemed to have disappeared under the burden of describing them. Through the rear view mirror he could see Rosco pick his nose and rub his finger on the upholstery.

Mrs Williams clucked a lot but did concede that the scenery was nice, especially the purple backdrop of the Shenandoah mountains. Her husband was silent most of the time, not wanting to commit himself even to an opinion about the scenery. He was waiting for the bottom line. He reminded Bob of the Fed he'd met in the State Department, a gentle easy-going man who liked his comforts and never suffered the trauma of decision. He knew suddenly there would be no sale.

He showed them the accommodation units, the swimming pools and the indoor recreation facilities. Then he drove them back to the main building and led them into the lodge-style reception area.

'Now, why don't you folks relax here with a cup of coffee and mull over this material?' He handed them printed sheets setting out the financial details in simple point form. 'I'll get out of your hair for a while.'

He met his boss, Sonny Winter, in the bathroom.

'Got a good prospect out there, Bob?' Sonny inquired, zipping his flies. He gave him a canny, appraising look.

'Don't think so,' Bob replied. 'Another Fed.' He combed back his dark hair, which had singed coils of gray in the sideburns.

'You're lucky,' Sonny complained. 'They've stuck me with a diplomat. The guy won't even be in the country for more than two years. Plus he's been around the world several times and has two vacation homes already.' He sprayed breath freshener into his mouth and blew into his cupped hand. 'Sweet as pecan pie.'

'The computer must've sprung a leak,' Bob suggested.

'I'll come by and give you a hand,' Sonny offered with a wink on his way out, straightening his tie.

'All right.' Bob didn't care one way or the other; he never really liked Sonny's cynical approach. He suddenly felt depressed and didn't want to leave the bathroom. In fact if he had a choice he would have curled up in one of the stalls and locked the door. He was tired of gimmicks and cheap shots, of pimping for space/time concepts. Most of all he recoiled from the thought of trying to manipulate that ordinary, decent Williams family. And he suddenly knew why. The canny spark that lit the edges of his deals, that jumped between the principals, had gone out. But, good Christ, he had to go on; there was nothing else he could do. He splashed water on his face, took a few deep breaths and walked out.

'Well, have you folks had enough time to consider? Can I answer any questions for you?' He loosened his tie and swivelled his neck for relief.

Mr Williams had plenty of questions and Bob tried to deal with them one by one.

'But what happens,' Mr Williams pressed, 'if someone else wanted to book the same unit at the same time? Hypothetically speaking,' he added hurriedly.

'If you go for the super deed warranty,' Bob explained, 'you get priority. You get bumping rights. That's why it costs a little more. But even at fifteen grand it's still very good value. And don't forget the easy payment plan.'

'Mmmm...Mmmm...' Mrs Williams intoned. Maybe the idea of bumping rights appealed to her.

A reflective silence followed during which Rosco spilled his coke on the table. Some of it dripped onto Bob's pants, his best ones.

'I don't know,' Mr Williams said. 'The whole concept is new to us. We'd certainly need more time to consider. I could call you in a few days.'

Bob knew from past experience that people never called back; they had to decide there and then. He was trying to psych himself up for the hard sell when Sonny Winter came by on cue.

'Could I help expedite a decision here?' Sonny inquired with a smile. He took a gold pen from his inside pocket, wrote a lower figure on a piece of paper and pushed it under Mr Williams's nose. 'I can offer that discount for an instant decision. But,' he warned, 'it's like an instant sale. The special offer doesn't last. Right, Bob?'

'Yeah, sure.' Bob had a headache. He'd been through this routine so many times and he knew what the next step would be. He had never felt so out of it before and it frightened him. The rhythms were gone, the synchromesh shot.

'I ... I just don't know,' Mr Williams responded. 'The whole idea is so new.' He looked to his wife. 'I don't think we can decide right now. Do you, Hon?'

'Of course not.' It was clear they'd come just for the prizes.

Sonny changed tack. 'May I ask which government department you work for?'

'Education.' Mr Williams looked uncomfortable as if he had just betrayed a confidence.

'Education,' Sonny repeated. 'My, that's impressive. You really are the kind of people we want in our program.' He straightened up suddenly as if he had come to a bold decision. 'I know what I'm going to do. I'm going to offer you the status discount.' He wrote another figure on the paper. 'What this means,' he added conspiratorially, 'is that you get another fifteen hundred off the last price. But,' he warned, 'you've got to keep it between us. We don't want other folks complaining about special treatment. Bob here can tell you how exceptional this offer is.'

'It's pretty rare,' Bob said dully. 'Pretty rare.' Sonny looked sharply at him.

'Why can't we call you back on this?' Mr Williams asked almost plaintively. 'Tomorrow, even.' The offer seemed attractive but he wanted some time to check out the whole deal with a lawyer friend.

Sonny shook his head sorrowfully. 'Rules. Company policy. You know what it's like. The discount expires the moment you walk out that door.'

Mrs Williams, who had been scolding Rosco for shredding his coke cup, interjected sharply, 'That's ridiculous. I can't stand the hard sell. Give us our prizes and let's get out of here.' Her husband shifted in his chair and looked embarrassed. Sonny had no further interest in them and left.

At this point, and in accordance with the manual, Bob should have made a final conspiratorial pitch but he hadn't the stomach for it. Instead, he checked their pre-selected computer numbers against the prize numbers. He returned with a gent's digital watch and a camera.

'We won an item in category B too,' Mrs Williams said sharply.

'Sorry.' He went and fetched a bracelet from the stores. He could see the swimming pool through the window and imagined Robbie's sleek body cleaving the water like an otter. They used to have such fun together in the pool. He didn't quite catch what Mrs Williams was saying.

'Pardon me?'

'I said this is a bracelet. There is no bracelet in category B.' Her voice was like a skewer, augering its way through raw beef on a butcher's block. She had done her homework all right.

He returned with the brooch. Again he saw Robbie, this time diving from the side of the pool, his slender body jack-knifing, re-surfacing with a brilliant smile, shaking his head and popping his ears. He could hear him laugh and call out, 'Let's stay longer, Dad. Just a little longer.' What came to him then was the wonder and the danger of innocence. Pain milled through him. The brooch missed the table and fell at Mrs Williams's feet.

'How dare you!' She yelled for the manager.

The stud partition rattled as Sonny slammed the door behind them.

'Boy, you've done it this time,' he fumed, throwing himself into the swivel chair behind the desk. His parboiled face had a surprisingly intelligent nose above which sat a frown in the shape of a tuning fork.

'The brooch ...?' Bob felt punchy.

'Not just the fucking brooch,' Sonny raged. 'I've been watching you on and off for the last few weeks and looking at your sales figures. You've been asleep at the switch. I tried to bail you out just now and you gave me no support. We're supposed to back each other's play but you just don't give a shit. What's with you?' He passed a hand over has bald head, which was covered with sheddings of dead skin; dandruff without hair seemed monstrously unfair.

'I've a lot on ...' Bob began, but suddenly decided he wasn't going to ask any favors. 'The Williams family didn't want to buy. Do you understand? They just didn't want to buy.'

'Bullshit,' Sonny spat out. 'Another ten minutes and I'd have had them eating out of my hand.' He glared at him across the desk and then relented a little. 'Do you realise what a great product we have here? We're right at the front edge.' He warmed to his theme. 'We're talking second industrial revolution. Mass production is a thing of the past. The punter now wants custom-made stuff, he wants to be different, get it? Individualism is back in town. The worker doesn't have to punch a clock anymore, he can stay home in his electronic cottage and use the air waves. He wants custom-made leisure too. That's what we're offering. We're selling freedom.' He nodded to himself at the aptness of that and repeated it to make it doubly apt. 'We're selling freedom.'

Jesus Christ, he's not playing with a full deck, Bob thought. Did he really believe that garbage or had he fallen in love with his own spiels over the years? The man was sitting there talking about forcing freedom on people. He couldn't let it pass.

'And I thought we were selling MDDWs.'

'Smartass.' Sonny was avuncular no more. 'You know what your problem is? You've lost your balls.'

'You're out of your mind.' Bob paid him back in kind. 'You've never known anything about selling. You couldn't sell water in a desert. A cynical blowhard like you doesn't know the first thing about people.'

'You ... be careful.' Sonny pointed a quivering finger at him. 'You've had it good here. But you're close to the edge now. Your job's on the line ...'

'Good,' Bob said. 'I quit. And you know why? I couldn't work within an ass's roar of you because your breath stinks worse than a Turkish wrestler's jock.'

There was a controlled vengeance in him. But it felt good; maybe it was a prelude to action. At last. The listlessness was gone. He could always go back to selling shoes at Tyson's Corner, kneeling in front of assorted feet, shoe horn in hand. It didn't matter. Only one thing mattered.

Chapter 9

'This won't help,' Art counselled, watching Bob drain his fifth martini in the Gattopardo.

'It's not every day you lose a job selling freedom,' Bob said. The liberation he'd felt at kicking over the traces hadn't lasted very long and the fever that had brought him that rare glimpse of what he did for a living had broken, leaving him spent and hollow.

'Oh come on. Don't get victimy,' Art said. 'It's not your style. Anyway you told me you quit. Thanks, Hon,' he added as the barmaid leant across the counter to straighten his bow tie and then pat him on the cheek to show it was better that way – but better than what, for even in his tux he managed to resemble and over-stuffed laundry basket.

'Some men seek redundancy. Others have it thrust upon 'em.' Bob looked askance at his empty glass that reflected in its crystal the exhausted green of the club. He moved aside to let a waitress through to the bar to announce a complicated drinks order in a breathless patois, decipherable only by the head bartender who had his diploma in mixology prominently displayed among the lustrous bottles and the framed cartoons of the club's better-known clients. 'Art?'

'What?'

'It's not the lousy job. It's the inaction. I'm behind the eight ball ... Robbie. You know what I mean?' He turned his bleary eyes on him.

'I know,' Art said sadly, folding in his rubbery lips. 'But this is no good. You've got to amalgamate the faeces. Work out a plan.'

'That's what I'm gonna do. But first I'm gonna get smashed. The lush before the storm.' He started to laugh, pushing his glass across the bar for a refill.

'Hey guys, try to keep it down back there,' Frank, the emcee, called from the stage. 'This is amateur night ... '

'You can say that again,' Bob heckled, listing slightly on his perch.

'Come on now,' Frank tried to cajole him. 'Let's give the newcomers a break.'

'How about giving us all a break?' Bob threw back, getting a few nervous laughs from the audience. He knew Frank quite well; he could handle himself on stage.

'It's always good to have a plant in the audience,' Frank responded. 'Even a potted one.'

'No, no, no,' Bob slurred. 'You've got to sell a gag, Frank. Give it more oooomph.' He didn't notice Art going backstage.

'Sell a gag, huh?' Frank appealed to the audience at large, a strained smile on his face. 'All salesmen think they're comedians. Course some of 'em don't even have jobs. Hey, Bob, do you want my job?'

'Job?' Bob repeated with phoney incredulity. 'You mean you get paid for this?' The cocktail waitress circled carefully away from Bob, hoping he wouldn't make any sudden movement. He saw the blur of pink umbrellas, swizzle sticks and assorted fruits floating in liquor and knew that he was quite far gone.

'Isn't he a pistol, folks? I wish he'd go off.' The audience chortled. The fear of embarrassment receded; the emcee was in charge. The drummer gave a late riff.

'Hey Frank, if I went off you might get shot. What difference would that make? You're dying already.' Bob got some appreciation from the audience; it was heady wine.

'This guy used to be a comic, folks,' Frank explained to the audience. 'And if his nose gets any redder he's going to make a comeback. With Ringling Brothers.' He was reaching, and his timing was off.

'And if you get any more boring you're gonna drill yourself into the floor.' Bob's head began to swim; he hadn't any shots left in his locker. He felt a hand on his shoulder. It was Art. Who else?

'Ease up, Bob. They're already running late. Linda wants me to drive you back to her place.'

Bob tried to focus on him, 'Is this … an arrest? You want me to … come peacefully?'

'I'm not going to fight you,' Art said.

'OK. You win. It was only … a bit of fun. I wanted to see if I still … you know …'

'I know.' Art helped him off the barstool.

'There he goes,' Frank announced with relief, 'the smashed hit of the evening.' He wasn't particularly gracious in victory.

When Bob woke the next morning he could hear Linda in the shower. He was weak as water and his eyes felt hot and raw as if they'd been sand-blasted.

Linda came into the bedroom draped in a towel. She stood looking at him, her head to one side, hands on hips.

'Oh God,' he groaned. 'Don't look at me like that. I feel bad enough already.' He burrowed under the bedclothes.

She started to laugh and did a little tap dance of amusement.

'You mean I didn't screw everything up?' He peered out over the top of the sheet.

'It was funny, actually,' she said. 'Corny but funny. But we were scared it might escalate.'

'And it didn't?' he inquired eagerly.

'No. We got you out in time.' She finished towelling herself and began to dress. Shorts, T-shirt and flip flops were run to earth and plucked from the unlikeliest places. Her lack of censure was refreshing.

'Thank goodness,' he sighed with genuine relief. 'Now I've only got my head to deal with.' He propped himself up on an elbow, a major feat in his condition.

'OK. Into the tub,' she ordered, jerking her thumb in the direction of the bathroom. 'You were no breath of spring last night.'

'Are there any foreign bodies in the tub? I'm not sure I could handle that.' He eased himself gingerly out of bed and pain surged to the top of his head as the spirit-level fluids of his body rushed to a new equilibrium. Like a nurse in a geriatric ward she helped him into the tub where he disappeared under the cumulus of suds, holding his nose; the craters marking his entry closed slowly over him leaving only his buckled knees in view like fence posts in a snow-drift. Resurfacing, he scooped soap from his eyes and face, impatiently flicking it away in dollops, and sat a little mesmerised, staring at the palisades of jars, deodorants and spray cans that lined the glass shelves. Linda sat on the edge of the tub scrubbing him with a wash cloth, fermenting a denser lather on his chest and shoulders until his entire body was rutted with streaks of foam and straight-slicked hair.

'How does that feel?' She looked down at him, her charge, with a grin.

'I'm still dying. But there's just a chance I'll make it.' He wasn't sure why he was being flip; the memory of his corny behavior haunted him still.

Splayed talons snatching, she shampooed his hair with a vigor that nearly took his scalp off and made unfathomable the softness of her breasts against his bent back. Penitently, he submitted to the ignominies of rinsing and blow-drying until her critical eye finally pronounced him cleansed, whole and shriven.

From these close ministrations that left him reeling and spacey, their love-making began, light-hearted at first but growing more earnest until they reached that moment of appraisal, almost like a farewell before senses strike out on their own with no apology for surrender. Linda stopped abruptly, her face showing conflict. 'I've got to get ... my diaphragm.' Her voice rued this sad practicality. He was about to release her but something snapped in his mind. He heard a voice; it was, amazingly, Sal's: For we are born in others' pain ... and perish in our own. A cruel loss rose up in him, bringing in its wake the blackness of a saint's despair and the threat of extinction. The fugue returned his own voice from a distance. 'No!' he cried out. 'I want ...' Desperate to cross a burnt-out wasteland, his movements had the fury of desolation, and the blindness '... a child.'

She clutched him, then tried to push away. 'We can't ...' She clung to him again, torn and helpless.

Realising the source of his insane urge, he pulled away and lay on his back suffused with shame. His heart rocked violently. The beast, revealed, was out stalking; there was no return. He stared at the ceiling, stricken, his breath coming in rasps.

'I'm sorry,' he said to the ceiling, the words sounding empty and inadequate.

She turned his face towards her until their eyes were on a level. 'You know I want to ... You know that.'

He nodded. 'Soon.' But not a clone, he thought grimly. Christ, what had happened to him?

'Yes. When everything is ... clearer. *Spero di sì.*' She held him tightly as if to make up for less than absolute conviction.

They went out for a late lunch to a nearby Italian restaurant. The Maitre knew Linda and of course her brother, Aldo, and was suitably deferential, guiding them to the best table and flicking imaginary dust off the upholstered chairs. After they were seated Bob noticed a flicker of concern in Linda's face, a tilt of the eyebrow that spoke volumes.

'Come on, what's the matter?' He put down the mural-sized menu and locked his fingers together, for as long as it would take.

'It's nothing.' She turned aside just enough to avoid his gaze, and nibbled absently at a cheese-stick.

'Tell me.' He reached across the table for her hand.

'There's so little I can do ...' she began hesitantly. 'I sometimes feel powerless, out of my depth.'

'That's crazy. You know how I rely on you.' He smiled, trying to reassure her. It was odd because he was the one who normally needed reassuring.

'There's more involved.' She faltered. 'It's Robbie. I can feel the strain you're under. It's killing you by inches.' No more than an hour earlier, in that forsaken moment, she had felt the hidden violence of his grief.

'Oh, I don't know,' he said lightly. 'Old salesmen never die. They only lose their wares. Or maybe their balls after all,' he added, remembering Sonny Winter's comment.

'Don't humor me,' she said sharply. 'What are you going to do about Robbie? I know you. You'll come apart at the seams unless you do something.' She wondered if she'd overstepped the mark. She didn't need reminding that Robbie was his son, that the problem concerned his family. But she couldn't hold back her feelings. Her practical wisdom told her that he would have to get Robbie back before he could make any commitments. He could not divide himself and she needed all of him. Loyalty was a double-edged sword.

'I guess you do know me,' he said quietly. 'To tell you the truth, Linda, I'm at the end of my rope. The problem is finding Robbie. London's a big place. We have no number, no address. Nothing to go on. It's a huge zero. I want to do something. I'm desperate to do something. Anything. But where do I start?' He looked past her, lost in thought, chewing the ends of his mustache.

'Maybe you don't have to find him. Maybe he could find you?'

'But he doesn't want to. That's the whole point.' He looked at her in surprise. For a moment he wondered if she really understood the situation.

'I remember when we were kids in Naples,' She scanned the menu in the candle glow which softened the emerald in her eyes, 'my brother, Aldo, ran away from home. He was sixteen or seventeen, no more. All we knew was that he was somewhere in Rome. Rome is also a big town.' She paused, looking steadily at him.

'Go on.' His chin rested in a cupped hand. 'We're not ready to order,' he said to the hovering waiter.

'Mamma was desperate. But she's a clever lady and nothing was going to stop her.'

'So what did she do?' He felt a tingling sensation in the pit of his stomach.

'She knew Aldo was crazy about his father. So she concocted his obituary and published it in a Rome newspaper. Aldo was back home in two days. But the consequences ...'

Bob's chair fell over as he jumped to his feet. He leant across the table and kissed her on the mouth.

'You're beautiful!' he said.

Chapter 10

'Mmmm, that's good coffee, Sal,' Father Molloy observed. His bony Adam's apple bobbled over his collar as he swallowed, like an egg about to fall off a shelf. His wan smile showed a discolored nerveless tooth. 'Still no news of Robbie?' Genuine concern showed in his gaunt face.

Sal shook her head. A thought had been fermenting for weeks so she decided to come to the point quickly. It was a question she could never have raised with Bob.

'Do you think it's ... a punishment?' The question seemed ridiculous and trite but she had to ask it. She had written articles on the concept of a loving God but had never in her heart of hearts quite convinced herself. Beneath her question lay a plenum of guilt that she had never adequately dealt with or discussed with anyone else except Father Molloy, and then only in the confessional.

Sal had been fifteen when her mother died after a lingering illness. After the funeral her father drank even more heavily than usual. One evening he came to her room, demented, literally out of his mind from grief and alcohol. He told her how like her mother she was, his beautiful Sally. The rest was unreal, beyond the pale of sensibility. Her mind voided the horror; she had blocked all feeling and could not, if her life depended on it, recreate the terror of that night or of the subsequent abortion which the doctor insisted was a clinical necessity. Maybe she had been catatonic and felt nothing; she would never know for sure. Her father avoided her for the remaining six years of his life, most of which time, including vacations, she spent on campus.

Having expunged all memories, a capacity she still had to some degree, the brute facts remained but could not be fully comprehended without tears. Thus she could never truly assess the extent of her own accountability. Or innocence.

'Punishment, Sal?' Father Molloy leant back in his chair. He wanted to be kind, to put a constructive gloss on it. 'Your sin, insofar as we understand it, has been absolved through the Sacrament of Reconciliation. Nevertheless there does seem to be a certain ... irony about Robbie's disappearance.' His words were as delicate as his own moral sensibility.

'A life for a life,' Sal breathed, expecting the worst verdict.

'I wouldn't put it like that,' he rebuked her gently. 'But there may well be a lesson; something may grow from it. Mysterious ways, you know? One thing you can be sure of,' he interlaced his fingers under his chin, 'is that the event is not without point.' He meant well, but he fed her guilt. In a way she needed that. He kept her at a level of acceptance, helping her maintain her outward composure by absorbing and metabolising blame. His very kindness punished her; his presence was a constant reminder, a drip feed of regret. Guilt and personal accountability were the corrals in which he unwittingly kept his flock. He could no more change his moral stance, the product of long training and intense prayer, than he could break his own vows. He was a Godfearing man in the most traditional sense of the term.

'Bob thinks I'm crazy even to think along these lines.' It was a question rather than a statement.

'He hasn't got the benefit of faith or of grace.' The priest was nothing if not fair. He looked at her kindly. 'And you haven't really confided in him ... about your difficulties in dealing with your past. He is your husband, you know.'

'But not for long.' She refilled his cup and passed the cream to him.

'Ah, no. That's too bad.' The priest had often in the past waited for her to confide in him about her marriage but she rarely did. He didn't press her. Both of them were in a sense more concerned with big principles, the God picture, than with the specifics of an individual case. He sipped his coffee reflectively.

'You wrote,' Sal pressed, 'in one of your recent articles about the nature of divine benevolence. I got the impression that you were very close to the charismatic view.' She was still chasing the specter of blanket forgiveness.

'Reasonably close,' Father Molloy agreed. 'But the charismatics don't have it quite right. It's not a question of automatic forgiveness. We don't have carte blanche. Getting blissed out on Christ, as the kids put it, is dangerously close to the cultic notion of self-deification. The process of forgiveness cannot be assumed to be painless. On the other hand a fatalistic approach to bearing one's cross through life, without hope of reprieve, is not quite correct either, but it is closer to revealed truth. Faith is stronger on the cross.' He frowned into his coffee cup then looked at her, his friend and colleague, more than a friend if the truth be told, wishing there was more he could do or say. He sometimes had the impression that she was too scrupulous for her own good and he was no stranger to that sinister form of perfectionism. He too had suffered from scruples; in the seminary thirty-odd years ago they had gnawed at him, making him feel unworthy to forgive sin and perform the Eucharist, almost costing him his vocation. He had prayed fiercely over that and he would pray for Sal.

The door flew open as Bob came rushing in. 'Hi, Father,' he greeted breezily, throwing his copy of the *Post* on the hall table. 'Enough talk about acceptance and resignation. We're moving on something.'

Sal protested when Father Molloy said he would take his leave, but he insisted.

'It's better that I leave you two alone,' he whispered to her as if they were young lovers no longer requiring the services of a chaperone.

'You almost forced him out of the house,' she said coldly to Bob after the priest had left.

'He could have stayed. Sorry anyway. The point is I've got this great idea. Just listen to this.' He fanned her with his hands, preparing her for a revelation. 'What we do is this. We put an ad in the London *Times* saying Robbie has big money coming, an inheritance, say. The cult may send him over to collect. What do you think?' He flung his jacket over a chair. 'It's worth a try, huh?' He stood in front of her, breathing rapidly.

'I doubt if those people read newspapers.' She wasn't too disparaging, however. Anything was worth a try. It was one of his better ideas in fact.

'Are you kidding? Those gurus play the stock market. Maybe we should put an ad in the *Financial Times* too.' He nodded his head, trying by postural echo to get her assent. She thought for a while as she put Father Molloy's untouched chocolate crumb cookies back in the jar.

'All right. Let's do it. There's nothing to lose, I suppose.'

They sat down at the dining table together and she started to draft the notice.

'We've got to make it plausible,' she said. 'Who's died?'

'What?'

'Who left the inheritance?' She idly bounced the pencil on its eraser tip then twirled it between her slender fingers.

'Your Uncle Dave. He's got a bundle.' He leant his elbows on the table watching her in the throes of composition.

'Good choice,' she agreed. 'He's Robbie's godfather too. Still. Poor Uncle Dave. He won't like the news of his own demise.'

'He won't know,' Bob said. They laughed for the first time in months. Her strong teeth showed through lips that were defined by a delicate seam. The smile had the effect of heavy drapes being flung open on a good morning. She read the draft aloud for his benefit.

'That's good,' he said. 'That gets it exactly. I like the bit about getting all the beneficiaries together. They're bound to send him over for that.'

'Maybe. If they read it. And if they swallow it.' She had a vision of casting a baited hook across the Atlantic. It seemed impossible. But still ...

Ma Bell transmitted the ad and Amex paid for it. The whole exercise was completed in just over an hour. Their spirits rose on the wing of a possibility. And they had done something. Together.

Chapter 11

There was a run on rope-soled sandals from Taiwan. Bob was doing fairly well in his new job in Tyson's Corner but his earnings were well down compared to his last job. It took eighty pairs of shoes to give him the same commission as a single MDDW, even without bumping rights. That was a lot of shoes.

The shopping mall was almost like a space laboratory, completely self-contained and on three different levels with long wide passageways flanked by glossy store fronts. Here and there were lay-bys furnished with easy chairs and massive tropical plants thriving in the pasteurised air that came purring out of hidden ducts and sometimes took a child's helium-filled balloon, emblazoned with 'I love Virginia', and sent it floating upwards to lodge in the geometric cross-hatches of the ceiling, or further up into the hidden labyrinth of plant and generators that quietly and relentlessly did nothing less than neutralise the seasons.

At every corner of these indoor streets was a computerised direction finder. If you keyed in 'footwear' the screen rapidly produced a menu of shoe stores. If you then chose 'The Stride Rite Bootery' you got a map with arrows leading to that emporium. The mall was patrolled by security men dressed in black environment suits lacking only laser guns. It was the front edge of consumerism, designed to make the extraction of plastic money comfortable if not pleasurable.

The worst part of Bob's job had, not surprisingly, to do with feet. This summer almost every male customer under thirty came in sockless in sneakers and Bob had to provide them with socks before they could have a fitting. Feet were extraordinary in their mutations. Some had calloused skeletal toes with serried ridge-like bones running up the instep; others were gross featureless nerf balls of proud flesh. He spent much of his time kneeling before feet, shoe horn in hand, tending those ridiculous organs. He began to understand the humbling biblical rite of washing feet. But he didn't really care; it could have been worse. Proctology.

Sal had consulted the London *Times* in the local library which got the British papers one day in arrears, and satisfied herself that the notice had been carried, as agreed, for three days. She wasn't very hopeful; there was still that maundering listlessness of waiting, though at least now there was something to wait for. After a week passed, however, she gave up hope.

Close to mid-summer the heat grew intense. Bob took it better than Sal who cowered indoors, aestivating, not stirring from the house until that fierce monstrance of sun fell from grace each day. Then she would scurry in her breezy linen smock and open-toed sandals into her air-conditioned car to deliver scripts to the presbytery or pick up some instant comestibles for the microwave.

Just by walking four times daily through the acres of shimmering cars outside the mall, across the boiling asphalt, Bob developed a deep tan. But the combined effect of humidity and poor appetite had shrunk and hardened him to the consistency of adobe. Indeed he had taken on a lean, smoked Mexican look that Linda found attractive, though she was not blind to the gauntness that lay behind the leathery exterior. Bob went about his job like a man in a dream. The controlled environment of the indoor city seemed to confirm the unreality.

From one of his colleagues he heard of an upcoming TV program on New Age cults which was being made by a local station. He called the station and volunteered himself. The producer said he would get back to him but instead he called Sal and invited her to take part. Taken by surprise, she asked how they had gotten her name and number.

'You husband called us,' the producer said. 'He heard we were dealing with this theme. But actually we want to do it from the mothers' viewpoint, the affective side, as it were. Fathers would be off concept.'

Blood on the carpet, that's what they want, she thought. She had seen some of these 'At The Scene' programs before. The whole series was an electronic tabloid that fed on public displays of emotion; more phoney than docudrama, it had earned the tag, 'realsoap', justifiably in her view. Did Bob not know this? She declined with as much grace as she could muster. The producer gave her a chance to re-consider then said, 'OK, not to worry,' he would go elsewhere to make up the panel. She went back to her work shuddering.

'You turned them down?' Bob said later. 'Why? We could get something out of it.'

'Damn it, Bob, it's not an appeal to release hostages. They just want a bunch of women to sob into the camera. It's confessional TV ...'

'So what? It would still be an opportunity to warn other people. Maybe get ideas from other parents in the same boat. The publicity could lead to some decent legislation. Who knows?' They'd got Moon for tax fraud, after all. He still had a hankering to believe in the system, open democracy, voices raised in public. Maybe they could in some way discredit Paajit over the air waves.

'You're clutching at straws.' How could he be so benighted when he prided himself on his own savvy?

'Sure I am.' He stood with his head bent forward, looking at the bottom of the wall, at the crack between the floor and skirting board. This was his shape these days and that was as high as his vision could go.

'Don't do this,' she said. Her eyes warned him off. 'It's a private matter.' She was going to say 'family matter', but that would have missed by a mile. The thought of Bob unburdening himself on screen, in every living room across the state, appalled her. She sat under the lamp with her knees together, the legs tapering down at an elegant angle to the Indian rug, an open book in her lap, the pages idly rising in their curves. A membrane of anxiety lay over her face and her eyes seemed filmed with glycerine.

'I'm sorry,' he said. 'But I'm going to call them back.' He felt sure he was right. He had some sense of the premium she put on privacy but that would have to be sacrificed. The stakes were too high.

'They won't want you anyway. It's the maternal angle they're playing up.' Her voice was disparaging for the most part but carried a note of entreaty too.

The producer confirmed what she'd said, but Bob's selling instinct hadn't completely deserted him.

'What about Iran? The Chaikha Rani are tied in with those space cadets, maybe with the Black Muslims in this country too. That should help your ratings.'

'Well, that's all a bit speculative,' the producer said. 'Besides, it's not a political show. We're more into personal reactions, the whole experiential bit ...'

'Listen, you want emotion? I'll give you emotion. Do you know what it's like to lose a kid to those mind-fuckers? What it's like to wander around from week to week like a fucking zombie not knowing where your boy is or what those creeps are doing to his head?' It had started as a ploy but now his voice shook and he couldn't stop. It came pouring out of him, all of it, and for the first time. To the disembodied voice of a total stranger.

'I'm sorry, but ...' the producer tried to cut in.

'Don't be sorry. Do something about it, for Christ's sake. You media guys make me sick. Always on about free speech and integrity and all the rest of it. But when it comes to the point you're just as crooked and conniving as all the other cons and four-flushers. It's just the bottom line. That and nothing else. Don't talk about themes and all that shit. You're just selling a line like every other goddamn door-to-door salesman in the country. Except they're more honest about it. I have a right to be on that program. Do you hear that? A right. You don't own the fucking air waves ...'

It worked finally. Coming unhinged, live, clearly had potential.

'My God,' Sal said looking grey in the face. 'I can't believe I heard that.'

'You heard it.' He was as grim as death.

'Sometimes you disgust me.' A lacquered hatred like a sheet of glass separated them.

'Too bad.' He unclenched his fists. He didn't need her blessing this time. 'Just as well you won't have to put up with me much longer.' He walked out.

Two days later Bob found himself being led by a floor manager through a studio as big and bleak as an airplane hangar with criss-crossed steel struts dangling spotlights from the ceiling, miles of cable snaking across the composite floor, headphoned technicians like a scrambled ground crew setting up their positions, cameras nosing hydraulically towards their marks. All these metallic actions, and the huge hollowness that was like an empty astrodome, made him waver. But he took his position with the panel on carpet-covered bleachers as if they were posing for a team photo, and smiled nervously at the other players, all women. The studio audience, maybe a couple of hundred, drifted in sheepishly, not even trying to give the impression that they had something better to do, and sidled into rows of seats opposite.

The host, Danny Matheson, more human than he seemed on screen despite the heavy make-up, warmed them up and indicated the kind of questions he would put. It was a team talk of sorts and he was a glossy coach, telling them to ignore the cameras and all that other technical junk which meant nothing to him either, to be themselves as if they were in their own living rooms having a fireside chat.

During a break in the warm-up Bob took his opportunity, 'Mr Matheson, I thought you'd have some people here from the cults. Representatives.'

'We did invite some of them,' he answered, 'but they declined.' He turned to the producer who'd come down from his lofty booth with a batch of suggestions. The producer gave a quick knowing look in Bob's direction as if to say: You talked you way in here, now we expect you to deliver. When he left, Bob took his next shot. He had to squeeze everything out of this.

'Excuse me, Mr Matheson. Did you manage to contact anyone from the Chaikha Rani?'

'I've absolutely no idea.' He turned to the panelists in the lower rows. 'Remember now, honesty is the only game in town. Don't be afraid of your feelings.' He looked at the studio clock. 'Four minutes to action. Then we kick the tires and light the fires ...'

'Mr Matheson?'

'What is it now?'

'Could you please ask one of your assistants about the Chaikha Rani? It's very important.'

Danny Matheson turned in exasperation to a willowy girl who had been standing between him and one of the arc lamps. 'No,' she said. 'We couldn't locate that particular group.'

Prompted through his headphones, the stage manager asked the panel to close up on the bleachers. Danny Matheson had a hurried word with the number one cameraman and had a quick run through his cue cards. Then he stood in front of the tiered panel, holding a clipboard in one hand while smoothing down the front of his jacket with the other. 'It's only a twenty-minute slot,' he reminded them again. 'So stick to the point and don't pull any punches. Get right into it.'

When the cameras turned he came alive. He gave his homely, concerned intro to three different cameras, turning smoothly on cue from one to the other, following the teleprompter. He spoke of the New Age cults, of the anguish of loss, the ecstasy of recovery. Then he turned to the panel like a lion-tamer wheedling his perched pets, giving a touch of the goad here, a sugar lump there. From time to time he went among the studio audience to take a question and turn sharply with it in the hectoring manner of his idol, Phil Donohue, to challenge his panel into a response. And they were ready enough to respond, to him, to the audience and most of all to the camera they were supposed to ignore. Whatever was the inspiration of that nosey lens – as it snuffled out truffles of the heart – several panelists became heated and some broke down.

From the overhead monitors Bob could see how the camera lingered over the tears and Matheson's words of comfort. He became uneasy because he sensed the message was being lost and because Sal would be proved right. Again. He also felt that his own few words, fairly calmly spoken, might as they say, end up on the cutting room floor.

The time sped by in a fever. When he saw the floor manager give the one-minute signal he fought for an innings. '... Warn the kids not to fall for this communications jazz. It's a con ...'

Matheson interrupted him but Bob went on doggedly, 'They make phoney promises. It's a slave trade ...' But he had more to say. The important bit that had brought him here. He had planned to leave it to the end but the end was coming up fast and Matheson had switched away from him again. Despite the blinding arc lamps Bob could see the wind-up signal. Desperate now and sweating through his shirt, he raised his arm. It was a matter of seconds. He had to make his pitch that he had rehearsed over the last two days. It came loudly, uncontrolled, 'If anyone knows how to contact the Chaikha Rani here or in London please call this station.' He didn't know if he had shouted or not, but at least it was in the can.

Matheson signed off. The floor manager drew his hand across his throat. It was done, a wrap. The camera lights went out and for a while there was a feeling of deadness as if all the nursery toys that had come magically to life at night had, at dawn, been found waxen and still. In a trance the crowds melted away. The panel was shepherded to the hospitality room for one drink, courtesy of the station. The numbness passed, indeed was transformed into that fevered state of excitement that follows an ordeal or a harvest barely gathered in before the rains. Bob mingled with his thawing-out co-stars.

'Has your boy been gone long?' an elderly woman asked him. She had a frank round face which could, if humor came, resolve itself into dimples.

'Over three months,' he said. Jesus, that long?

'What have you tried?' She touched her glass to his and sipped her drink which looked like a pink gin.

'We put an ad in the paper ...'

'Money coming? It's been done before. Mind you, it's better than the alternatives. If it works, that is.'

'What alternatives?' He looked keenly at her. This woman had the kind of quiet confidence that came from knowledge, and a practicality that suggested she would chop wood for fuel in an oil crisis.

'Oh, heavies.' She said it with an impish smile. He was right about the dimples; her face puckered rather than creased. 'I've heard of people using gangs, the Mafia, even mercenaries. To get their kids back.' She picked some lint off her green stretch cardigan and pill-rolled it from her fingers. 'We didn't have to go quite that far. My oldest two are line-backers with GWU ...'

'The Mafia?' he repeated. He'd heard it from a little woman, probably a grandmother.

'Oh yes. When the authorities won't help what else is there?' It was a rhetorical question. She was no Ma Baker but she had that pioneering self-sufficiency that put fire in the belly and bread on the table. She made him feel guilty about his own inaction.

'My problem is that I don't know where they've hidden him,' he said almost defensively.

'Ah, yes. Sorry I can't help you there. But if you do get him back you'll need a deprogrammer.'

'I've heard something about that ...'

'There's a good one in the DC area, Calvin Stritch. Unorthodox but he gets results. We've used him. He's in the book.' She drained her glass, touched his arm when she was leaving and wished him well.

He filed it all away. He'd got something out of the deal – information was power. Maybe. And she'd put skids under him, strengthened his resolve. But to do what? Mercenaries, heavies, the Mafia ... was it real? Shipping out of Vietnam in the mid-seventies, he thought he was returning to peacetime ...

When the program was aired he watched it with Sal, though she feigned disinterest. The slot had been cut to ten minutes, sandwiched between commercials for roach motels and Orkin men – it was the season when pests and creepy-crawlies broke through the concrete skin of the Washington swamp. The editing had been severe with a definite bias towards the lachrymose. His plea for information at the end had been cut.

'Bastards,' he grated. 'Don't say I told you so.' He gave her a blighted look, disparaging a response.

'What did you really hope to achieve?' She was slightly relieved that he'd got such little exposure. But still, anyone looking in could hardly have missed him and it was close enough to prime time.

'Just call it a shot in the dark,' he said with little grace.

'Oh.' She switched off the TV by remote control; there was the usual crack of the power being cut, followed by a hiss as the screen went blank.

'What's that supposed to mean?'

'Seeing you there in full view ...'

'Ah, the neighbors again. What does it matter if the whole world knows? It's not our fault that Robbie was conned. It doesn't reflect badly on him or on us. Anyone could be taken in by them. Anyone.' He paused for breath. Even her silence could get him going.

'You don't understand.' She knew it hadn't cost him a thought to bleat out his woes before the world, those peppered banalities that drove her to distraction. But was it just that he was thick-skinned?

'No, I don't have your sensibilities, etc. etc. But I know this much. You can't take it because of guilt and that's your issue.' He paused to let an intuition develop through the sullen intelligence that lay on the air. 'Where the guilt comes from I don't know. How could I? You've never confided in me. Not really.'

She blanched and deftly moved ground. 'TV trivialises everything. It's all so cosmetic now.' It was true that she sighed for older values, substantive discussion of issues, real wood in furniture. Even the smell of new car upholstery was sprayed on nowadays. She sometimes felt that she was born too late, into the wrong age, although she couldn't quite rule out the possibility that the anachronism was somehow rooted in herself. She shrugged. 'What can you expect with a movie star in the White House?'

Easily deflected, Bob went for the decoy. 'At least Reagan made it in the film industry. He was good at his job, a success. Maybe you'd prefer a peanut farmer ...'

Unknown to them and beyond their wildest hopes, the insertion in the London *Times* had, like some invisible interplanetary probe, done its work. The cable that came two days later said,

'Will visit on 14th. next. TWA flight 403 arriving Dulles 15.30. Robbie.'

Bob sat down until the congestion of adrenalin resumed a steadier flow. He re-read the message several times until he finally believed it.

'Thank God,' Sal breathed, fighting back tears of relief that welled up behind her eyes. 'Thank God.' She looked from the cable to the calendar near her message pad on the kitchen wall. 'That's only three days from now.'

Bob jumped up. 'I've got to contact the deprogrammer immediately. What's his name? Calvin Stritch ... I hope to God he's free ... And go to the bank.' He tapped his pockets for car keys and wallet. 'There's so much to do.' He began to laugh, relishing the action and even the panic. 'At last,' he shouted. 'At last.' It was strange how different a racing heart could feel.

'Take it easy.' She helped him on with his jacket.

'Thanks.' He looked at her gratefully. 'Call the shoe store,' he threw back as he flung open the screen door. 'Tell 'em anything.' A mile down Old Kirby Road he had to pull over and collect himself before venturing on to the more hazardous Parkway.

Chapter 12

They stood on the observation deck at Dulles watching the 747 circle and make its approach. The landing gear was down, the lights on; it was only a matter of time before the floating shrine entered its glide path. Bob's mind was blank except for one thought that repeated itself in different ways: Robbie's on board ... he's coming home ... in ten minutes we'll meet ... the plane has only got to touch down. Nothing could go wrong now. All the energy in the world was committed to that moment of landing.

Sal was breathing quickly. Her hands fluttered at her throat, freeing her neck from the collar of her blouse. As the plane landed a puff of silent smoke came from the wheels. A spirit descending.

'He'll ... be changed,' she said under her breath to brace herself.

'I know,' Bob answered vacantly. That didn't matter much to him; the important thing was getting Robbie back.

The mobile lounges drove out to the aircraft and surrounded it like offspring at the belly of a giant mammal. Five minutes later, filled with passengers, they started the return journey. Bob and Sal rushed back to the arrivals lounge and took up a position at the front of the crowd which waited behind the customs area.

They saw him before he saw them. He was in a brown robe and his head was shaved. His eyes, hooded like Sal's, were expressionless in their deep sockets.

'My God,' Sal cried. Her hand flew to her mouth.

'Don't. Pretend to notice ... nothing.' His voice was tight, constricted by the effort of control. The shaved head was too real a symbol of what they'd done to him. Worse, he noticed a small triangular mark on the forehead that wasn't painted on but etched into the skin – a brand, dear Christ! That was the final obscenity. They watched the customs man go through his canvas duffel bag item by item and finally clear him through with a dismissive jerk of his head.

'Over here, Robbie,' Bob called. 'Here we are.'

Sal rushed to embrace him but he stepped back clutching the duffel bag. Her hands fell limply to her sides. Another brown-robed figure came into view.

'You must be Robbie's parents ...'

'Who are ... you?' Bob asked in a choking voice.

'I am Paajit, his temple leader.' He took Robbie's hand in a proprietorial way. Robbie smiled into the face of the slightly older man whose olive skin was pock-marked like pumice and whose eyes were black and piercing. His indigo, shaven head was pointed like a torpedo.

'We ... we expected Robbie to come alone.' Bob fought for composure, oblivious of the stares of onlookers. 'It's a family matter ...' His mind was reaching frantically for a new plan.

'We never journey alone.' Paajit smiled, looking protectively at Robbie. 'Company shortens the road.' He took Robbie's hand again.

Bob never knew what bad vibes meant until that moment. But what passed from this man to him carried the stench of gangrene. It was one of the few times in his life he felt afraid; a pure distillate of funk spread through him. In that second he learnt something that in two years' active service in Vietnam he had never fathomed, that killing could be justified. It took everything he had to keep the plan on course. 'We've a cab waiting,' he said. The deprogrammer, Calvin, was behind the wheel posing as a cab driver. Maybe he would know what to do.

When they sat into the car he caught Calvin's eye in the rear-view mirror.

'Where to?' Calvin asked neutrally.

'Eighteenth and H, North West,' Bob said. It was the address of the Gattopardo. Maybe they could off-load Paajit there. Art would help.

'Sure thing,' Calvin said without a flicker, going along with the change of plan. Two minutes into the drive a road sign gave them away.

'Don't you live in Virginia?' Paajit asked warily. Robbie nodded slowly. Paajit demanded the driver's ID which was not on display on the dash-board.

'Purple aura! Robbie, it's a trap. I warned you about this ...'

Calvin braked hard and slewed the cab off the road. With Bob's help he dragged Paajit from the car.

'Robbie, if you break faith you will die!' Paajit called out. 'You are one of us. They will return you to Lakhryon, the outer world ...'

'Shut your fucking mouth.' Bob hit him with a left hook, knocking him to the ground. He took his bag from the back seat and threw it at him.

'One down, one to go,' Calvin said grimly as he gunned the car away from the scene, skidding on the loose gravel of the hard shoulder.

'It's OK, Sal,' Bob said, trying to calm her; she seemed to be in shock.

'We're in the clear now.' They took the next exit and headed for Virginia.

Robbie was as pale as death and rigid with fear. He started to chant, 'Paajit, Chaikha Rani, Swaminathan Rani, Rani ...'

'Cut it out!' Bob shouted. Maybe he was in shock too. 'Robbie, please don't. It's over. All that's over and done with.' He tried to put his hand on Robbie's shoulder and noticed that the knuckles were bleeding.

'Rani, Rani, Chandavakaar muthuswami ...' Robbie wrung his bony hands and rocked from side to side. 'The Mutawa will help. They guard the Sharia. Paajit will not desert me. It is written. Swaminathan Rani, Chaikha Sedanthur Chaikha Rani ...'

Bob couldn't stand it. He looked to Sal who seemed to come out of her trance.

'Robbie. It's us. Your family ... It's all right, you're home.' She tried to take his hand, sick at the thought of how Paajit had held it.

'No! Satan. Lakhryon ... Paajit warned me ... Rani, Chaikha Rani, Thakur Rani ...'

Calvin pulled over, let Bob take the wheel and sat in back with Robbie.

'We're going to help you,' he said. 'Help you get your mind straight. You've been brainwashed. You must snap back ...'

'No. Kill me ... must prepare for death ... Bahram Rani, Nihad Chaikha Rani ...'

'Shut up.' Calvin spoke sharply. 'Your head's full of garbage. Your mind's been raped ...'

'Jesus, have mercy.' Sal said under her breath, her heart still lurching violently.

'Lakhryon, Prince of Darkness!' Robbie shrieked and smashed his fist against the window. Calvin struck him across the face with the back of his hand.

'No!' Sal cried. 'Don't hit him.' Was it just a few months since that barbecue on an ordinary day in an ordinary yard when she wanted Robbie – God grant forgiveness – to be different?

'I know what I'm doing. Have to scare him straight ...'

Bob put the accelerator to the floor. There was a squad car following.

'Move it. Go!' Calvin ordered. The cab lurched into top gear.

'They couldn't ...' Sal interjected fearfully.

'They could.' Calvin said. 'Goddamn law. It's kidnapping.' Knowledge of the ghetto was in his black eyes.

Bob drove like a maniac, weaving between lanes, his mind divided between the road ahead and the siren-wailing squad car that took up the chase.

Robbie looked out the back windscreen, 'Paajit, I knew you would ... come for me.'

'It's no good,' Sal cried. 'They're gaining on us.'

Bob sped past a line of traffic, two wheels on the median, then he cut over to the hard shoulder to pass a truck. 'Come on, you bastard,' he spoke dementedly to the lumbering cab. 'If I can make the Beltway I can lose them.'

But it was useless. The squad car closed the distance and edged him off the road. Bob slowed down and then instinctively made to swerve out again.

'No.' Calvin shouted. 'It's no good. Pull over.' The police car came to a stop in front, trapping him on the hard shoulder. The cop approached the cab, 'What the hell do you think you're doing?'

'We're rescuing our son.' Bob fought to control his voice.

Paajit rushed up. 'They've kidnapped one of our priests ...'

'He's lying.' Sal interjected. Calvin started to say something. The officer silenced them.

'Keep it down,' he ordered, weary from crazy excuses and from trying to make sense of chaos. He painstakingly examined IDs and drivers' licenses. His movements were agonisingly slow and deliberate, the law taking its ponderous course. Robbie stared at Paajit, incredible wistful hope and fear in his face.

Finally the officer asked if Robbie wanted to go with his parents.

'No.' Robbie cried. 'I belong to Rani ... Paajit.'

'We're his parents, for Christ's sake.' Bob's voice was desperate, pleading for reason to prevail.

'You also assaulted this man.' The officer nodded towards Paajit.

'He brainwashed our son,' Bob said. 'Don't you understand? Don't you see ...?' He jumped out of the cab gesticulating wildly.

'Come on, man,' Calvin urged. 'Give us a break.' The officer, who was also black, asked Calvin what his involvement was. Calvin answered him truthfully.

'A deprogrammer, huh? Yeah, the name rings a bell. The fact remains, you're taking this kid against his will ...'

Sal couldn't stand it any longer, 'You don't understand,' she sobbed. 'He's my child ... my child ...' she broke down, her face contorted in anguish.

'Officer,' Calvin said evenly, 'we're trying to free this boy, not kidnap him. Come on, man.' He spread his hands almost in supplication.

The cop rubbed his chin, 'You stay right here.' He pointed a gloved finger at them and went to confer with his partner in the squad car. Bob fought back a powerful urge to make a break for it.

The officer returned at length and spoke to Calvin, 'My partner's heard of you. I guess you helped a friend of his ... I really should take you all down town for a statement ...'

'You've got all our addresses,' Calvin put in quickly.

'You just be on call anytime.' He turned to Bob, 'If you ever drive like that again you're going to go down for a long time. Now get outta here. This hasn't happened. None of it. Understand?'

As they drove away Robbie scratched and clawed at the rear window, watching Paajit being bundled back into the squad car. 'I'll come for you.' Paajit called out. Then he disappeared from sight.

'That was closer than you think,' Calvin said.

'I know,' Bob's voice shook. He turned to Robbie who had passed out.

'Let him sleep,' Calvin advised. 'He's been deprived of food and sleep. When we get to the house we should put him straight to bed. When he comes round, make his favourite food.'

'Lamb cutlets,' Sal said vacantly, touching the shaved head of her son whose sanity returned only in sleep.

Chapter 13

They put him to bed in his old room. He was still out cold.

'You might as well get some sleep too,' Calvin suggested. 'He'll be out for a while.'

'No, we'd like to sit with him,' Sal said quietly.

'OK, well call me when he comes to. It'll probably be around dawn.' Calvin went to the guest room where he had already stowed his gear.

Bob sat on one side of the bed, Sal on the other. They couldn't talk for fear of waking him. It was a sad tableau which, during the deep silence of the night, could not but remind them of how, through no fault of his own, he had come between them, for they had responded so differently about how he should be raised, educated, formed in faith. Now he still lay between them and they were enjoined to silence.

Sal sat with her arms folded, frustrated at not being able to tend to him in some way. She was aghast at his appearance, the hollow cheeks, shaved head and wasted body which made him look uncannily like her own father during his last six months. But that had been the result of fifty self-indulgent years ...

She trembled at the thought of what Professor Simpson of Georgetown University had told her some months earlier when she went on her own to consult him. He had held nothing back. He spoke of techniques beyond brainwashing, the kind that led parents to murder their infants at Jim Jones's command in Guyana. Much of it she didn't understand but she knew there could be a total loss of mind, complete dysfunction, like physical impairment. Victims were known to identify solely with the cult, unable to comprehend anything outside the belief set, because they had no critical faculty left.

The causes were less clear. But there was some consensus that intense experiences by sensitive people, like Robbie, could sever long-standing synaptic connections in the brain. Professor Simpson had described the brain as a living product of information; without the life blood of information it could be totally disrupted.

Sal's optimism was guarded. In a way she envied Bob his hope, but she could not escape from her own fatalism.

Bob's reflections were rather different. He didn't fully understand the damage that might have been done to Robbie and was simply excited at having him back home. There would be a chance to make good his own past mistakes. That was all he wanted; a chance for Robbie to become himself again, this time with the support of his family.

Bob himself had had no youth. His folks, especially his old man, had equated innocence with ignorance and set about making him worldly wise. Bob desperately wanted Robbie to regain his innocence. It was something that had never occurred to him before. He had a strong image of Robbie as a child – before he developed his jaunty walk – with a shiny face and shy smile, his direct eager manner, taking everything on trust without any reason not to hope.

His thoughts went further back in time, to when Robbie was born. He had watched the tiny wrinkled form through the glass of the incubator, fighting for his life. He couldn't believe it. His son. An infant invaded his heart saying: Here I am if you want me ... When they brought Robbie home he would stare into the basinet for hours at a time in disbelief, his feelings then and later beyond words; the salesman dumbfounded when price and value are suddenly measureless. In a way he had been scared by the depth of his feelings, of straying beyond the conventional parameters of love that had been laid down for him when he was a kid.

A sliver of dawn light came through the drapes and Robbie stirred as Calvin had predicted. Calvin had insisted on being alone with him for at least the first few days. His techniques were rough and experience had taught him that the presence of emotional parents was destabilising. Bob and Sal reluctantly left the room as Robbie woke up.

'... The golden age of Esalen ... the Aquarian dream ...' Robbie murmured before he was fully awake. Then he became frightened, 'Sleep spirits ... will devour me.' He cowered away from Calvin, clutching the headboard. 'Water ... Must have water ...'

'Not on your life,' Calvin said. 'They used water to keep you awake, didn't they?' He had to show him he knew the score to establish credibility. But the Chaikha Rani was a new cult and Calvin, whose own experience had been with the Moonies, knew that he would have to improvise.

Robbie shrank further away like a beaten dog, his eyes wide and staring.

'Sleep spirits destroy ... inner force ...'

'Bullshit.' Calvin held his arm. 'They've screwed you up good, kid. But you don't con me. I've been there. Don't surrender to that mind fuck. Fight it. Fight!'

Robbie tried to pull his arm away, 'I obey … therefore I am … No power outside the temple …'

'Sure you have. Why don't you leave your body and go to Paajit? Go to that sick bastard if you can.'

Robbie tried to get up but Calvin restrained him and he fell back weakly, feigning sleep: *Rani Davarkaar, Subhar Rani … Lakhryon approaches. He is near at hand. I have surrendered to you, Rani.*

Bob entered the room timidly with a tray of food. He whispered apologetically, 'We didn't have time to get lamb cutlets. Is he asleep again?'

'I don't think so,' Calvin said. Bob left the tray on the bedside table and withdrew quietly, closing the door after him.

'OK, Robbie. Chow time. Come on. You're not fooling me.' Calvin held a plate of ground beef under his nose. Robbie sat bolt upright, turning his head aside.

'No food … until …'

'Until when?' Calvin probed. 'Until after the ceremony? Is that it?'

Robbie nodded slightly. Something was coming back, a faint glint of recognition.

'You mean until Paajit's counted the money, the day's take?'

'Offerings,' Robbie said weakly. 'Must be sacrificed …'

'The food must be sacrificed? I get it.' Calvin caught on quickly. 'They probably told you that unsacrificed food is touched by the serpent. It's a con. Don't you see it? They starved you to make you receptive. Come on, eat.' He offered the plate again. Robbie looked at the meat and began to gag.

'You think it's cannibalism? You might be chewing on some poor bastard who came back as a bull calf? No such luck. This is half soya bean. But it's good. Good Karma.' Calvin was still probing; it was difficult to piece together the elements of the cult's belief system.

Robbie had gone into a trance again, this time with his eyes wide open: *Satguru Paajit, Avatar of Rani … I wait for you to come … You said I could be perfected too, become one of the Christs. Don't abandon me …*

'Maya … Withoutness,' he moaned aloud.

'Alienation from God, from Rani?' Calvin seized on this. He had to break through the exclusivity of the beliefs; if he could prove that he, too, had been there and back then he might have a chance to explode those insane fantasies. 'It's the other way around, kid. Here you're at home. This is where God reigns, not in the cult. I know there are wonderful kids in your temple. I know they love you. But that's how the leaders put the fix in. They use love to trap you …'

Robbie didn't seem to be listening: *Rani, Azarnihad. Withoutness is death. Prey of Lakhryon. Lord Rani take me. Save me from this black Adversary, Visuki, Lord of snakes, Consort of Eve …*

Calvin knew he was praying or chanting. He had to stop it because it was a form of self-indoctrination. He ate some of the meat, chewing noisily.

'It's good. Mmmmm, very good.'

Robbie's eyes grew wide, horror-stricken, 'Stop!' He made a feeble effort to grab the plate. When he failed he opened his mouth and curled his tongue back towards the uvula. Calvin caught the significance immediately, 'That doesn't purify you. It's not divine nectar. It's post-nasal drip. You can't taste Rani. Why? Because he doesn't exist. Everything they've told you is garbage. When they wipe out your past they have to put something else in your head. So they make up all this stuff about Rani, reincarnation, enlightenment and of course, what's-his-face Lakhryon. Oh yes, you definitely need him to scare you straight, to keep your mind right. But it's all junk, Robbie. Believe me. I've been there.'

He ate some more of the ground beef and Robbie feigned sleep again.

'No, you don't,' Calvin said. 'I know you're listening. God made animals to give us food, you damn fool. Think, man. Think. Don't fear your past. It's real.' He had to get him to start thinking again, to destroy the idea that reason was deception and that cosmic awareness was the only realm of God. This notion was shared by all the known cults and Calvin felt sure that the Chaikha Rani was no different.

Robbie closed his eyes tightly, screwing up his face. He chanted aloud for a while and then said with surprising clarity, 'Rani into the garden comes ...'

It struck a chord with Calvin who asked, 'That's what you sing after Paajit counts the take ... sorry, the offerings?'

'Hit and go, hit and go,' Robbie said vacantly. 'Witnessing for Rani ...'

'I'm with you, kid. That's what we said too, when we were pushed out of the van to work the street or the airport without food or sleep. Don't you see how they used you?' Calvin's own bitter memories returned. He offered the plate again, this time forcing some meat into Robbie's mouth. Robbie's eyes turned white as the pupils went back in his head and he passed out.

Calvin paced the room, passing his hand over his close-cropped head. He switched off the tape recorder. He would go over the tapes later to improve his understanding, to search for a way into Robbie's mind.

From a dyslectic kid in the ghetto he had come a long way. The Moonies had in a sense done him a favor by changing him from a drug user with no future to a deprogrammer who had made the inside of *Time* magazine, if not the cover. He was not as famous as Ted Patrick – Black Lightning – but he was getting up there. He was expensive but he was good. And it was rewarding work. When the snap-out came it always gave him an incredible sense of achievement. He lived for that moment when the subject suddenly came back from nowhere and started to relate to his surroundings. He could tell by the eyes when the snap-out happened. But Robbie was far from that point; his thousand-mile stare was so vacant and yet so intense. Calvin knew the power of the cults only too well. He still had recurring nightmares, one of which related to a movie he'd seen as a kid. A medieval king was being entombed alive; he disappeared piece by piece as the wall was built up around him until, finally, only his wild frantic eyes were visible. Then the last stone was cemented in ...

'He's sleeping. For real this time,' Calvin said, joining the others in the family room. He offered Sal a cigarette, a Black Russian, which she declined.

'I guess it's too soon to expect ... progress,' Bob said diffidently though with a trace of hope in his voice.

'It's very early days,' Calvin replied. 'I've seen better cases and I've seen worse,' he added non-committally.

'You're not telling us very much,' Sal said quietly, laying her book aside. She resented being excluded and also had reservations about Calvin. She wanted to test him, 'Do you think it's a metabolisation of new sensory data or a dysfunction proper?' Bob looked at her in surprise, unaware that she had researched the subject. Calvin knew he was being tested; since he had no formal qualifications it was not an unusual experience for him. In fact most of his clients were educated and tried to get a similar reading on him.

'I'm doing the job the best way I know how,' he answered evenly. 'But I don't think anyone has definite answers. We're at the front edge, especially where the Chaikha Rani are concerned. No one knows for sure. Theories don't count, only results.'

'You're dealing with a mind,' Sal pressed.

'I've been through this myself, remember,' Calvin responded. 'I've felt it. I know what I'm doing.' He was edgy, sensing waves of disaffection from Sal.

'Do you?' Her voice sounded cavalier but there was a calculating look in her eyes.

'Look, my success rate is good.' Calvin was angry with himself for being defensive. 'I'm sure you've checked it out. But,' he added, spreading his hands, 'if you want me to quit there are others out there who need my ...'

'No. Of course not,' Bob interjected. 'We're all under strain.' He looked across the room at Sal and guessed that she had said her piece. 'I have a question though,' he added.

'Shoot.' Calvin had calmed down; in any case he didn't feel threatened by Bob.

'Well, it's his eyes. I mean he looks so ... spaced out ...'

'I see it all the time.' Calvin was on firm ground now. 'Brainwashing affects peripheral vision. Until they snap out. You've probably also noticed that his voice is high pitched and his beard is almost gone. Symptoms of the same thing. But the important thing to remember is that it can be reversed.'

'What can we do to help?' Bob asked. Like Sal he felt frustrated, though he accepted the fact that Calvin needed to work alone for the first few days.

'What we need is a hook,' Calvin said, stroking his chin with black slender fingers. 'Something that makes the past real to him so that he starts to think again. His mind is seized up. He's got to think again ...'

'I don't understand,' Bob interrupted. 'How can they stop someone thinking?' It didn't make sense to him.

'They made every decision for him.' Calvin spoke slowly. 'They probably held his hand all the time and even blew his nose for him. I'm serious. It's called "love-bombing". But the effect is that you become totally dependent and unable to decide anything by yourself. You come to believe that free-will is Satanic and so you conform completely to the group. They probably used humiliation tactics too. Humiliation followed by "forgiveness" is strong medicine. It reinforces the desire to conform. You literally stop thinking for yourself. Everything they do is designed to prevent thought – the rituals, chanting, sensory deprivation, even the use of the Hindu belief in a shared soul. That's why we need a hook to get Robbie thinking again.'

'What kind of a hook?' Bob asked. He was still somewhat confused. Calvin's explanations were scary but on the other hand it didn't seem to be such a big deal just to get Robbie to think for himself. And they now had all the time in the world to work with him.

'Something he can relate to,' Calvin explained. 'An old hobby or project. Something that he really liked.'

'Let us think about it for a while.' Bob looked at Sal who nodded.

'OK. I'm going to jog around the block. Holler when he comes to. I'd also suggest,' he looked towards Sal, 'vegetarian meals for the next few days.' He went to his room to change into his running suit.

After he left, Bob asked Sal why she'd been hostile.

'I'm afraid of charlatans,' she said glibly. But the truth was deeper than that and reflected her own pessimism. In addition, she didn't like the idea of a deprogrammer living in her home, jogging round the neighborhood, telling her what to cook and charging four hundred dollars a day.

'He's the best around,' Bob said. 'What's the alternative? Have Father Molloy sprinkle holy water on Robbie? Anyway,' he relented, 'what about this hook? I'm going to have a look at those home movies again.'

They both watched the little flickering screen. The first shots were of Robbie playing Little League baseball in McLean. They watched him sliding to base, unnecessarily, in a cloud of dust, trying to be impressive. There were shots of his batting. He was afraid of the ball ever since the time he'd been hit and cried openly in front of everyone. In this game he had also been hit by the ball because of his tendency to turn his back rather than duck. Bob watched the scene come up. The ball had hit him hard on the shoulder. But this time he hadn't cried. There was footage of Sal running to him, of Robbie turning away, not wanting help or sympathy. He shrugged off her outstretched hand. Bob had been pleased at the time but now he wasn't so sure. The sight of Robbie biting his lip in pain and turning away repeated itself over and over in his mind.

There was some footage of Glacier Park which they'd visited when he was about ten. They watched him sitting in a field of wild flowers surrounded by glacier lilies, bear grass, Indian paintbrush, with snow-capped peaks behind him. Robbie was smiling, his cheeks bunched and dimpled, hovering on the verge of an outright laugh. He held in his lap a richly ornate medicine shield that they'd bought from the Blackfeet Indians.

Robbie loved the stories of the Indians which Bob, too, had heard when he was a kid growing up in Montana. They'd picnicked on Thunder Bird Island, so called because the Indians believed that it was the home of the giant bird that caused thunder by the flap of his wings and lightning by the gleam of his fierce eyes. Robbie had also been fascinated by the thought of the Indian chiefs going alone into the mountains to meditate.

'Painting,' Sal said. 'Remember how he loved the Indian paintings? And the set of water colors we got him later on?'

'That might just be the hook we need,' Bob agreed. He switched off the projector. They went to look in on him as he slept. Unlike the night before when he was out cold, his sleep was restless and fitful. Sal could hardly bring herself to look at his gaunt face which was thinned down to the bone, as if he had no reserves left of youth or comfort or protection; the mould had hardened. How could he be touched again, or feel, through that skeletal structure? Pure structure. She moved to put her hand on his forehead but Bob restrained her gently. 'He has to sleep.'

'Dear God, give us your help and protection,' she breathed. 'Restore him to us.'

He wondered momentarily whether there was any difference between her prayer and Robbie's chanting. What was so damned hard about just living? Maybe if they'd all lived in a dirt-poor country and had to scratch for food they'd have managed better.

Sal went to answer the doorbell. He heard her say, 'Can't do it today, Marge ... Next week maybe ... Yes, a rain-check ...' She would keep the neighbors out while they tried for a miracle in the secrecy of their home. It was unreal.

As Calvin jogged along the sidewalk he was conscious of the covert glances of neighbors and he felt like singing out: Don't worry about your property values, folks. I'm just passing through. Washington was eighty per cent black and yet here in Langley, just six or seven miles out of town, there weren't any blacks to be seen apart from the odd African diplomat, although most of them preferred Bethesda and Chevy Chase. Apartheid, US style, was administered by the realtors. He didn't really have a chip on his shoulder about it anymore. It was strange how a growing income and reputation could dampen one's revolutionary zeal. Anyway, the blacks now had the Spics to kick around. It seemed to him that everyone, including the cult leaders, needed someone to dominate.

He wasn't, however, cynical about his job and he thought about Robbie as he ran, trying to get a picture of the belief set they'd implanted in him. There were elements of Shia and Hindu, even Christian, but how did it all hang together? The odd thing about all the cults he'd come across was that, despite the fantasy, there was usually a certain logical consistency woven through it all, as if the cult leaders recognised the mind's insatiable desire for some kind of unity. It had often struck him that the mind could accept almost anything as true as long as the re-inforcing effect of unity was present. But what was this Chaikha Rani theme, how did it scan?

He recalled the news item about the Shia fundamentalist who, back in 1983, drove a lorry-load of dynamite into the US marine complex in Beirut, killing over two hundred American soldiers and of course himself. Further back, the Al Jihad group had assassinated Sadat in broad daylight. Was the Chaikha Rani some kind of training ground? He didn't know, but there was no point in taking any chances. He would have to bring Robbie out fast.

Chapter 14

There was paint everywhere, not just on the canvases but on the book-lined walls of his bedroom and on the panelling of the family room. Hardened lumps of red and purple acrylic were ground into the shag pile of the beige carpeting.

They watched helplessly as Robbie used and abused the painting materials they'd provided. But they couldn't intervene because somewhere in the mayhem of color, somewhere in the random daubs and splashes, might be the insight they sought, and the touchstone of reality that he so desperately needed.

As time wore on the shapes became more defined, but the images were wild and unreal: half-finished demons and mutants, landscapes with no horizons, voids of maroon peopled with tiny specks of yellow.

The following evening Sal was passing through the den armed with bags of groceries. She paused at Robbie's shoulder and gazed intently at his latest 'work'.

'That's very good, Robbie. It's almost ... a real scene. Where is it?'

Bob and Calvin immediately gathered round.

'I ... don't know,' Robbie answered.

'Let's see.' She laid her shopping aside and peered closer. 'Mountains ... trees?'

'Lodge-pole pine trees,' he said suddenly, correcting her.

'My God,' Bob said excitedly. 'It's Glacier Park. It's coming back to him.' He looked from the painting to Robbie who nodded slowly.

'This may be the beginning of a breakthrough,' Calvin whispered.

'You remember Heavy Runner Mountain ... and Thunder Bird Island ... and the mountain goats jumping from ledge to ledge ...?' Bob asked eagerly, forcing the pace.

'Thunder and lightning. Yes, the Indians believed in a giant bird ...' There was consternation in his face as if the glimpses of reality were so unexpected as to shock. Gradually, in small discrete shifts, his face muscles relaxed and he went back to his painting.

Calvin watched closely and said, 'I think this is the first stage. Next, we have to teach him not to be afraid of reality. Sometimes it can be a process like this rather than a snap-out.' He turned to Sal who gave him her gratitude in a smile.

Calvin's judgment was confirmed over the next few days as Robbie returned slowly and with a sense of nostalgia, sometimes tinged with fear, to himself and his surroundings. He regressed from time to time but there was no doubt that the general trend was positive. Dressed now in jeans and T-shirt, with his hair beginning to grow and his eyes becoming more aware, he looked almost normal; they planned to have a plastic surgeon look at the mark on his forehead. Even Sal was impressed and she began to revise her opinion of Calvin, indeed looked for ways of apologising to him.

'It's like waking ... from a dream,' Robbie said one night as they sat around in the den after dinner. He looked from one to the other as if seeing them for the first time.

Calvin was quick to respond. 'It was a bad dream. But they made it seem beautiful, didn't they?'

'Yes, they were all so ... caring. It was impossible to believe it was just ... a means to an end.' He nodded grimly to himself, feeling ashamed. He had gone there for enlightenment and been conned instead.

'Caring?' Sal repeated, unable to let it pass.

'It seemed so. At the time,' Robbie said. After a while he asked, 'I presume Uncle Dave is alive and well?'

'We had to do that,' Bob said. 'We were desperate. I wonder how he'd take it if we told him?' They all laughed; the sound was almost novel.

Sal leant forward. 'Do you feel up to telling us why you went to them in the first place?'

Robbie gave a slight shrug, indicating how dumb he'd been. 'I really thought they'd something to offer. About relationships. Love, I suppose. And,' he gave something of that shy smile, 'I thought I could help you and Dad in some way.'

'Did we not ...?' Sal faltered, not knowing exactly how to put it. But she knew the answer. They had not filled that lacuna in his life, so he went elsewhere. It hurt. But the pain was lost in the miracle of having him home again.

'Robbie, I want you to know,' Bob said earnestly, 'that we truly appreciate what you tried to do. You weren't to know it was a set-up. These people are pros. But your motives were fine, really fine. And I promise you, things are going to be different around here from now on. Very different ...' His voice started to shake so he quit while he was ahead.

'It's OK, Dad. I know what I put you through and I'm sorry. But college doesn't seem such a bad idea now. So maybe something came of it after all.'

'Don't worry about that.' Bob gave a magnanimous sweep of his hand. It all seemed so trivial now. 'There's plenty of time and we all have some living to do.' He glanced towards Sal who nodded in agreement.

'Well, I do have to get on with my life sometime ... Avatur Satguru Nihad Rani, Chaikha Mutuswami Rani ...'

'Please don't do that!' Sal sat bolt upright. He gave her a look of offended dignity as if he were truly a priest disturbed in a holy rite.

Calvin rowed in. 'Chanting is part of the technique they used, kid. Manipulation by remote control. Just cut it out and they'll have no more power over you.' He reached out and turned Robbie's face towards him.

'You're right,' Robbie said. 'It's just a habit I have to get rid of.'

'Sure,' Bob said.

The reassuring buzz of talk stopped dead as a window shattered. A stone came to rest at Robbie's feet.

'It must be the kids next door,' Sal said.

Bob went to the window. Through the enveloping dusk he could see a van parked outside the house. Paajit was not alone.

'Call the police!' His throat was dry.

'No,' Calvin cautioned. 'We're on thin ice. Just sit tight and bolt the doors.'

Instinctively they moved closer to Robbie, surrounding him. A faint echo of chant came from outside and gradually grew louder.

'Make them stop!' Sal put her hands to her ears. Then, to her horror Robbie started to answer, slowly at first, 'Muthuswami Rani, Bahram Nagathur, Paajit the Satguru comes ...'

'Cut it out,' Calvin barked. But some switch had been thrown and Robbie continued answering the sick caterwaul, on a louder higher register. The chant outside grew more confident, gathering into its insistent rhythm a high nasal mocking tone and a sense of triumph. The madness was becoming real. Robbie started to sway from side to side as his responses rose in pitch and rhythm.

Calvin reached back and hit him across the face with such force he would have fallen if Bob had not been holding him. 'Ignore it! You must close your ears to it. It's not holy. It's just a technique. It has no meaning. Do you understand? No meaning.'

Robbie looked at him and stopped. Another switch clicked into place. 'What's Paajit doing out there?' he asked. He was back with them again.

'Good man,' Calvin said. 'Now, close your ears to it. You're here with your family. Nothing out there matters.'

For what seemed like hours they sat listening to the chant outside. The tree frogs and crickets were strangely silent but startled birds broke cover and filled the night sky. Fireflies glittered in a strange firmament. The night was rent by lunacy. The chanting became less shrill but more intense and more frightening. It developed the beat of primitive drums pounding out dire threats. They were trapped in the clearing of their own home, encircled and cursed by sound. Other families were watching Johnny Carson or 'Tic Tac Doh' or repeats of 'Cheers'. Robbie was silent but he was jumpy. Bob noticed the drawn face and the white knuckles of the hands that pressed against his ears. What if he went over the edge again? The hatred he felt for Paajit brought bile to Bob's throat. He jumped to his feet, blood rushing to his head.

'It's a fucking siege. I'm not having it. Where do those crazy bastards get off?' He rushed upstairs and grabbed his hunting rifle from the closet. Cornered, with madness ascending, his actions were instinctive. They were trying to take Robbie away again. Action was all that counted, a matching violence. He was back in the swamps and napalmed ilex trees of Tongking, looking for a way out.

'Oh, no,' he said aloud, ramming two rounds up the spout. 'Oh, no. Not this time, friends.' He smashed a window pane and got Paajit in his sights through the glass of the van. 'Here's yours coming,' he grated. With any luck the round would do for the other guy too. Clear out two twisted brains with one shot, the ultimate in brainwashing. He steadied himself on one knee and felt the comfortable curve of the trigger ...

'No!' Sal cried, rushing into the room. 'For God's sake, Bob.' She grabbed his arm and fell trembling on her knees beside him. 'You mustn't ...' She was on the verge of hysteria. The rifle dropped from his grip and he slumped against the wall.

Calvin burst in, 'What's going on? I heard ...'

Bob looked up at him as if he'd never seen him before, then he noticed shadowy figures moving in the front yard.

'Get back downstairs fast!' he called out in a choking voice.

But it was too late. The window was smashed and Robbie was gone. So was the van.

PART II

Chapter 15

She knocked up against the green practice wall, her forehand shots skimming the white line that represented the net cord. She was in control of direction and rhythm and alternated her shots at will, making the ball return to her backhand, then forehand again, hitting it early on the rise each time. She was glad she'd taken her doctor's homely if unscientific advice: 'Get out and about and above all keep busy.'

The practice session heaved up memories of college tennis tournaments played out under cloudless skies, spinning rackets for side or service, friendly handshakes at the net, the feel of the starched white dress flapping against her thighs. A defined crisp sport that gave a welcome break from textbooks.

She thought of Bob's first attempts at the game, how he kept lofting the ball clean over the wire, unable to comprehend a game that required more than strength, how he finally, and no doubt with some embarrassment, put down the sport as one for schoolgirls and faggots.

It was over two weeks since Robbie had gone. They had checked out the airlines and were certain that he had gone back to London with Paajit. But where was he in that city of ten million people? They were right back where they started, but more lost, poorer – for Calvin hadn't come cheap – and no wiser.

For Bob it was even worse than that because he had seen Paajit, felt his presence and his shadow, and could not imagine a greater threat.

'I should have killed him when I had the chance,' he said to Sal one evening when they had calmed down enough to discuss it. They sat in semi-darkness because a tornado in Great Falls had taken out the power lines.

'Don't be ridiculous.' She sat under her lamp but because of the power outage couldn't read or work on the magazine.

'I mean it.'

'I don't want to discuss it.' Her next comment shook him to the core. 'Are you sure Robbie didn't go with him willingly?'

'What do you mean? Robbie was coming out of it, for Chrissake. Even Calvin said so. The chanting was just a reflex. Sure, it was scary but it didn't mean a damn thing. He was coming back to us. You must have felt it. We all felt it.' He paused. 'I just don't know what's eating you these days.'

She didn't respond; he fought the silence for a while and then left.

'Sal, is that you?' The club pro who had just finished a lesson, hailed her from an adjoining court. 'You're really socking 'em. Come and hit some to me.'

He stood at the net, volleying them back to her. She tried lobs with top spin and passing shots, and though he returned most of them, she was stretching him and they both knew it. She had hit her stride.

'Atta, girl,' he encouraged her breathlessly. A small group formed outside the court behind the umpire's chair watching them play. Sal moved easily around the court, hitting up and through the ball, feeling the satisfying impact that was something between a punch and a caress. She was light on her feet, flexed in anticipation, playing with controlled intensity. Her concentration was honed as never before. She was in that trance-like state that pros and pundits called the O-zone and which they tried to analyse in terms of positive reinforcement. Answers came in each stroke of the ball. She could do nothing wrong. She took risks, attempted shots that had always been beyond her, and gradually drove Don back from the net.

'Way to go,' an onlooker cheered.

'Don't encourage her, for God's sake,' Don groaned, barely retrieving a passing shot with a miss-hit lob.

Then it happened. Sal was reaching up to make the smash and suddenly she seized up. There was too much space; she felt lost in the infinite sky. Her heart missed several beats and she stumbled. Filaments of blinding light seared into her aching brain. She thought she was having a stroke.

'Are you OK?' Don rushed to the net. She mumbled something about having to leave. Her lips were compressed to prevent vomiting.

The drive home was a nightmare. She could barely see the road ahead and her hands were so numb that she couldn't feel the steering wheel. Traffic lights were blurred, the colors garbled by flashes of white and gray. She had some residual memory of a previous panic attack, after her mother's death which happened suddenly after a fun-filled day of shopping together. It was as though she could never afford to feel good because it tempted providence.

When she finally got to the house she groped her way to the medicine cabinet and took three librium, chewing the capsules to release the powder quickly. She sat rigidly on the toilet seat, trying to steady her breathing and regain control.

Gradually the sedative took effect, her eyes began to focus again and the vise around her forehead loosened its grip. She took several deep breaths and went out to park the car properly; in her urgency to get into the house she had left it blocking the sidewalk.

She began to clean the house, especially the daubs of paint which Robbie had left on walls and rugs; the rooms reeked of turpentine before she'd finished. But keeping busy had little therapeutic value; it could not still her mind.

For several days she tried to convince herself that the panic attack was some kind of aberration which would not recur. But she sensed deep down that it was a sign that her defences had crumbled, that she was losing her grip. What plagued her night and day was the thought that she hadn't even had a chance to talk to Robbie, let alone reach him in any real way.

She fought the urge to drink for a long time but finally gave in. Fate had given her a genetic need – and a good excuse. One bright afternoon she sat in her bedroom at her desk, which was littered with galley proofs and past issues of the parish magazine. She had been researching the Gnostic heresy, tracing the history of evil incarnate. Satan, she discovered, was a Judaized version of Ahriman whom the Persians regarded as the enemy of Light. Later on the Israelites invented Satan to rationalise their dashed nationalistic hopes. It was ironic how the figure of Satan had entered Christianity almost as a scapegoat to absolve the triune God from the evils of the world. She brooded in her cups on this awesome possibility.

But the fruits of her research became less unpalatable after her third gin. She watched the sunlight being refracted through the liquid in her glass. She began to understand how her father had needed that feeling of numbness, of floating. The anodyne brought her to a safe haven of feeling; in fact she even began to feel good ...

She remembered the same sensation on their seventh wedding anniversary when she and Bob had gone to a pretentious French restaurant in the district and got well and truly stoned just for the heck of it. The Maitre d' had rattled off a list of special dishes which weren't even included in the encyclopaedic menu. His French accent complemented the *mise en scène*, which included murals of Normandy chateaux and prints of French impressionists, interspersed with royal crests and fleurs de lis. The interior decorator had clearly worked from a tourist brochure.

They started with martinis and bread rolls wrapped in warm towels. Ordering was half the fun and Sal was determined to take her time. After two martinis she still hadn't decided. The Maitre hovered.

'Is Madame ready to order yet?' he inquired politely with some strain in his French voice.

'*Non,*' Sal replied. '*Nous ne sommes pas prêt. Mais J'ai une question concernant les cervelles ...*'

'I ... beg your pardon?' The Maitre looked uncomfortable.

'You're not French, are you?' Bob asked delighted.

'Non, Monsieur. Romanian.' He looked crestfallen.

'Well, don't worry about it,' Bob said with a glint in his eye. 'Now, do you have anything on a bun?' Sal covered her mouth with her hand.

'No, Sir ... May I recommend the langoustines to start and then, perhaps, the filet mignon?'

'Have you got anything on offer?' Bob asked. He slathered butter on a bread roll and knit his brows into a most serious expression.

'The prices are on the menu,' the Maitre said poker-faced, pencil poised over pad. Educating the stomachs of Americans was an uphill struggle all the way.

Bob turned to Sal. 'Do you have any coupons in your purse?'

'Only for Big Macs,' she spluttered. 'He's not cheap,' she announced to an inquisitive woman at a nearby table, 'just frugal.'

'Tell you what,' Bob said, 'bring us a couple more martinis to oil the wheels of decision-making.'

When the drinks arrived he appraised her through his raised glass. Her eyes danced; she was good fun when she gave herself half a chance. 'Here's looking at you, kid. Still carry a torch for the old Gipper, or has the good Father Molloy cut me out?'

'No contest.' She thought of how wary she had been of him at first. True, he didn't have too many social graces but his obvious respect for her was compensation enough. Also he was handsome and she never felt that she was all that pretty. She believed that his deference to her gave her the right to mould him a little. His strong sex drive, finally revealed, was not scary because she could control it through his respect for her. She had always assumed that if she married at all it would be to an older man, quieter even than herself and perhaps a little owlish. Instead, in Bob, she got an outgoing man who kept her on her toes and laughed at her imagined fears until she began to let go of them and share, diffidently at first, his huge sense of fun.

The Maitre returned several times, once to recommend with some desperation the sole bonne femme.

'*Non, je ne pense pas*. It give me ... how you say? ... ze gas ...' She croaked into her handkerchief. He turned away with a swish of his claw-hammer tux, shrugging his shoulders in the direction of the kitchen from which the chef peered grimly.

Bob had been looking at meals being served to the table on his left; the portions seemed tiny. 'A robin would starve in here,' he said.

'I know,' she replied. 'It's the nouvelle cuisine.'

'But it's a rip-off. And it's phoney.'

'I know. Would you believe I've got steaks in the fridge?'

'Then what are we doing here?'

'Nothing. I just wanted to see the place. Marge raved about it. She said the Republicans were moving here from the Sans Souci and the Twenty-first Amendment.' She grinned ruefully, admitting her curiosity, which had been duly satisfied. Bob paid for the drinks and said they were leaving. It was hard to tell from the Maitre's expression whether he was insulted or relieved.

After dinner and several more drinks at home they fell into bed and made love in a playful way.

Next morning everything was different. Sal was up early, showered and dressed, and looking very spruce.

'You've some capacity,' Bob said admiringly as he shuffled around the bedroom holding his head.

'I didn't have much to drink.' She sat in front of the mirror, brushing her hair with long sweeping strokes, grimacing a little when she hit a snag.

'Oh, come on now,' he said, mildly disparaging.

'You're mistaken,' she said icily, laying down the shell-backed brush.

He looked at her in disbelief. 'Last night was fun. Sure, we went too far. But when was the last time? Our wedding day? Come on, you're entitled.'

'*You* had too much to drink,' she insisted. 'Your judgment was impaired.' Her expression which came to him through the mirror was glacial.

'How can you deny last night, the fun we had? How can you do that?'

She didn't answer ...

Yes, she had denied it then. But the time for denial was now past. Sitting at her desk in a limbo of the senses, twilight filtering through the window in the scented evening, she knew the addiction was taking hold. She tried to do some copy-editing but reached for her glass instead.

Chapter 16

Bob filled his days differently. At work he performed by rote, carrying shoe boxes and foot rests, shoe horn at the ready. There was a run on snow boots, people laying away for winter.

In his spare time he saw Linda but he didn't frequent the club much. Instead, when she was working, he gravitated towards his old gym on Sixteenth Street. It was an old fashioned boxing gym with sawdust on the floor, the air reeking of sweat and embrocation. There was no stainless steel equipment, or slinky ladies doing aerobics in leotards, just the whiff of soured hopes.

Art was with him on one occasion, leaning against a wall that dripped with condensation. His hat was pushed back on his head, which was as big and lugubrious as an Easter Island statue. He was faintly amused by Bob's frenetic energy.

Bob threw the skipping rope aside and worked for a while on the seventy-pound bag. His taped fists thudded into the wadded canvas, which winced but hardly moved as it absorbed everything he threw at it. He was pumping; there was a menagerie in his chest, primal and rhythmic, as he danced and hit. There was, however, little satisfaction in punching out an inanimate object.

So when he was invited, he stepped willingly into the ring to spar with Danny Hughes, a cocky young heavyweight who was starting to build a reputation. The sparring session turned into a bout and then into a fight. Bob was eager for this; having a real opponent was such a relief from fighting shadows. He stood his ground and slugged it out with Danny who was becoming more and more serious. Bob landed a few good punches at first, but Danny began to dance out of reach and return with flurries of one-twos to the head. Bob didn't realise he was taking such a beating. He felt his head being snapped back several times and guessed he wasn't rolling with the punches. But he didn't know that his guard was slipping or that he'd lost his gum shield. He felt little pain; it was more a sensation of weakness. His legs began to buckle. They felt spindly like a new born colt's. But he wasn't going down.

'... That's enough. Enough!' He vaguely heard Art. Then he was helped to his corner.

'You goddamn fool,' Art said, sponging his face. 'Do you know what you've done to yourself?'

Later in the locker room Bob was surprised when he saw his face in the cracked mirror. His lips were swollen and shredded, one eye was closed under the weight of puffed raw tissue. There was congealed blood in his nostrils and a deep gash over a cheek bone. Art applied petroleum jelly and band-aid as best he could.

'Did I win?' Bob gave a crooked leer through his pulped face.

'You're mad,' Art said heavily. 'Totally fucking mad. He had your balls for bookends and you didn't even know it.' He stood back, appraising his medical handiwork.

'But it felt good, Art. You know?' Bob gingerly touched his cheek with a gloved hand.

'No, I don't know,' Art said sternly. He looked carefully at him. 'Do you know where you are?' He felt his ribs under the sweat-soaked singlet.

'Oh, come on, Art ...'

'Well, where are you?' Art insisted.

'I haven't lost my marbles. It's Rick's lousy gym on Sixteenth. Right next door to the Center for Adult Delight. There's a Pizza Hut two blocks down the street and a metro station ...'

'OK. I'm just checking, that's all.' Art folded in his lips and shook his head at the insanity of it all. He had the weirdest feeling that Bob was training for something.

When Bob got home he caught Sal off guard. She had been drinking and hadn't expected this intrusion. She covered up by going on the offensive.

'Have you been brawling?' she asked accusingly.

'No. Just working out at the gym.' He threw his Adidas bag into the closet in the hall. But she couldn't leave well enough alone and followed up sharply.

'Tried to shoot anyone since?' She stood to her full height, palming a peppermint into her mouth. By ignoring the taunt he goaded her. 'So you were conned. The salesman sold a pup. That's rich.' She wasn't very steady on her feet so she sat down again.

'What're you talking about?' he asked wearily. He thought for an instant that she was referring to the fight.

'Calvin,' she spat out. 'He took you. He didn't even give us a chance to talk to Robbie. He really took you …'

'Lay off. I'm going to bed.' Exhaustion had overcome him. But she couldn't let him escape; she had to lay her own guilt on him. Like many gentle people she was bad in drink. 'Anyway, Robbie's gone for good now.' She sipped her coffee which was laced with scotch.

'No, he's not,' Bob said flatly. He poured himself a cup of coffee but couldn't drink because of his bruised lips. 'I'm not giving up.'

'That's your ego speaking.' She gave a sickly smile, trying to be condescending.

'I don't give a damn what's speaking. I'm going after him.' He kicked off his shoes, recalling how close they'd come; he still had Paajit in his sights, the pock-marked face was etched on his mind. There was only one way to erase it and the time would come.

'You're mad,' she slurred. 'It was never meant to be.'

'Shut up. I'll find him.'

'What am I supposed to say? Oh, my hero?' She sank back in an armchair, a glazed look in her eyes. She scooped back a strand of hair and looped it behind her ear. Then she held her hands, pinioning them because they were so restless. 'You don't have the crusade franchise.' Everything about her was coiled tight and the knots which burned into her could no longer be dissolved in gin.

'I don't give a shit what you say. I've decided. That's it.' He knew she was smashed, not that it mattered one way or the other. He got a glass of cold water from the fridge to take to the bedroom.

'You're wasting your time.' She recalled her mother's Alanon prayer: Let go, Let God … Give me the courage to accept the things I cannot change. She looked blearily at him. 'You can't control another human being … Can't manipulate. Not even salesmen …'

'What about the Chaikha Rani?' he demanded. 'They seem to be good at it.'

'They know what they're doing,' she threw back with the force of a ricochet.

'And I don't? Christ Almighty.' He looked at her in pained surprise. 'I don't want to talk about it anymore. I've made plans …' He drummed his fingers on the table as he passed, then stopped, remembering how he used to do it for Robbie, horses coming into town then galloping away, the hoofbeats fading – and the smile that shone with recognition.

'Oh, more plans?' She twisted the knife, not quite sure why she was being so vindictive, but unable to help it. 'You're such a take-charge guy. I'm impressed. Really. You have such a thorough grasp of the inessentials.'

What the hell was happening to her, he wondered, to this woman whose elegant poise used to make him feel inadequate? Well, this wasn't the time to talk it out. He started up the stairs, carrying his glass of water and his shoes as if he were sneaking into the house after a late-night party.

'Can't you see it?' she called after him. 'Do you not see what's happened?' She couldn't let him get out of range that easily.

He paused on the stairs. 'Say it.'

'He's not our son anymore.' She knew she'd gone too far; that was never meant to be uttered.

'How dare you say that.' He turned round, stooping slightly. 'How can you abandon him?' It suddenly came together in his mind, what he had to do. She had goaded him to action sooner than he'd planned. Maybe it was for the best.

'I'm leaving tomorrow,' he said slowly. 'You mightn't see me again. But if you do, Robbie will be with me.'

'You're moving in with that woman,' she blurted out. 'Admit it.' She peered down at the coffee cup on the floor. Had she thrown it ...?

The next morning Bob packed a bag. The waiting was over. There were many details to be worked out but these would fall into place, in the slipstream of his decision.

As he left, Sal sent her parting shot. 'Suppose he's not brainwashed. Suppose he hates your guts.' The door closed on her regret.

She was surprised how lost she felt when he was gone. Her last claim on serenity went with him; she had lost her poise. He was necessary for that, a buttress, even a mere presence. It was incredible to think that she had once been the nucleus of the family. Nothing now revolved around her. She poured her drink down the sink. Scared. Memories of her father. A sleeping pill later perhaps, to get through the night. Dalmane. She had some in her purse.

His first port of call was the bank. The assistant manager, Joseph Hayworth, showed him to a chair in his office which had a stars and stripes in a corner behind a rubber tree plant and a glossy photo of his family on the desk.

'I think I can guess why you're here, Bob,' Joseph Hayworth said.

'Oh?' His eyebrows lifted in surprise.

'The TV program.'

'You saw that? Well then you know why my account is in such poor shape. Deprogrammers don't come cheap and I ...'

Joseph raised a hand. 'Bob, let me stop you right there. It's a hard time for you and believe me I sympathise.' He could have been talking to a dirt farmer who had just lost a crop and needed to borrow the seedcorn. 'But we have strict guidelines from the Fed and shareholders snapping at our heels. Our loan officers are having breakdowns because refusals do offend. That's why I stopped you. I don't want you to ask.'

'Well, I am asking,' Bob said doggedly.

'Oh, shit.'

'Look, fifteen grand isn't going to break you. It's chicken feed.'

'Bob, it's the principle. We have Feds in every second week going over the books. With Reagan splurging on defense they have to throttle back on lending to the small man. What it comes down to is that you and I are paying for Star Wars.' It sounded to Bob's practiced ear that Joseph had made this speech before. 'Every unproductive loan they see on our books they go berserk, even fifteen grand, believe me. They could pull our ticket. You have to have a project at least ...'

'I have a project. Rescuing my kid.'

'Bob, please don't make this hard for me. I'm talking about financial projects, with cash-flow and pay-back periods ...'

'That's it then.' Bob got up heavily. To his certain knowledge this bank had lent some eight billion dollars to Latin America, most of which it would never see again.

'I'm really sorry.'

'Forget it.' He had a fall-back position. Of sorts.

Chapter 17

They sent out for Japanese food and Linda set the table. She lit candles and put a U2 album on the turntable. There was an unusual urgency to her movements which were fluttering and indecisive. She was conscious of a growing insecurity where Bob was concerned. His obsession with Robbie made her worry about where she stood with him. She didn't doubt that he loved her but she couldn't help wondering whether love could surmount the force of circumstance. He sometimes seemed so distracted, his energies directed to a goal which didn't involve her.

'You should have told me you were coming over,' she upbraided him mildly. 'I could have made veal or fettucini.' She knew how much he liked it when she cooked for him.

Bob took her hand when they sat down to eat. She became still, her silken hair falling forward over her face.

'Linda, it's time. Time for me to do something.' His grooved face looked intense in the somber candlelight.

'I know.' Her voice was low, almost a whisper. She wondered where it would all lead. 'Waiting around is not helping you ... or us.'

'I have to see it through,' he agreed. 'One way or another.'

'Are you going to hire Calvin again?'

'I don't think so,' he answered uncertainly. Maybe Sal was right in her assessment of Calvin. 'Anyway, I have to find Robbie first. Then rescue him.' He was breathing rapidly. 'If I can just get him back and talk to him ... We didn't have a chance the last time with that creep, Paajit, on the scene.'

'I hope it works out.' She meant it in more ways than one. She placed her other hand on his and looked steadily at him.

'I'm thinking of asking your brother, Aldo, for help,' he said diffidently. This didn't come easily to him, but months of selling shoes had softened his pride. Besides, there was no other way.

'Do,' she said immediately, feeling that this would keep her more involved in a familial way. 'I'll talk to him for you.'

'Thanks, Linda. I knew you would.' He hesitated. 'What do you think he'll want in return?'

'I don't know,' she said simply. The thought hadn't occurred to her.

'But something?' Bob pressed.

'He is a ... businessman,' she conceded slowly. 'But I'll work on him. Anyway,' she forced a smile, 'he's not the *capo di tutti i capi*. Talk to him.' She took his face in her hands and kissed him, wishing she had a stronger claim on him. Aldo could help them both and she had always been able to reason with him, even when he ran wild in the *vicoli* of Naples. The idea grew on her.

The cadillac pulled up on Twenty-first Street opposite the State Department at the appointed hour. Aldo Tognetti got out and asked his driver to pick him up in half-an-hour at the other side of the Lincoln Memorial. Bob had met him once before with Art, but he would have recognised him as Linda's brother in any case. He had the same smooth pampered features and his small frame moved jauntily. He wore a white light-weight suit.

'Good to meet you again, Bob.' He extended his hand then patted him on the shoulder. 'Let's walk. I need the exercise.'

They turned the corner into Constitution Avenue and passed by the National Academy of Science. Aldo stopped to look at the bronze statue of Einstein.

'What a man,' he remarked. 'You know what his theory of relativity really means?'

'No,' Bob said.

'Your viewpoint depends on where you're standing at the time.' He laughed softly.

Bob looked at the seated bronze figure, a huge pixie staring at his round belly with a smile of beguiling innocence. He liked Aldo for liking it. But he was still on edge.

'If we all had minds like that ...' Aldo raised his hands in a parody of admiration. 'We wouldn't have to hustle.'

'Maybe. Maybe not.' Bob was tight-lipped. Aldo glanced at him, 'You're thinking mob? Old-fashioned stuff like that?'

'No. Brainwashing,' he said slowly, taking his eyes off the shaggy sculpted head.

'Yeah,' Aldo sighed. 'The brain is a wonderful but delicate mechanism.'

He looked at Einstein's statue once more. 'Linda explained the situation. Too bad.'

They walked in silence for a while, crossing the Mall where a group of kids were playing softball. Aldo looked sharply at him. 'What gets me is why Linda would want to help you out. Can you explain that?'

Bob hesitated, feeling very uncomfortable, then said simply, 'We're having an affair.'

Aldo laughed raucously and slapped him on the back. 'Got you didn't I? You thought I'd hit on you for messing around with my sister? Come on, admit it.'

'It had crossed my mind.' He felt relieved. Some buzzard-headed marines jogged past in khaki shorts, their singlets stained with sweat.

'She's a big gal now,' Aldo said. 'She can do as she pleases. Women's Lib. Can't fight it anymore.' He stopped abruptly at a roped-off section of cultivated ground which bore a sign, 'Care, Tulips Sleeping'. 'Hey, that's cute. I really like that. I hope Reagan doesn't fire the guy who came up with that sign. That's what we need in this administration. More imagination, more flair. What do you think?'

'I guess so.'

'Of course, we have too much government,' Aldo went on, 'And Reagan can't trim the fat much more. I read an article by Milton Friedman recently. He blames it all on air-conditioning.'

'Oh?'

'Sure. Before they invented air-conditioning the congressmen stayed away from Washington all summer long and the country was much better off. Good government is lazy government, just like Reagan. Laziness and flair, the Italian way. Don't just stand there, undo something. I believe that.'

'It's a point.' They'd reached the sun-washed steps of the Lincoln Memorial. Tourists milled around aiming cameras through the giant portals at the massive statue inside.

'Every time I come here and look at this ... shrine,' Aldo said 'I get goose-bumps. Know what I mean?'

'Sure. It's impressive.'

They walked by the reflecting pool. Brightly colored kites were flying around the top of the Washington Monument. The dome of Congress, like Kafka's castle on the hill, beckoned all the supplicants, with lobbyists in tow, down the huge corridor of the Mall.

'Right. To business.' Aldo clapped his hands as if summoning a troupe of dancers. 'What do you need from me?'

Bob was more than ready. 'A loan of fifteen grand and a contact in London.'

Aldo lapsed into silence and stared at the ground for a while. Bob's heart began to pound.

'You can't manage it?'

'It's a question of demarcation. I'm the legal counsel of the firm, not the financial controller.' He rubbed his chin; there was more to it than that. It would mean making contact with the operations side, the regime in New York, and that not only ran counter to his policy but also, in a way, played into the hands of his brother, Meo. Still, it was a small thing and it was the first time Linda had ever called in her markers. 'I'll get back to you,' he said.

'When?'

'Hey, if it's that urgent, tonight, OK?' He turned sideways to let a roller-skater jive past. 'Damn kids with their headphones and heavy rock. Give me Pavarotti anytime.'

They stopped by the Vietnam War Memorial, its black marble slabs almost hidden from view, buried in the Mall which was once a swamp. It showed in its black interred lines a deep ambivalence of half-remembered valor and shame. Aldo nodded towards it. 'Any of your marine buddies inscribed there?'

'Yes.' Bob remembered all too clearly the fate of his chopper pilot and the day, eight years later, at the unveiling, when he came almost by stealth, to search for his name on that half-hearted plaque.

'I'll call you tonight,' Aldo said. 'Nice meeting you. I hope it goes well.' He waved down the cruising cadillac, sat in and disappeared down Independence Avenue.

'So do I,' Bob said after the vanishing car and wondered how Aldo knew about his tour in 'Nam. He was intrigued by something else Aldo had said, 'Your point of view depends on where you're standing at the time.' He was standing in the inner showcase of the nation's capital, surrounded by shrines to freedom and sleeping tulips, having to prepare for his own private war.

Waiting was becoming a habit these days but it didn't come any easier to Bob who sat all evening by the 'phone in Linda's apartment. She was at the Gattopardo. It was ten when it rang.

'Aldo?'

'Yes, we can do it. On the financial end the best I can manage is seven points above Fed funds rate.'

'That's OK.' He didn't even think about it.

'Good. Now, on the manpower end, I think you're cutting it too fine. One of our guys recalled a similar operation in LA a couple of years back. There can be complications, especially if you're dealing with fanatics. I would suggest two guys in London ...'

'Whatever you think,' Bob said in relief. 'Thanks ...'

'And,' Aldo interrupted, 'you should take Art with you.'

'Why?' Bob was surprised and wondered if it was Aldo's way of keeping tabs on him.

'It's always good to have a friend on a job like this. Besides, Art is sound. He has it front and center. Plus, I don't know these guys in London. They're just friends of friends.'

'All right.' The idea of having Art along grew on him. He then put the inevitable question, 'What's your end of the deal, apart from the interest rate?'

'We can talk about that later, after you get your kid back.'

'I'd rather know now,' Bob said firmly. 'Up front.'

'Nothing ... heavy.' Aldo sounded hurt by the question.

'You're not telling me much,' Bob pressed. He had to know what he was getting into.

'You could be a contact, a friend hopefully. Maybe you could oblige us sometime with a little courier work ... what's there to say?'

'A bagman?' Bob held his breath.

'For Christ's sake. You've seen too many movies.'

'OK, a courier then. But carrying what?'

'Papers, confidential material, maybe cash ...'

'Laundered?'

'Look, every well-run firm avoids tax, especially under this administration. It's just creative accounting.'

'But nothing more than that?' Bob pressed further, aware of the strain in Aldo's voice.

'No. We don't want your goddamn soul. Deal?'

'Deal. And Aldo, thanks.'

'*Prego*. Good luck. Art will have the details. Give those Mullahs one back for the hostages. Fly the flag. *Ciao*.'

Bob stood up. It was set. The first stage anyway.

Chapter 18

Bob sat into the cab, grateful for Art's company. This woolly and world-weary sadsack had watched Linda tearfully kiss Bob goodbye and wish him luck.

'She's some kind of gal,' he whistled softly and shook his St Bernard head. 'Of course, I've never had any luck.' On that doleful note they set off for National Airport circling the tidal basin where some cherry blossom still lingered.

Robbie had always liked to visit the area during the few days a year while the trees were still in bloom, before the blossom disappeared suddenly in a spindrift of color. Once they had left it too late and witnessed only the blizzard of falling petals. Sal had reminded them of the biblical reference to souls spiralling to purgatory in similar profusion.

Art was a Jeremiad also except that he could sometimes, and almost against his will, get a kick out of things in his own droll way. He was more direct too, less blocked, and thankfully there were no sides to him.

'I'm glad you're coming along,' Bob said sincerely.

'Aim to please,' Art grunted. 'Goddamn cults. Do they really believe all that junk? Lost city of Atlantis and all that. Should be shot with their own turds. The lot of them.'

'That's what I like about you, Art. Your open-minded approach.'

'Well, I mean why can't these disturbos go off on their own and meditate? Why do they have to snatch kids off the street? I don't get it.' But of course he had a theory about it, as he did about most things.

'They make a fortune out of it,' Bob replied. 'But I think it's also a question of power. I guess power over people is the ultimate. Slavery, Hitler, mass hysteria. That's the big turn-on.' He was surprised at how calmly he could discuss the matter. It was partly because he was now doing something about it. Action somehow freed his mind. 'You know,' he added reflectively, 'when I make a good sale it's not just the commission that counts. It's partly that I've convinced the buyer; I've persuaded him ...'

'But that's hardly brainwashing,' Art countered. 'Anyway, how could they have suckered Robbie into it? I mean he's so bright.' He lolled his big head and answered himself, 'I guess bullshit baffles brains every time.'

Bob thought of the salesman's dictum: The secret of success is sincerity; if you can fake that you've got it made. The Chaikha Rani had sold his son a bill of goods. He looked out the window of the cab as they passed Fourteenth Street Bridge and thought of the Air Florida crash some years back. He reminded Art about it. 'Remember what was on the black box? The co-pilot said, "Larry, we're going down. We're going down, Larry." And the pilot said, "I know it." And that was it. They just augered into the frozen river taking some of the traffic with them off the bridge.'

'Yeah, yeah,' Art said uneasily, his curt agreement designed to cut off further conversation. It had the opposite effect.

'Of course they still haven't done anything about National Airport,' Bob remarked. 'It's still as dangerous as ever.' The cab driver followed the blue arrow towards the eastern terminal.

'It's not dangerous,' Art said shifting in his seat. 'Because the pilots know its reputation and they take no chances.' He fidgeted with the raincoat in his lap.

'You got to understand the psychology of pilots,' Bob observed. 'They're trained to fly. That means being in the air. So they don't worry too much about take-off conditions. They just want to get the crate airborne.' He exaggerated to make his point. 'The engines could be shot to hell but they're still going to go for it ...'

'Knock it off,' Art said abruptly.

'What's the matter?' Bob looked at him in surprise.

'Nothing. Just leave it alone.'

'Are you scared of flying?' He noticed the stolid face beside him, the normally slack pouches tightened into knuckles of flesh. It was answer enough. 'OK,' he said, trying not to smile.

After they'd checked in it was Bob who suggested a drink. He had a beer and Art had two double manhattans, finally pronouncing that they'd hit the spot. They walked on to the shuttle with five minutes to spare and were soon winging their way round the dome of the Congress, then along the meandering trail over the Potomac.

'The shuttle isn't so bad,' Art grunted. 'It's just a hop. If anything went wrong we could glide into La Guardia.' The manhattans had clearly given him a rosy view of aerodynamics.

'That's the spirit,' Bob said. 'Take it a piece at a time.'

In less than forty minutes the Manhattan skyline with its deep marquetry came into view and shortly after that they landed with scarcely a bump. There was the usual shouting match between dispatchers and cabbies, but finally they sat into a cab and headed for Kennedy. The cab driver told them a story about a drunk he'd picked up recently off a Concorde flight who wanted to throw up. The driver had stopped at the nearest toll plaza. His disoriented passenger mistook the exact-change basket for a sink and upchucked his Concorde cuisine into the basket, fouling the barrier mechanism and causing one of New York's worst ever traffic jams.

'Never met a New York cabbie yet who couldn't spin a yarn,' Art said afterwards as they were being checked in. 'Don't believe a word of it, naturally.'

When they boarded the aircraft a professionally smiling stewardess showed them to their seats.

'Why do all these feisty little dames smile at you?' Art asked with some pique. 'Is it that mustache or what? I never get a second glance.'

'You should wear tighter pants.'

'Naw, give me comfort every time.' He let out the seat belt to match his girth.

'You feeling all right?' Bob inquired.

'So far so good,' Art said. He sounded a little tense and his hands gripped his knees. 'I have some duty-free anyway.' He kicked the bag under the seat in front and heard the reassuring clink.

'I can hardly believe this is happening,' Bob said as the 747 soared powerfully into the sky, heading out over the Atlantic which was like a vast expanse of silver chain-mail, white-plumed here and there by sea-going vessels.

'I know what you mean.' Art nodded slowly. 'What's your game plan when we get over?'

'Nothing very specific as yet. Meet with Aldo's contacts. Get a list of Chaikha Rani hang outs. Narrow it down. Move in. I've got Robbie's name on my passport. That's the most the State Department would do.' His eyes had an eager gaze but he knew it was a long shot. Nevertheless he felt a sense of excitement, of going up against unknown odds. There was comfort in commitment, however ill-conceived.

'Assuming you get Robbie back home, what then?' Art pushed his seat back, trying to relax.

'He'll come around,' Bob said. 'He's got to. This time it'll be different,' he added, half to himself. He lapsed into silence, which Art respected. A stewardess announced that dinner would be late.

After a while Art said, 'Tell me to mind my own business. But where does Sal fit into all of this?'

'I don't know ... She's retreated into herself. I don't know where she's coming from anymore.' He paused to gather his thoughts which were breaking new ground for him. 'It's as if her mind has also been got at ... Does that sound crazy? Anyway I'm not sure I ever really knew her. She's much smarter than me ...' He couldn't pinpoint when they'd gone off track. They had for a while tried to make out just as friends but it hadn't been very successful because real, unspoken issues were piling up with the speed of multiplying cells. Sometimes when he simply felt like holding her she would fear it was a prelude to love-making, make some comment about whisky breath, and go to help Robbie with his homework. On a few occasions Bob tried to talk it through with her, but she was usually busy with the magazine, the PTA, the tennis club, unmarried mothers and other causes promoted by the redoubtable Father Molloy. When Bob was free she was up against deadlines; when she was free he was out wheeling and dealing. They'd hit white water and were floundering badly.

He'd felt inadequate in the light of her growing abilities and confused by her detachment. Sometimes, unwittingly, she made him feel like something she'd walked in. He hit back, of course. There was that scene at a dinner party she gave for her editorial committee, including Father Molloy. With a few drinks under his belt, Bob did a passable impression of Don Rickles at one point in the evening. It was a little risqué and Sal tried to change the subject, but not before someone asked who Don Rickles was. Bob reacted badly. 'No, I guess you don't know who he is. Well, neither do I really. I never even watch the boob tube. I'm such a smartass I listen to Bach fugues all the time ... That's when I'm not writing articles on how to rehabilitate murderers and rapists and all those other unfortunate rejects ...'

The memory of that scene was still painfully fresh. It was strange how the bad memories upstaged the good.

He shifted his feet, one of which had gone to sleep. They didn't give you much leg-room in these economy seats.

'Education kills by degrees,' Art joked lamely. He fiddled with his seat belt, wondering if he should open it; he decided to leave it closed.

'It's probably more my fault,' Bob went on. 'Not understanding enough. Robbie was much closer to her than to me. Sensitivity or something.' He shrugged, feeling that a full explanation was beyond him.

'Fault, fault. It's nobody's goddamn fault,' Art said vehemently. 'When I was on the force I arrested more kids than you've had hot dinners. Kids from good homes. But their folks would beat their breasts and wonder where they'd gone wrong. It's not their fault. They just got short-changed by the system ...'

'System?'

'Look, what most of those kids needed was a good old-fashioned hiding. But the system wouldn't allow it. Teachers, cops, even parents were prevented from laying a glove on them. Dr Spock had the whammy on everyone.' He warmed to his theme, having momentarily forgotten his fear of flying. 'Those four-flushing liberals put us all behind the eight ball with their constitutional rights, protection of the individual, probable cause, exclusionary rules, all carried to extremes. Result? A generation of kids who were rich pickings for crazies like the Chaikha Rani, Charlie Manson, Jim Jones. My God,' he went on becoming almost agitated, 'that guy Hinckley who shot the President got off on temporary insanity. Every TV in the country showed the guy pull the trigger. And he'd planned it for months. Those shyster lawyers used the system to save his hide. "Poor Hinckley," they said, "he was disturbed. It wasn't his doing." Christ, it's like blaming the mirror for pimples.' Art's facial isometrics intrigued Bob who had never seen him so exercised. 'Washington is full of gold-bricking lawyers feeding off the system, making chump money hand-over-fist. Every second guy in Washington is a lawyer or a lobbyist. The other half are politicos and buccaneers. And what happens when the forces of law and order try to straighten them out? Remember Abscam? And all the bent politicos? No, that wasn't "fair". The FBI was accused of entrapment. The villains must be protected at all costs.' He took a vengeful swig of his drink. 'So don't give me your guilt. It's the system that stinks.'

'What can I say?' Bob was grateful and felt exonerated to some extent. But there was another question at the back of his mind. 'Is that why you left the force?' he asked quietly.

'Mainly.' Art's voice subsided to its normal even register. 'It was one frustration after another. That's why some cops went on the take. I never did that. I just got out. I'm not proud of the organisation I joined but at least there's no hypocrisy about it. My last job on the force was staking out a known killer. He had the gall to accuse me of harassment. I was suspended for six weeks without pay. That was it. The last straw.' He hung his head, staring at hands that had become fists.

'Does Aldo … own you now?' Bob asked pointedly.

Art answered with a series of rhetorical questions. 'Who's free? The president surrounded by bodyguards? The working stiff punching the clock? The salesman scratching for the almighty buck? Everybody has markers they can call in. You know what's really funny?'

'No.'

'Capitalism. Christianity. We're all supposed to be individually unique. Free to go our own way. Jesus Christ, if you ask me, we're not even robots. Not even clones of a robot's armpit.'

'I guess you've a point.' Bob looked out the window. They were above the clouds which were curdled and convoluted like brains – cerebral cumulus – brightened by the sharp disk of an early moon. He was fascinated by the endless variety of cloud formations. After a while they became wispy and stretched out like flax, then they became dense and smooth like rolling sand dunes. 'America the free,' he mused aloud. They were all caught in one way or another, trapped or controlled. Sailing through the infinite sky the idea seemed out of place, almost impossible.

'You know,' Art said lugubriously, 'sometimes I feel like cutting loose, kicking over the traces. But to do what? I'm going on sixty and have a bad stomach. I'm used up. Jaded of earth and laden with sin. What have I to show for anything?' He fingered a sagging dewlap in worried reflection.

'You've a fine family,' Bob said. 'I've seen you with your wife. No problem there. And your kids are doing well. You've beaten the system, you old con.'

'Well, it wasn't easy,' Art conceded with doleful reluctance. 'I have this theory about kids today. They envy us for the sixties, I reckon. We tried to change the world. They can't aspire to that. So they try to change themselves instead. You have to give 'em just enough rein …' He stopped abruptly, realising what he'd gotten himself into. Tension always made him talk too much. He decided finally to unfasten his seat belt. Just then a bleep sounded to indicate an announcement from the flight deck. Art cupped his ear, straining nervously to hear the garbled message.

'Holy Christ!' Art sat bolt upright, clutching his stomach.

'What's up?' Bob asked in alarm. Art gagged, unable to answer. He clawed frantically through the seat pocket for the barf bag and vomited with great raucous heaves. Finally he wiped his mouth with the handkerchief Bob gave him.

'What's the matter?' Bob asked again.

'Didn't you hear? … The fucking engines … are out.' He rummaged for the emergency leaflet.

Bob broke into convulsive laughter. 'It's not the engines,' he chortled. 'She said ovens. The ovens are out. Dinner will be delayed. That's what she announced.' He covered his mouth and pretended to groom his mustache.

'Oh Christ, why do they do this to me?' Art complained. His anxiety turned to annoyance rather than relief. As if insult were added to injury he added, 'Who can eat dinner now? They can shove it.'

Bob rang for a stewardess who took away the barf bag, holding it by a corner with a napkin under it to collect the seepage of manhattans. Her head was averted and her nose had a pinched look about it. Art rummaged in his bag and took a long swig of Pepto Bismal. 'Can't even get a decent plane anymore,' he grumbled. 'We should have gone Concorde. But no. Aldo's counting the pennies. Recession, he says. Reaganomics.' He wiped his mouth with the back of his hand. 'Reagan should piss or get off the pot if you ask me. The whole goddamn system's going down the toilet. No one cares anymore ...'

Bob listened to the tirade, trying not to crack up again. Aldo was right. Art was good company despite himself, a bitter tonic. But how useful was he going to be when the going got rough?

The stewardess returned with a glass of water for Art. The plane yawed a little and she spilled some on his pants.

'Oh my God,' he groaned. 'Why don't you just get a hatchet and finish me off?'

Bob winked at her to soften the insult. But unwittingly she came back for more. 'Dinner will be served soon, Sir. Would you care for the steak or chicken?'

'Miss,' Art said with a pained expression, 'I have just spilled my guts out because of your oven failures and your gobbledegook announcement. I almost spat a ring out of my mouth. That ring is my ass. If I hadn't kept it down I would now be inside out. Then you tried to drown me. And now you want to poison me. Will you please butt out and let me die in peace.' He folded his arms and jutted out his lower lip.

'Don't take it too badly, Miss,' Bob said, trying to keep a straight face. 'His bark's worse than his bite.'

She didn't, however, need such consoling, for she retorted, 'You mean his barf's worse than his bite.' She left in a huff.

'You see what I mean?' Art demanded in a parody of indignation. 'Do you see now? Feisty little bitch, badmouthing a man who could be her father.'

'Oh, come on,' Bob cajoled him. 'Cheer up. We're still in one piece.'

'No thanks to British Airways,' Art grumbled. He paused for a while listening to the rumblings of his stomach. 'If you get the chicken I might just try a forkful.' He made it sound like a concession, from a man who was in thrall to his liver.

After dinner they slept for a while. It was dark outside when they woke up. The captain announced that they had to stack up over Heathrow for a while because of an industrial dispute. Art spread his hands and raised his straggly brows as if appealing to a jury. Bob watched the play of moonlight on the city. Further east the sea was gray with a metallic sheen. Strings of orange lights etched the coastline and the Thames estuary. The arteries and aura of the city glittered as if lit from within by diagnostic lasers. Robbie was down there, somewhere in that huge complexity.

Art was speculating that the traffic controllers were probably on strike. 'We'll be going in on a wing and a prayer,' he said nervously, attacking his bottle of duty-free liquor. 'Murphy is right: if anything is likely to go wrong it will.'

They traded some Murphy's laws while they circled the airport.

'The one I like,' Art said, mellowing from his duty free, 'is a Smith and Wesson beats four aces.' Bob didn't feel like laughing; their mission was beginning.

It was nothing short of miraculous, Art said afterwards, that they got through British customs without being strip-searched and anally probed.

Chapter 19

Next morning Art came through the adjoining door into Bob's room in the Cumberland Hotel. He had just showered and had a towel stretched around his large sagging gut.

'How're you feeling?' Bob was fully dressed and had ordered breakfast for two to his room.

'Bit jetlagged. But OK.' Art looked at his plate as he sat down at the table. 'Holy mackerel, do they call this a breakfast? Bread and jam?'

'It's a Continental breakfast,' Bob explained. 'What did you expect? Hominy grits?' He hadn't slept well and had a headache.

Art spread butter on a roll and said, 'I called our contacts. The head honcho is Frankie and James is his back-up man. We're to meet with them at eleven in a place off Oxford Street. They're roughly in the picture. I briefed them and Aldo had sent a cable.' Art was surprisingly businesslike.

'Good.' Bob felt a tingle of excitement. It was beginning at last.

'Is this tea or coffee?' Art asked.

'Taste it and see,' Bob said vacantly. Thoughts raced through his mind; he sifted options as calmly as he could.

'I have. That's the trouble.' Art's face wore a distasteful look.

Bob looked at him in surprise, wondering what he was talking about. 'Get dressed, Art. I want to meet these two guys on time.'

They walked through Hyde Park. It was a gray tolerable day. Some horse riders cantered past on a nearby bridle path. A small crowd sat round a gazebo in which a brass band played military tunes.

‘I’d like to see the changing of the guard at the palace.’ Art walked with his head craned forward. It was a legacy of when he used to brush his thinning hair over his bald spots; he had to bend into the wind to prevent his flimsy thatch from being lifted clean off his temples.

‘We’re not here to sightsee.’

‘No.’ Their conversation was staccato, almost breathless. They turned into Oxford Street, passing pubs and Wimpy bars and the canopied front of Selfridges. The street was a strange mixture of gaudy store fronts and stolid granite buildings of a past age. Black hump-backed cabs lumbered by, honking at the red double-decker buses that stopped frequently for passengers. A barrow boy offered them hot chestnuts. They declined, but a bowler-hatted city gent bought a little bag; it seemed absurd.

‘They’ve got Kentucky Fried Chicken here,’ Art observed.

‘You’re some tourist,’ Bob said. ‘Where to now?’

Art consulted a piece of paper. ‘It’s just here, The Pig and Whistle.’

In the gloom of the wood-panelled pub two figures rose to meet them. Art made the introductions. Frankie was stocky and had darting perceptive eyes; his nose was in direct line with his forehead as if he had walked into a door. He was third generation Cockney. He reeked of cologne. ‘How do, mates,’ he greeted them. James was tall and rough hewn, originally from Pittsburgh. He had completed marine training in Quantico and seemed quietly competent. Their well-cut suits didn’t quite disguise the fact that they were heeled.

They sat down together at the marble-topped table. All but James had tea; he had a beef extract called Bovril, a sausage and two gherkins. Bob looked on as Art paid them in advance, peeling off hundred dollar bills from a wad that he pulled from his marsupial jacket. Bob had the impression of a meter running.

‘Art tells me you know the situation,’ Bob said, keen to get started.

‘Yes, mate,’ Frankie said, squirreling away the bills in his wallet. ‘Your lad’s been nabbed by the Chaikha Rani. And you think he’s in London. It’s not much to go on, is it?’ Despite the Cockney sprightliness there was a curious wariness to him.

‘No,’ Bob admitted. ‘But they can’t have too many hang-outs over here. They started in LA only three years back.’ He looked hopefully from face to face.

Frankie sucked in his breath, ‘Not sure about that. Those yobs are springing up all over the place. And the Greater London area is a big patch.’

‘Well, how can we help track him down?’ Bob wondered if Frankie was one of those types who imagine obstacles to alibi their own failure. He had a mordant sense of doubt about the whole operation.

Frankie rubbed his forehead and turned to James. ‘Who was that bloke from the Yard we used in the Garfield caper last year?’

'Cummins, wasn't it?' James spoke with quiet authority.

'Right. Nip up to the office, James, like a good lad, and see if he has a list of Chaikha Rani temples ...'

'And see if they've anything on a guy called Paajit,' Bob interjected. James walked to the back of the bar, chewing the remains of the sausage, and went upstairs to make the calls.

'Your office is upstairs?' Art queried. 'I always wanted an office over a pub.'

'It's handy enough,' Frankie concurred. 'But the firm is going through a sticky patch right now. How is it for you blokes?' He obviously regarded Bob as a member of the organization. Bob wondered what Aldo had told him in the cable. The pub began to fill up and two extra barmen came on duty to cope with the lunch-time trade.

'We're taking a pasting from the recession,' Art replied and went on to detail some of the business problems as if they affected his own pocket directly. Frankie countered with horror stories of his own; he was a good match for Art in recounting financial and personal setbacks. Both of them seemed to agree on a general conspiracy theory with domino effects thrown in for good measure. Comparing the styles and habits of their respective leaders, they disagreed about Aldo's strategy of keeping his distance from the Caporegimes. Frankie, who from his insights seemed better connected than Art and much closer to the Consiglieri, did worry, however, about reactionary elements coalescing round Aldo's rivals. Bob became edgy listening to these idle, speculative exchanges; they were going nowhere fast.

'So, you're a salesman?' Frankie included him in the discussion. 'So was my old man. He used to have a stall in Petticoat Lane.' He recalled how the rozzers finally caught up with him in Dirty Dick's with his fence. 'They threw the poor sod into clink. He died there doing porridge. He deserved better than that.' He exuded such an injured air it was hard to be sympathetic.

'Too bad,' Bob said impatiently, not sure he followed the story. 'Shouldn't we see how James is doing?' He wondered how good Frankie was going to be; first impressions didn't inspire confidence. But there was that hint of a hidden side. Anyway, James was no lightweight.

The upstairs office was tidy and functional with heavy metal filing cabinets lining the walls, tubular stacking chairs and a couple of old-fashioned black bakelite telephones squatting on the steel desk. James was just replacing the receiver when they entered. He stood up to brief them. 'Cummins thinks there might be a guy called Paajit who used to run with an anarchist group in France. A real shit-disturber who also turned up in Iran after the coup. Then he went to the States.' He paused to consult his note pad. 'Cummins thinks he got into cults in LA but broke away and set up on his own in New York where he got his tail caught in the wringer. He is in London now.'

'Where?' Bob asked.

'He doesn't know.'

'If we sweeten the pot?' The run-down on Paajit's sinister history made Bob wary but even more determined.

'It wouldn't do any good.' James spoke with quiet authority. 'The trail ran out in London. The law lost interest in him because cults are not illegal.' He ripped the page from the pad, crumpled it in a large fist and threw it in the waste bin.

'So what do we do now?' Art asked. 'This info and five cents wouldn't buy you a cup of coffee. We've got nothing.' He tipped the hat back on his head and sat looking up at the panelled ceiling lights, framed behind plastic honeycomb fixtures.

'We could use the media,' Frankie suggested. 'An advert might ...'

'We've done it,' Bob interrupted. 'He wouldn't fall for that again.'

'Then we'll just have to put the word out to our chaps,' Frankie said. 'It'll mean a lot of shoe leather.' He shrugged; it wasn't his best ever idea.

Bob had visions of waiting again. In that killing desert where the horizon went out and out beyond imaginable space, leaving him lost and paralysed. He couldn't go through that again.

Art sat quietly, his rubbery lips sucked in. 'Why not rope in the police? Their patrols could keep an eye out.'

An exasperated sigh escaped from Bob. 'You haven't been listening, Art. The cops are not interested.'

'They don't have to be interested,' Art replied.

'Come off it, mate.' Frankie turned aside dismissively and sat in thought on one of the stacking chairs. Bob, however, saw something in Art's face that he had seen before, good openers, a pair of aces at least. 'Go on, Art,' he said.

'Well, the way I see it is this,' Art began, knowing he had the floor at last. 'The cops don't have to know why they're looking for this guy. All you have to do is put the fix in right. Give 'em Paajit's description and just sit back and wait.' Frankie was about to interrupt but Bob silenced him. 'Mind you, I hate doing this to the boys in blue,' Art continued, 'but the end justifies the means. Right?' He scanned the waiting faces for confirmation of this principle.

'Right,' Bob agreed. 'But how do we put the fix in?'

'Find a dispatch officer who has a price. Get him to put Paajit's description on the wire, an APB maybe, with orders to locate not apprehend. It's been done before.' He sat back basking in the silence.

'He's not just a pretty face,' Frankie said. 'James, what about that duty sergeant at Bow Street Central Dispatch?'

'It's worth a try,' James said. 'Although he's been lying low recently.'

Art took out the wad of notes. 'How much do you reckon?'

More waiting. And wait he did, trapped in the hotel room overlooking Marble Arch, playing poker endlessly in shirt sleeves on the bed, afraid to leave the phone, subsisting on papery sandwiches and warm beer. In this hothouse he nurtured hatred for Paajit, that failed anarchist and hypocrite who peddled his wares in the safety of a cult. Though the enemy was now personalised, Bob couldn't say that he knew him. There were still too many pieces missing. But he knew enough.

It would have been much worse without Art, though even he could be infuriating at times, so fondly pandering to his stomach, constantly carping at various aspects of culture shock, itching nevertheless to see the sights, and always ready to pass some inane remark about the social mores of the host country. 'Jeez, the British sure go crazy about soccer. It's a sort of compensation.' Their conversations were light and inconsequential with a forced whimsy, a sort of mumbled incantation to fend off fear until they had to face it. Being closeted with him proved one thing: Aldo had not sent him to spy on Bob.

On Thursday morning just after seven, persistent ringing drilled into Bob's sleeping brain. He groped for the phone with a sluggish reflex, but became instantly alert when he heard Frankie. 'We might have something. A panda car spotted some nutters peddling trinkets at Lords. Lot of West Indians in town for the cricket. Could be a false lead but it's the only one we've got.'

'I'm not with you ... Was Paajit identified?' Bob sat up and flung off the bedclothes.

'Maybe. A sort of make. The plod followed them out to Kilburn.'

'That's where they live?'

'I don't know. But they work the streets there, selling literature and stuff. It's a long shot.'

'It's something,' Bob shouted into the receiver. 'Get over here fast.' He jumped out of bed and pounded on the adjoining door to Art's room as he pulled on his pants.

Chapter 20

The VW beetle careered through the cobbled streets of Georgetown with the hood down, and the brown-stone houses flashed past in a blur of terracotta and leaf green. Barbara, who was trying to get her legwarmers off after a dance class, gave up and grasped the dashboard. Her dog, Si, crouched in the back seat, wind ruffling his shaggy fur.

'The stores stay open till six,' Barbara said timidly, tightening her grip on the dash.

'So?' Linda's hair was blown forward over her face as she turned sideways.

'Nothing. There's no ... rush. That's all.' Barbara decided to leave it alone. They made the green arrow into M Street and were slowed by the traffic and promenading crowds.

'I'm glad you could come.' Linda liked to go shopping with Barbara who was good fun and had excellent dress sense. Her dance spot at the club gave her the money and time to pursue her first love, modelling.

Linda slewed the car into a parking space at the shopping mall and they made straight for Bloomingdales. They passed the cosmetics counter where customers dabbed perfume on wrists and tested lip gloss in small powerful mirrors that turned eyes into lakes and pores into craters. This scented bower sent eau de cologne wafting all over the store. Linda groaned when the mesmerising vista of dresses came into view. Thank God for Barbara who had already taken the plunge and was waist deep among the revolving racks, lifting a hem here, reading a tag there, like some tropical botanist searching for a rare species.

Linda entered the maze from a different direction and worked her way towards the center. A couple of dresses caught her eye but, on holding them up against her front and to the light, she changed her mind. She and Barbara worked in silence, bent to their grim task, sullen as cotton pickers under a blazing sun.

Eventually Barbara straightened up with a triumphant look in her eyes. 'I think I've found something.' She detached a russet flouncy number from its hanger and held it at arms' length in expert appraisal. 'Yes, I think it's you.'

'I don't think so ...' Linda demurred. 'The color doesn't seem quite right.'

'Try it,' Barbara insisted, looking at the hem and halter-neck stitching. The finishing was the key.

Linda always felt a little foolish coming out of a dressing room and parading in front of a mirror in new duds. It was an odd quirk since she had little fear of appearing on stage. She didn't have much confidence in her own judgment about clothes. Her mother had never been interested and her family had other priorities. Linda grew up on hand-me-downs and so hadn't much opportunity to choose. She knew what to wear for her act but off-stage she preferred to be casual rather than chic; it was safer that way.

Barbara circled her in serious thought, a forefinger tapping her lips. She caught the garment by the page-boy shoulders, raised it a little and let it fall into a more natural sweep.

'What's the verdict?' Linda asked in a strained whisper.

'Mmmmm.' Barbara nodded slowly as the picture came together. 'Yes, it's you all right. No question about it.'

'Good. I'll get a couple of these.' Linda turned to retreat into the privacy of the dressing room.

'No, you won't. I've spotted a different model. You've got to try it. And you need some accessories.'

Much later, when the assistant was wrapping up the purchases and taking a credit card stencil, Linda said, 'Thank God that's over.'

'It should be fun,' Barbara remonstrated.

'I suppose so. But I couldn't go through this without you. You have great taste.'

'Well, modelling is my business. Or will be. I have two choices. To dress this skinny frame or undress it. And believe me I'd prefer the former.'

They took their bearings from a direction finder in the mall and set off to explore a new boutique. They passed a coffee shop that had a window display of schwarzwald cake, pecan pie, mille feuilles, and gooey eclairs arranged like spokes of a wheel. These and other creamy comestibles were laid out on doyleys in the landscaped window, the centerpiece of which was a huge layer cake with a wedge cut out to show its anatomy of sponge, cream, fudge and marzipan.

'Barbara, don't stop here for God's sake.'

'But I can't move. I'm rooted to the spot.' They laughed, looked stealthily around and plunged in. The decor of bamboo, wicker and rubber plants had a touch of Eden and was suitably decadent.

'We must be compensating for something,' Barbara said, biting into cherry pie and hot chocolate sauce. Linda laughed at the irony. Barbara was hardly sex-starved. She played the field and put alphabet-soup ads in the *Washingtonian*: "SWF, ISO SM with sense of humor and savoir faire. J pref." J was for Jewish and W for white; the specification did not exclude black gentiles.

'Well, are we going to double-date tonight?' Barbara asked, delicately licking off a long-nailed finger. 'You'd like David. he's cute, and very physical.'

'I'll take a rain-check.' Linda really wasn't interested in casual encounters. Blind dates meant too much fencing and trying to impress; the men were usually gauche, self-centered and pushy and they took themselves so seriously.

Before Bob she had had a couple of serious affairs which at the time seemed magical and full of promise. It was odd how the feeling could be the same and the men so different. Maybe she allowed herself to be taken over too much. She sometimes wondered at how the pain of separation could wane and finally disappear. Did it mean that love itself could be outgrown? The thought of transience saddened her.

She had never met Sal or even seen her but she was scared of her in a way, almost sensing her brittle courage, and the effort that went into that studied poise, drawing fully on her Puritan WASP reserve. Maybe she should meet her to see if she was quite so formidable. In a way she sensed that Sal was her own worst enemy.

What worried Linda more was the possibility that the impending divorce had contributed to Robbie's unhappiness. Maybe joining that idiotic cult was his way of hitting back at his warring parents. Did Bob feel this in some shape or form? Linda didn't want that kind of responsibility.

'Si, come here. Sit!' Barbara patted her dog's rump and made him sit under the table.

'How can you call him Si?' Linda knew that Si had been a former boyfriend.

'Because Si, the creep, was hairy too and shed all over the rug. Also there were doubts about his pedigree.' Barbara laughed but there was a trace of bitterness in it. She changed the subject. 'How's Bob? Any word from London?'

'Not yet. But I'm sure it'll go all right.' She had complete, almost childish, faith in his abilities. Nothing was beyond him once he put his mind to it, so her heart bragged, and his strong face, which now floated up for her, was verification enough.

Barbara herded the crumbs of cake into a neat pen with her fork and said without looking up, 'You really complicate your life, don't you?'

'Meaning?'

'You know. An older man, married. That son business. The whole can of worms.'

'Barbara, it's not something you plan. It happens. They're the breaks.' There was no need to go further in defending Bob or herself. She didn't put ads in the *Washingtonian* or engineer tacky affairs with specified ethnic males, flaunting their credentials. A real relationship meant taking the rough with the smooth.

'I guess I prefer simplicity. Clean lines.' Barbara's hands moved out and down as if tracing the flare of a classical gown. 'No complications.'

'Sounds like skating over the surface to me.' With her ingrained memory of narrow Neapolitan streets, ragged kids and families living cheek by jowl in the Bassi, Linda found Barbara's prescription flat and antiseptic. A real man had callouses and complications and the fates snapping at his heels; how else would he acquire strength?

'Maybe.' Barbara's expression dealt with a sad memory. 'Once bitten and all that. At this time in my life I don't want anything heavy. Who needs it? I'm doing what's right for me now.'

Linda touched her hand. 'I hope it works for you.' She was intrigued though at how Americans in general regarded their lives as being completely within their own control, to change at will; it wasn't selfish, just a matter of private ownership, inherited wealth that should be invested wisely for their future. Why, after all, feel shy about changing your life when you owned it?

'Still,' Barbara persisted, 'be careful. You could get hurt. You're twenty-eight years old. Look what you're taking on ... To be honest I don't see much of your old sparkle ...'

Linda bridled and said abruptly, 'We all have to grow up. OK, I'm in a complicated situation. Bob's son ...'

'But it's not just the son,' Barbara interrupted as gently as she could. 'If Bob is the man you say he is don't you think he's going to want to help his wife through that awful business?' She shrugged apologetically; maybe she'd gone too far, but it had to be said.

Linda didn't answer. It wasn't as if she hadn't thought about this, but hearing it from someone else ... A shadow fell over her; what started out as a shopping spree had turned into a bleak and harrowing appraisal.

In her dressing room before the club opened she went over some song scores, pencilling them in her own shorthand for breathing pauses and grace notes. Maybe it was too soon to try out 'Memories'; she'd been having difficulties with the phrasing and the range was a little beyond her. A couple of notes off the top would help. She hadn't quite decided, when Aldo barged in.

He cleaned off a chair and sat down heavily. 'God it's a mess in here.' He hooked his well-shod foot under a fluffy wrap and kicked it on to another chair.

'Make yourself comfortable,' she ribbed him though she guessed that something was bothering him.

'Does that cleaning lady ever come in here?' he asked truculently. 'Do you know what the payroll is for this joint?' He snorted with glum satisfaction at the unresponding silence.

Linda turned round from the dressing table to face him although she could read Aldo blindfolded. 'What's the real problem?'

He swivelled the chair for a while tossing his head, then ground a fist into an open palm. 'It's Meo, our dear brother. What a flake.' He sniffed some more as if the air itself were conspiring against him. 'He's getting into some shady deals. I said no, you can't put the clock back like that, the old way is gone, *passato*. But will he listen?' It was rare for him to discuss business with Linda, though they were close in other ways. He had leant on her a lot when their father had his first heart attack and spent ten days on a knife edge in intensive care. She folded her arms. 'Go on.'

'This is *nascosto.*' He tapped the side of his nose. It was their childhood word for a confidence. He waited until she nodded.

'You know I want to move with the times. To get the best legal and financial brains on board. Information is power now. Silicon chip revolution and all that. Right? So there's no need to go outside the law. There's plenty of opportunity out there without taking risks. Insider trading, asset-stripping, leveraged buy-outs. It's all fair game, especially under this administration. Free enterprise is back in town.' He brushed some ash from his trouser leg and watched it flutter to the ground. 'I mean look at those juicy defence contracts and those beltway bandits out in Virginia and Langley. My God, we're talking megabucks, drowning in gravy. But Meo can't see it. He just cannot see it.' Aldo grimaced at such culpable ignorance and held his head as if to retain his sanity.

'Or maybe he doesn't want to see it,' Linda offered. Knowing her two brothers she had no doubt that Aldo was right. His pained extravagances didn't cut any ice; she had learnt many years ago to see through the fancy web. Deep down he made sense.

'Well, whatever.' Aldo waved her contribution aside to get back to the real issues. 'This you won't believe. He's making contact with people in Colombia. And you know what that means. Christ, the narcs are crawling all over the Caribbean basin and Miami. Who needs it? It's crazy.'

Linda studied her hands which rested in her lap. 'Why do you think he's doing this? It doesn't make much sense.'

'Maybe he wants to impress the people in New York. And they don't impress easily. Meo's heading straight for shit city.' He stood up and let his hands fall to his sides.

'Did you fight with him?' She remembered the time shortly after his tenth birthday when Aldo accidentally started a fire in a deserted warehouse they used to play in off the Via del Duomo. Meo, who was the last to leave, exaggerated the damage and threatened to tell their father. He kept that hold over Aldo for almost three years.

'A bit. Shadow-boxing. Christ, he's stubborn, *ostinato.*' He appealed to heaven with outstretched hands.

Linda knew all too well the unstable chemistry between her brothers; when they were younger she had often been forced to mediate. Meo almost died once because Aldo dared him to climb down a simmering crater in the volcanic region of Pozzuoli. She guessed they were still over-reacting to each other like phosphorous and water. 'I think you should let it lie for a while. Sleep on it.'

He stopped pacing and gave an abrupt laugh. 'You always say that. Just like Mama. The sky is falling. Sleep on it.'

'It's good advice. What else can I say? I don't know the business. But I do know what Meo is like. Remember when he took on that huge *poliziotto* at the Festa di Piedigrotta just because you said he couldn't? There's only one way to stop him.'

'How's that?' He leant against the wall and looked keenly at her.

'Agree with him.'

He gave a snort of derision. 'Knock it off.'

'You know him,' she insisted. 'If you say black he says white. It's sibling stuff believe it or not, *rivalita*. He always wanted Papa's attention. And to be seen as his own man. Being the oldest wasn't easy. He worked fifteen hours a day in that *forno* when you were at college. Then you graduated and got all the credit.'

'You're breaking my heart.'

'Aldo, I mean it,' she said sharply. 'You should at least try to see it from his point of view. He doesn't have an education. How do you think he feels being surrounded by your Ivy League types? Threatened, that's how. The feeling that it's all slipping away from him. That's probably the reason he wants to go back to the old ways.'

'Have you been talking to him?' he asked suspiciously.

'No, of course not.' She frowned at the implication. 'It's all so obvious I'm amazed you can't see it.'

'If I'm so smart why did the *Padrino* send for him to come to Washington. And leave the company to him?' It was a token point, more churlish than convincing and Linda read it as such.

'You know the answer. Meo is the oldest.' She suddenly felt sad, not just at the rift between brothers, but remembering their childhood in Naples, the anxious striving and pathetic schemes to escape the patronage of better-off relatives. On every birthday Padrino Hitti would come in his car from Rome to collect them.The whole family, who had been ready and waiting for hours, would come tumbling out of that little tenement flat in the Bassi and bundle into the shiny black car. They would usually stop for ice-cream on the Via Manittima and then go swimming at Margellina or take the chair-lift to Pugliano. They enjoyed those outings and treats but there was always a feeling of being indebted and this in turn brought them closer, inspiring the need to join forces and work out their own future. Despite the largesse of the US, her first months in Washington had been miserable. She felt homesick and disconnected. In fact she never fully regained that sense of belonging until she met Bob.

Aldo stroked his chin and smiled slowly. 'Maybe I will sleep on it.' He opened jars of cream on the dressing table and absently smelt the contents. 'Any word from London yet?'

'No. Give him a chance. It's early days.' She resolved there and then to tidy the apartment for his return and plan some celebration.

He looked sideways at her and put the jars back on the table. 'There's no future in it for you.' It was his turn to give advice. 'On that I do agree with Meo.'

'You've discussed it?'

'It came up,' he said silkily.

'Well, don't. I make my own decisions ...'

'Is he using you?' Aldo looked her in the eye. He wasn't really expecting an answer, just putting out a probe to make her think.

'Don't be ridiculous,' she snapped. Nothing was further from the truth, yet strangely she couldn't deny the fact that she felt used. Used by circumstances. Her timing had been badly off from the word go. So maladroit that the fates or birth signs must have conspired against them both.

'You're self-sufficient, we all know that,' Aldo said. 'But some situations ... well, you just have to walk away from them. Don't be confused by loyalty. You're not helping him. How could you? No one could. Think, Linda. Think it out.' He tapped the side of his forehead.

'Shut up, Aldo. For Christ's sake, enough!'

'All right. OK.' He backed away, raising the palms of his hands defensively. 'Sorry. Forget I said anything. You can give me advice. But I can't ... OK, I'm finished.' He paused for a while to let the temperature cool down. 'Hey, you're worse than Meo. Black!'

'White!'

They laughed and walked to the door, where he paused. 'Anyway, you care for the guy. The way you talked me into sponsoring his trip. I should be so lucky.'

She moved closer to him and touched his arm. 'Don't look for a pound of flesh. He's got enough problems. Remember how we used to hate waiting for favors to be called in?'

'Phew, I thought I was the advocate in the family.' His face spread in an easy smile that made him a kid again. 'I'll do what I can. But Meo's the oldest. Right? *Il maggiore*.' He patted her shoulder. 'Come for dinner Sunday, a good old Napoli *banchetto*.'

'Sure.' After he left she turned back to the music sheets, a smile on her face, and decided to try out 'Memories'. But then she changed her mind – for reasons that had nothing to do with vocal range.

Chapter 21

They drove through the heavy commuter traffic out towards Maida Vale, West Hampstead, passing Lords Cricket Ground, thronged even at that hour. Art drew attention to the heavy West Indian presence and the groups of Jamaicans with dreadlocks, nursing beer bottles at the entrances to the ground.

'I didn't realise the Rastas were into cricket,' he remarked. 'I thought it was a sort of posh game.' He needed badly to talk, but none of the other three men in the car rose to the bait.

They turned finally into Kilburn High Street, tattily revealed in weak morning sunlight.

'This is a pretty rough neighborhood,' Art observed, a flatfoot connoisseur of street life.

'You're not wrong, mate,' Frankie said. 'I wouldn't come here on a Saturday night. Bloody National Front mixing it with the Pakis. Queer-bashing is back too, because of AIDS.'

'Why would a cult try to recruit people here?' Bob was worried that they'd been misinformed.

'Lots of strays and runaways live here too,' James said, looking at Bob in the rear-view mirror. 'Kids who can't afford to live down town.'

They drove up and down the high street scanning both sides. The pubs were closing for the afternoon and groups of brusquely-evicted drinkers formed on the sidewalks, blinking in the sunlight. They dispersed slowly, some going to bus stops, some to bookie shops, others seeking out clubs which had special liquor licenses. There were the customary shoppers and street vendors and, yes, James was right, there were many poorly dressed teenagers and young adults promenading or hanging out at corners and billiard halls. But there was no sign of the Chaikha Rani.

They parked for a while outside a seedy run-down pub called The Old Bell. Bob's heart began to sink. It suddenly seemed incredible that at this moment and in this place, five thousand miles from home, he could locate his son. He was also aware of the possibility that Paajit could have hidden him away in some other corner of the huge sprawling city. Frankie lit a cigar and filled the car with smoke.

'What do you think?' Bob asked, losing confidence. 'A bum steer?'

'Cummins knows his onions,' Frankie answered. 'Give it another while.'

They waited in silence. James switched off the engine and put twenty pence in the parking meter. A town hall clock boomed the hour of four. Art opened the back window to let the cigar smoke out.

'Well, I'll be blowed,' Art said. 'Do they wear brown robes?'

Bob swung round, 'Yes. Where? ... Where?'

'Back there, by that filling station.' Art pointed through the back window.

'My God, I think it's them.' Bob felt a spurt of sickly sweet adrenalin. There were seven or eight brown-clad figures in the distance moving slowly in their direction. He heard tambourines and the hoarse sound of a conch shell, and eventually that all-too-familiar chant. His heart raced. 'They're going to come too close … Get over to the other side of the street.'

'Can't do a U turn here,' James said.

'OK, they don't know you. You stay here.' Bob rushed out of the car. He tried the door of The Old Bell but it was locked. He ducked into the butcher's shop next door and peered out the window through the dangling carcasses. Within minutes the slowly-jiving troupe came into view, like a weird mardi gras. Some girls at the head of the procession sold flowers and pamphlets to passers-by. They were followed by the musicians. Bob scanned each proud and vacant face. Robbie was not among them. But at the end of the procession, walking straight and slow, his arms folded inside his robe, came Paajit, like some evil genius parading his creatures before him. Bob waited until they passed the window.

'Can I help you, sir? The pot roast is good today.' Bob looked vacantly at the eager face of the butcher and raced out of the shop into the car.

'Robbie's not with them,' he said breathlessly; there was bile in his throat. 'But Paajit is. We can take him now. Get moving!'

'Easy on.' Art put his hand on his arm.

'We can't snatch him in broad daylight,' Frankie said. 'Just sit tight.'

'We could tail them now,' James suggested, putting his gloved hands on the wheel.

'No.' Frankie disagreed. 'When they reach the end of the street they'll probably come back up the other side. Just relax.' He puffed his cigar.

'Probably!' Bob repeated scornfully. 'We can't afford to take that chance. Take off. Move.' His nails bit into the palms of his bunched fists.

'Come on now,' Art reasoned. 'they'll probably cross over and work the other side of the street. Anyway, there's no point in grabbing Paajit. We've got to find out where they live …'

'We're losing them,' Bob cried frantically.

'All right,' Frankie said. 'If they don't cross at the next set of lights we'll go after them.'

Bob stared with deadly intensity through the windscreen. 'The lights are red,' he shouted. 'They're not crossing!'

'OK. Go, James.'

James had to go up a side street to turn the car. By the time he'd completed the maneuver the procession had disappeared from view.

'Christ, we've lost them.' Bob felt sick. 'You dumb bastards.' He gored them with a look of contempt.

'They must've turned right,' James said evenly. He cornered on two wheels, the steering wheel slipping through his hands like quicksilver as the car straightened out. There was no sign of them.

'I can't believe this,' Bob groaned. 'You turkeys. We've lost them.'

'They've got to be around here somewhere,' Art said in a strained voice.

'Go right on Sitwell Road,' Frankie ordered. 'There are some big houses down there.' James followed the instructions but to no avail.

'Try Golders Lane next.' Still nothing. Bob held his head; he had run out of abuse. Just a dire sense of failure.

Art put a hand on his shoulder. 'It's not the end. We can try tomorrow.'

'Pull over. I'll ask this bloke.' Frankie approached an elderly man who was washing his car with a hose. He wore fisherman's waders.They were engaged in conversation for what seemed like eternity. The man started to point and give directions, tapping his forehead with his finger. Frankie returned to the car. 'He said he saw some strange characters drive off in a van. Go, James.'

'A van,' Bob repeated. 'It could be.' His mind clutched at the hope. Frankie continued to give directions, this time with more certainty.

Finally they rounded a corner and saw a van up ahead moving slowly in the same direction.

'It's them,' Bob breathed. 'Got to be.'

'Pass them,' Frankie hissed. 'Keep going.' James swung the car out and accelerated past. Bob crouched down in the back seat almost lying in Art's lap. They came to a T-junction and had to turn. The van was now out of sight.

'Pull into that driveway and wait. You two in the back stay down.' Frankie got out, went to the front of the car and opened the hood. If the residents came out he could make some excuse.

The van took the same turn at the junction, passed them, and to Bob's profound relief pulled into a driveway farther down the road. The cult members got out and quickly disappeared into the house.

'We've got them,' Bob gloated. 'We've got them. Fifty-six Priory Road.' He repeated the address a number of times under his breath. 'We could move in now,' he said.

'No,' Frankie said firmly. 'We have to prepare … do it right.' They drove by the rambling Tudor house and headed back to the city.

On the way Art turned to Bob and said hesitantly, 'You realise that Robbie … may not be there. They may have moved him …'

'Just let me get to Paajit,' Bob said.

Chapter 22

The run of luck petered out. Bob was up at first light looking out over Hyde Park, a towel round his shoulders, thinking, today is the day. He was pumped up and ready, his mind clear and alert. It was that same cool detachment that stood to him in Saigon when the word to stand by came down the line to his marine unit. He was relieved that he hadn't lost it.

Then Frankie phoned to say James had been called away and the job would have to be put back.

'Something came up in North London,' was all Frankie said in explanation.

'What is this?' Bob asked suspiciously. He never trusted last-minute changes of plan; they often signalled some deeper flaw or even treachery. 'We can do it without James,' he said forcefully.

But Frankie would not agree. 'It's still on for tomorrow,' he assured him.

Art took the news a little better. They were sitting in the sunken coffee lounge off the lobby. 'One more day isn't so bad. Maybe I can get some sight-seeing in after all. They have these tours on double decker buses. Might be worth a try.' His pockets bulged with postcards for mailing. He had been up early writing them to his kids, nieces and nephews. He showed Bob the card for his one grandson, Jaimie; it had a picture of a leprechaun cobbling a shoe on a toadstool.

'Wrong country.' Bob smiled in spite of himself.

'Aw Jeez. Well Jaimie won't know that.' He looked at the card, head on one side. 'Wish it could be more. He's such a cute little tyke.'

Bob sized up this family-centered man, surprised at the envy he felt. For much of his life he had worried about being tied down by a family. Now he was fighting to save his. The irony drilled into him. There was something else that had been gnawing at him and now was as good a time as any to get it out in the open.

'Art, how come Aldo doesn't use you for anything heavy?'

'Who says he doesn't?' Art put the cards back in his pocket and smiled at the waitress who brought the coffee.

'Come on. You're like the old family retainer. No pun intended.'

Art shovelled sugar into his cup and put a cube into his mouth to suck. 'He reckons he owes me.'

Bob gave him a disbelieving look. 'You saved his life, I suppose?'

'No. I whupped him when he needed it. Hey, these scones are good.' He slathered on three pats of butter and a spoonful of blackcurrant jam, then pulled some tour brochures from another capacious pocket.

'You whupped Aldo ... a guy with his clout and his kind of connections?' Bob shook his head from side to side; if this was true he would believe anything.

Art's mobile face moved like a bellows as he chewed. He waved to indicate that he had to swallow first, then he answered, 'Yep. He was just a skinny kid at the time. But wild. I was pounding the beat back then. We were keeping a high profile on the street because of the race riots. Remember? Anyway, I caught Aldo hustling in a trattoria on Fourteenth Street. His family, Tognetti, weren't big then. Sure, I cuffed him. Brought him home too, and let my kids straighten him out.' He clasped his hands behind his neck and stretched massively. 'Aldo's all right. He says he got interested in the law because of me,' he added proudly.

Bob pushed the remaining scones and shortbreads across the table to Art. 'Maybe I'm cashing in on your good deeds.'

'Maybe. But Aldo doesn't have the final say. It's his older brother, Meo, who runs the show. He's so different. Now there's a go-getter.'

Bob absorbed this information and tried to figure out what kind of commitment he had made and what would be expected of him. Maybe he had sold his soul. His skin crawled. A soul for a mind. Some exchange.

The waitress came with more coffee and replenished the butter dish with a little cairn of engraved yellow pats. Art smiled gratefully at her and resumed, 'Since Aldo came on board things are much more legit. Condos, co-operatives, commodity dealing, stuff like that. Sure, they do a little OTB and numbers in south west DC, but that's on the way out.'

Bob had not heard him expand on the business like this before and wondered if it was because he was now on the inside.

'Actually,' Art went on, 'Aldo brought in some Ivy League guys, lawyers and investment analysts. He wants to cut down on the operations side and distance himself from the Family, capital F. I mean a complete break. Much safer that way, more on the up-an'-up. But he's ahead of his time and I don't know if he can bring Meo with him. Meo's a mover and a shaker. Likes to be in the thick of things. Well,' Art put his hands palms down on the table, 'are you coming on a tour or what?' He pushed his chair back, a little gilt bentwood job over which his considerable rump sagged like mule sacks.

'No. You go ahead. I'm not up to it.' He couldn't see himself riding around on a bus, listening to a guide, on the eve of rescuing his son. He wanted to wait it out alone; it seemed more fitting. Besides he didn't want to be too far from a telephone. Art put on his hat and let it settle far back on his head so that he looked like a comic-book detective.

'It'll do you good. You'll only brood here.'

Bob signed the bill. 'I'll stay put. Maybe I should brood for a change.'

His room was made up when he went back upstairs. He hung the 'Do Not Disturb' sign on the door, threw off his jacket and lay down. A day to kill looking at this high ornate ceiling, listening to pigeons communing on the balcony beyond those fluttering drapes, high above the muffled roar of London traffic. From the corridor came the faint sounds of chambermaids trundling hampers of laundry and linen.

He hated hotel rooms. Even when he was a rep on the road he never got used to them, the silent witness of four walls and the strangeness of whatever city lay outside, its blank stare cold against the window pane. There was the subtle exploitation of loneliness, too, the adult movie piped in for a buck, the pimping bus boys and the racks of glossy magazines. He always looked forward to the last day of the trip, knowing he would be home that very evening. Yes, there was a lot to be said for family – some coherence in the void and an enduring legacy when they put you six feet under.

There was still a chance. Linda knew what family meant. She said he would hit it off with her father who had always wanted her to find a mature man to keep a firm hand on her. Good Italian papa. Age didn't matter in Italy where the old folk presided and doled out the wisdom of antiquity and the lessons of moldering stone. Christ, he wasn't that old. Take it easy.

But time was strange; it passed in fits and starts. He felt he had lost a lot of time along the way, been cheated somehow. Vietnam maybe, which put him on hold but didn't compensate him afterwards because the meter had kept running.

Age wasn't an issue with Linda but it had taken him a long time to realise it. The summer before last they had rented a canoe from Fletcher's boatyard and taken it on the Potomac. Linda craned forward in the bow, the waistband of her jeans dipping in a vee towards her rump as she splashed about with the paddle, steering him towards rocks. She leant further overboard to examine algae and water lilies in a quiet inlet.

'They're lovely. *Vorrei comprarmene molti*! So delicate.' She scooped up some fragments and held them to the sun, water trailing from her fingers. Bob knelt in the stern, paddling slowly, watching the slender canoe nose through the water, leaving chevrons of rippling waves in its wake.

Down by the boathouses of Georgetown University some riggers were out racing, feathered oars skimming back over the water as the boat ran on effortlessly beyond the neat rows of whirlpools, the sources of their thrust. Linda shouted for the crew wearing green. 'Row harder. You're catching them. *Via! Via!*'

'Sit down,' Bob said. 'You'll capsize us.'

'Don't be such a worry wart. I want my team to win.' She continued to yell encouragement and waved at the cox who acknowledged with a salute.

'Why don't you go faster?' Linda called out.

'We're dying, that's why.' The cox grinned into his loud-hailer.

'That's no excuse. Put on a spurt. Quickly before the finish ...' She caroled on, then sat down heavily as Bob fought to balance the canoe. 'Oh damn. They lost.'

They clambered ashore near one of the boathouses where a group of students were strumming guitars. Linda got involved, singing and showing them new chords. She helped the green crew carry its rigger up the slipway and joined in the ritual of dunking the cox in the water. Bob felt a little out of it, but needn't have worried.

'Nice guys,' she said afterwards in a way that dismissed them as being fun but immature.

'I thought the cox was putting the moves on you,' Bob said to test her reaction.

'But he's just a kid,' she said with real surprise. 'Out to prove himself. Like those drivers in Rome.' He felt a new confidence.

Further downriver they had a picnic lunch. She had packed endless tupperware containers of chicken breast, salad, mayonnaise, spiced rice and coleslaw. She sat with her legs curled under her, sampling everything with a pensive air and licking off her fingers from time to time.

'You can really put it away,' Bob said in admiration.

'I know,' she agreed dolefully, then jumped up and threw off her clothes to have a swim. 'Got to burn off some calories.'

Bob looked round in alarm. Chain Bridge was already carrying a fair number of early commuters home to Virginia. 'You're crazy.'

'Who cares.' She stepped out of her jeans, minced towards the water and jumped right in. 'Come on in you stick-in-the-mud,' she gasped. 'It's good. *Che gioia*!' He cowered further back in the foliage, keeping an eye peeled on the bridge. He watched her swim right out to the middle of the river and perch like a mermaid on one of the half-submerged rocks.

When she came out finally it was with a squeal and a splash because a frog or something slimy had touched her. She dripped all over Bob and wanted to make love there and then. He held back, dithering and out of his depth, ashamed of being so straitlaced.

'You don't want to.' She was downcast and hurt.

He made a helpless gesture, 'It's just that ...'

She stepped away from him, her face flushed. 'You can't be ... *come si dice?* ... spontaneous.' She snapped her fingers disparagingly. 'You have no sense of adventure. *Che fastidio!*'

'You don't understand ...' he began wearily, searching for the right words.

'Now you tell me I am stupid. Ha!' She shimmied energetically into her jeans and zipped them up with a vengeance.

He moved towards her, leaving the relative seclusion of dogwood and maple trees. 'Come on. You know I don't think that ...'

She threw out an accusing finger. 'You are a stick-in-the-mud right-wing Republican with no imagination. No flair.' She tapped her forehead and splayed her fingers into the air.

'Does it take flair to go skinny dipping in a muddy river almost in the city center?' He was in deep now and felt sure he had left himself open to an attack on his middle-aged sense of propriety. But it didn't come. Instead she lectured him on what flair and spontaneity really meant as she threw all the plastic containers into the hamper and marched towards the car.

He grinned now at the memory of that innocuous and indeed reassuring row. From then on the age difference faded from his agenda as he realised that it had never been on hers. It took him longer to learn that her huffs left no after-taste of rancor, did not strike at the roots of their relationship, but were simply reactions that came faster than blinking, raw and unedited. He got hooked on her directness which had the speed and color of a tracer bullet. It was a relief to be with someone so natural, without inhibitions, angles, images or a yen to put a face on things. What you see is what you get.

Her directness had to come from inner security, a solid memory of family, perhaps. But it seemed more the prerogative of elderly people who had reached the age of indiscretion, had no axe to grind any more as they entered the long glide path home. Linda's claim on this quality set up an intriguing contradiction. Young and self-assured, unconcerned about the future; she had it all, happy in her skin.

Although Bob lacked it in his early life he did develop something like that same sureness of step when he arrived in Da Nang with the first marine unit in May of '65. He knew what he had to do, he believed in the mission and he learned not to think about the future. He had killed and been injured, coming out just ahead of the game.

His training had prepared him well; combat simulation left no room for unsettling imagination. Death and destruction were hazards of war. He had no illusions going, and consequently no surprises during the two rough years he was based in Saigon. As a gunner in a chopper, he did his job well, in a workmanlike way, keeping his head down, going by the numbers. He was mentioned in dispatches and promoted to marine sergeant in the field. They said he had a good war.

Long afterwards it amazed him how he became so acclimatised, even to the hourly prospect of death. The outrageous passed for normal. Once, flying over a paddy field near Tongking they were strafed by a unit of Vietcong firing from a copse of ilex trees. The pilot caught two rounds in the head. It was bad, a fatal wound. He slumped over the controls and the chopper went into a downward spiral. Bob did the only thing he could do. It wasn't until after the war that the agonising thought came – often in dreams – was the pilot really dead when he pushed him out to take over the controls?

But that was the function of training; the substitution of reflex for thought. In a way he had been brainwashed, not by the Vietcong but by his own people in Quantico, one hundred miles north of Washington. The questioning, fearful, imaginative part of his mind lay dormant for his tour of duty. Heroes were trained, not born. So he had first-hand experience of conditioning, circuits implanted in his head. His hope for Robbie derived from the fact that it was reversible; he had the image of dissolving sutures. Even his comrades who were worked over by the Vietcong, using techniques developed during the Korean war, reverted to normal when they came home.

He hadn't talked much about the war with Sal, sensing that her liberalism would pre-empt discussion. Having put his life on the line he didn't want to hear that it was all for nothing or that Kissinger had misread the Sino-Soviet split or that there were wider issues involved. He had done his bit the best way he knew how. Shortly after he came home he moved to a separate bedroom so that he could handle his nightmares on his own without having to explain his actions in the field. He didn't want her sympathy either. It would have made him cringe, since he had enlisted against her 'better judgment'.

When they finally, and almost by stealth, built the Vietnam memorial on the Mall, Bob went on his own to the unveiling and spent hours searching the black marble walls for the names of his fallen comrades. Although this was nine years after the war it was the first time he felt able to close the book.

It had taken him that long and he was hardly a sensitive soul or a deep thinker. Sal of course thought too much, that was her problem – analysis paralysis. Still, he did respect her careful, thought-out approach, although he was never quite sure what was going on in her head. You could drop a stone in her subconscious and never hear the splash. All he knew was that what she did say was only a minute fraction of what she had considered. It was mystifying and often unsettling; he sometimes had the eerie feeling of being judged and sentenced silently without even knowing what the charge was.

But he depended on her judgment in many ways as long as she didn't crow over him. He had no problem deferring to her as far as Robbie's upbringing was concerned. You had to trust someone who sifted everything with such care and who had an over-developed moral sense. She was a challenge too in a way. On that rare occasion he made her see something his way or differently – usually the same thing – it gave him a charge. It was rewarding in the early years to get a laugh out of her. It was an abrupt kind of barking laugh that surprised her as much as anybody; it was good to hear.

She was not amused by his salesmen friends who were typically roughcut, and a little of whose company went a long way. 'There's no substance to them,' she would say almost sadly after they'd left the house. 'All those silly jokes and pranks. It's arrested puberty.'

'It's a hangover from being on the road,' he would defend them. 'It gets so boring out there you have to do something to relieve the monotony.'

'They might consider growing up.'

Bob usually gave up at this point though he once offered the observation that we were all children in the sight of God. It did not endear her to him or to his knights of the road.

He had to admit though that her first introduction to them had been less than felicitous. Norm, his best man, took it upon himself to liven up the wedding reception. He and a couple of cronies, feeling no pain, made off with the three-tiered wedding cake which, during an argument about where to hide it, came to rest in a flower bed outside the hotel, face down among the petunias and gladioli.

He knew that Sal found him a lightweight, but he didn't set about changing his character. He believed in playing the cards he was dealt. He had said this to Art one night last fall in the Gattopardo, and Art asked him what kind of hand he'd been dealt. Bob thought for a while. 'I guess a pair of deuces.' Then he added, 'But I can bluff.'

'How about Sal?' Art warmed to the game.

'A full house.' Bob didn't have to think about it. 'But she can't bluff.'

Art laughed. 'And Linda?'

'Three queens.'

'Can she bluff?'

'No. But she could charm another queen out of the dealer. How about you?'

Art rubbed his chin. 'Jeez, I didn't even ante up.'

Sal was right, of course. He hadn't done much with his life to impress anyone. Apart from work he was easy-going, liked football, boxing and locker-room antics; his favorite color was red but he wasn't macho anymore, and he didn't want to be president. Lacrosse he could take or leave, and he had no views on the cold war except that he would prefer to be vaporised right off in the heart of the fireball rather than linger on with radiation sickness, growing mushrooms under the stairs. His most recent view was that since Reagan's toughness had called the commie bluff, the greatest threat to world peace now came from the Middle East. Apart from that he had few thoughts he could call his own. Like Art, if he finally earned that all-American title, 'regular guy', he could pass on in peace.

He wondered if being smart was wise. There were so many idealists out there who had brains to burn but didn't know their own shoe size. They threw themselves into causes, dazzled by their own brilliance, and sailed like lemmings over the cliff.

He would have liked Robbie to be more wily and street-smart for his own protection. But he wasn't and his school pal, Geoff, could buy and sell him. Geoff once traded Robbie a glass marble for a brand new fountain pen. When he got home from school Robbie proudly produced the marble, holding it up to the light and smiling. Bob felt sick at the thought of his son being conned like that and tried to explain it to him as gently as he could. Sal hadn't helped much, pointing out that the value one placed on objects was a subjective matter.

Robbie looked from one parent to the other and then at the marble which splayed the sunlight through its swirls of color.

As Robbie neared his teens an awkwardness developed between him and Bob; it was vague, wraith-like, a resonance in the air, but each felt sure the other was aware of it. The first inkling perhaps came when Robbie refused to join the McLean junior soccer league. Bob tried every trick in the book to get at the reasons, but Robbie was not forthcoming.

'… If it's the wheeze you sometimes get don't worry. You can play center back or even in goal …'

'It's not that,' Robbie said dismissively as if the wheeze had never been a problem, or that he was now too grown up to worry about such things.

'Well then what is it?'

'I just don't want to play. It's that simple …' His expression tried to trivialise the whole idea but there was also a pleading in his eyes not to go on with it.

'Robbie, please tell me. We can work it out.' Bob was conscious of a distance opening imperceptibly, a sense of fading into memory. 'Is it the locker-room. You know, changing in front of …'

'Aw Dad, come off it.' He winced and clamped his mouth shut. And Bob never did find out what seeds were growing in him. But he was anxious about this big gauche boy trying to make his own way and it somehow mirrored his own first sad steps to independence, when he too had grown a shell which would never be pierced. He couldn't make sense of what he felt, beyond knowing that Robbie would never again run to him with a grazed knee or a story from school. It was all too close and crowded for perspective. He still had that freeze-frame image of Robbie escaping with his secrets through the screen door into the sunlight of the garden …

The corridor was quiet now; the chambermaids must have finished the floor. Bob looked at his watch. Almost noon, probably the quietest time in a hotel, all the rooms vacated, empty beds wrapped tight in sheets, a funeral parlor pall in the palatial emptiness. Everything felt hollow and unreal. He got up and paced the room, tracing the design of the carpet. Time lay heavy on him. He wanted to call Linda. But then he should also call Sal … There was no news anyway. He shaved again for want of something to do. Seeing his face blown up in the round magnifying mirror he wondered whether it was strange or familiar and had no answer. Too close to know for sure.

He wiped off the rutted shaving cream, went down to the lobby and bought his first pack of cigarettes in twelve years.

Chapter 23

'I agree with Frankie,' Art said. 'It's best to wait for nightfall.'

Bob ground out a cigarette. 'Christ, another day to kick our heels.' He was weary from idleness and worried in case he couldn't retain that mental state of readiness he had worked to achieve. Athletes had the same fear of peaking too soon. There was something unreal about waiting in a plush hotel, staff pussy-footing by, very formal and polite, voices lowered, ageless dowagers in fur coats sitting over coffee. Sense deprivation in a rubber room inside a furry time warp. One could go quietly mad and feel no pain.

Art rocked on his heels in front of the graceful Adams fireplace. Lifts moved silently in the well of sweeping stairs. Across the lobby the oak reception desk, like a judge's dais, intimidated the sparkling chic boutiques that led to the dining room.

'The changing of the guard was great,' Art said. 'Those fur hats are something else ...'

'Haven't you done enough sightseeing?' Bob hadn't left the vicinity of the hotel for two days. When the confines of the room bore in on him and the cabin fever reached a climax he had walked around the block but no further. He knew every mews and elegant Georgian house, every Bentley and blue 'police notice' on the block. He lit another cigarette. They were beginning to taste like they did twelve years ago.

They finally compromised on a movie. Bob sat in the silver-vectored darkness listening to Art laugh and feeling his amused lurches which sent vibrations down the whole row of seats. His mind darted restlessly from action plans to memories and back again. He remembered another movie, *California Split*, his favorite of all time. He had forced Sal and Robbie to watch it with him on home box office the winter before last. At the point where the two drunks in the bar were trying to name the seven dwarfs Bob cracked up: Doc, Bashful, Grumpy, Snoopy ... No, not Snoopy. He's not one of them ... It got funnier each time he saw it. Sal just didn't get it though she laughed finally because he was so helpless. Robbie's reaction was also delayed and even more diffident, like a sycamore seed falling in a high wind. They just couldn't see the humor because it was all nonsense and of course they were right. But he was right too. The only thing was that he was out on a limb.

Half way through the movie Bob went out to the foyer and called Frankie to make sure it was still on for later. It was. The arrangements had been made as planned. He looked at his watch. It was still only three-thirty. He went back into the cinema.

Later, walking down Oxford Street, he said to Art, 'I bet there'll be a hitch. I'm not sure about Frankie.' There was little accusation in his voice because his doubt included himself.

'Relax,' Art said. 'It'll be OK.' He wasn't very convincing and wished he could take his own advice. Trying to distract himself by scanning passers-by, he remarked, 'They have as many blacks here as in DC.'

'So?' A hawker selling hot digital watches made them an offer and Bob shook his head absently.

'I just didn't expect it, that's all. Can't imagine the blacks have much chance of making it here. With the class system and all. Still, could be wrong ...' They stopped to let a group of schoolchildren enter Bond Street Underground station. They were being shepherded by two nuns; an orphans' day out perhaps. The distant roar and breeze of a train came up from the bowels of the earth, followed by the faint clang of automatic gates. A Cockney outside the entrance arranged evening newspapers on a little wooden table. They walked on. Bob's head was bowed and shadows moved in the twitching hollows of his face.

'The US embassy is just over there in Grosvenor Square,' Art said pointing. 'That's where we go if ...' He didn't finish. 'Pity it's not Sunday. I'd like to see those characters at Speaker's Corner. The tour guide yesterday said it's a gas.' He looked hopefully for a response and was disappointed. His stomach was beginning to churn. Unlike Bob, the closer it came to the appointed hour the more the anxiety would build. He wanted to talk. 'Look at all those folks leaving work already. And more in those office buildings over there just walking around. Maybe a late tea break. What do you think? Doesn't anyone do any work around here?'

Bob consulted his watch again. The evening was still too bright for the luminous paint to show the digits and too dark to see without it. 'What time is it?'

'Four-forty,' Art swallowed hard, flailed by doubts.

'We're getting there.' Bob was beginning to feel a little better. 'You all right?' He gave him a sidelong, testing glance.

'To tell you the truth my stomach's acting up. Maybe if I ate something ...'

They sat in a nearby Golden Egg in the relentless buzzing light that swept along all the chrome and glass facets of this palace of fast eats. Behind the counter the Pakistani chef, his back to the customers, skimmed ground beef patties on a flat steel grill, moving them along deftly, making room for the raw ones that went down with a hiss. Art tried a cheeseburger and a glass of milk. 'Once the system gets hooked on junk food you've had it,' he said belching slightly. 'You go into withdrawal in these good hotels. Sure you don't want a hamburger? Cheese is good for the bowels, binds you up. Well, you know that from 'Nam. It's the rennet that does it. Know how they invented cheese? The Arabs used to carry milk in a calf's stomach, or was it a camel's stomach? Milk is good too.' He held out his tumbler. 'Kind to the system. We're never really weaned. Right?' He broke off to re-set his loose dentures, covering his mouth with his free hand. 'Ever have that feeling, what am I doing here? It's strange, isn't it? Life ... Why am I talking to myself. Hey, Bob, your pants are on fire.' He put the cheeseburger down. His big fingers had left depressions in the sesame-seed bun crusts, crescents of brown skin open like eyelids exposing the white floury inside. He fiddled with a decanter of white vinegar. 'For Christ's sake say something.'

'It'll be OK, Art. Lighten up.' Bob smiled slowly, staring at the tiny grease spots floating on his coffee in a mug as thick as a kitchen sink. It was getting dark at last. The sodium street lights were coming on except for one just outside the café which sputtered like a caged canary and died. Offices and stores were discharging their hordes. It seemed a long time since Bob had punched a clock but he used to hit the streeet too just like that, breathing in the freedom, sometimes waiting for Sal and Robbie to pick him up. It was all of a life ago. Queues fringed the sidewalks, forming mysteriously, lengthening like sentences from a telex machine. Bowler-hatted city gents sat into throbbing cabs and opened their newspapers. Punks headed for the tube, past barrow boys, bobbies and traffic wardens who waited for this hour. Landlords took towels off beer pumps and lined up half tankards on the bar; their wives put out reheated sausages and scotch eggs left over from lunchtime.

Soon the street cadences would change and the West End would almost evaporate, growing impossibly quiet in that grey interregnum between end of work and beginning of play. Some raindrops fell intermittently, signalling a downpour. People scurried quickly and gulls wheeled and headed back to the Thames. The darkening ribbon of sky was a lead roof soldered to the granite and limestone buildings. The vibrant red of buses and telephone kiosks began to fade to grey.

'Let's get back.' Time at last had come for Bob. There was that same stirring in the bowels as when the word to scramble passed down the line in his billet in Saigon. Contact. Then and now. The chopper on the pad, primed and fuelled. He was ready.

'There's still an hour.' Art wanted to play for time. The milk hadn't helped; his stomach was a mess.

'Now.' Bob stood up.

Chapter 24

Sal had mulled over the idea for some time and, with Bob away, the opportunity presented itself. She wasn't convinced she needed help or that it would be forthcoming, but one session wouldn't hurt. The notion of paying to talk to somebody was chilling. Nevertheless a professional approach had something to recommend it. It would be easier than talking to a friend, less demeaning and safer. She had called Dr Lanyi and made an appointment.

She parked on Wisconsin Avenue and entered the building. The institute suite was right opposite the elevator on the fourth floor. When she opened the door she got a charge of static electricity which threw up the grim but whimsical thought of shock therapy. In the waiting area there was a hot-water urn and jars of ingredients for coffee and tea. Two women sat under a cork bulletin board displaying institute services and cartoons from the *New Yorker*. Sal sipped her coffee; her mouth was dry. She was acutely aware of the presence of the other women whose conversation had lulled. Was her neurosis showing? She lit a cigarette and crossed her legs. The women resumed their chat in low tones.

'So I told him straight out that I resented it. I'd never been so direct before. It's a good feeling.' The other woman nodded and said, 'I can relate to that.'

Sal felt uncomfortable. There was something precious about parading quirks and bleeding on the carpet; the desire to prove one's uniqueness was pathetic. She wondered what she was getting into.

Dr Lanyi ushered her into a sparsely furnished office and showed her to an armchair. There were cushions on the floor, probably for group therapy. He had a grey moth-eaten beard and brown steady eyes and was reassuringly old enough to have heard it all before. He wore corduroys and moccasins which he kicked off when seated. There was some form-filling and a short introductory spiel about confidentiality and the difference between therapy and analysis.

The conversation, when it began, was sluggish and hesitant, though easier than she had expected. Of course it was mainly at this stage biographical data, a safe outside narrative which helped prime the pump. She talked more easily, leaning forward, fingers interlocked on her knee. He nodded, bird-like, drinking in the information, making sympathetic sounds. Rogerian mirroring technique, she sensed. There were techniques for everything – communicating, listening, maybe even living. That bleak thought entailed Robbie and another stream of disconnected images that ranged from cults to psychocybernetics and a world where computer software replaces the human spirit and machine language becomes irresistibly user-friendly. Only religion remained, but it too was manipulated by TV hotgospellers, buffed and toupéed, selling the blood of Christ like detergent and slaying in the spirit, ten bucks a throw.

Sunlight through the window was sliced by venetian blinds. She removed the jacket of her suit. Dr Lanyi altered the angle of the plastic slats, nodding to show he was still listening.

'You're not giving. We're dealing with feelings.' He resumed his seat and rested his stockinged feet on the coffee table.

'I don't feel anything.' It was true at that instant, as if her heart lacked a memory.

'Your marriage is on the rocks. Your son has disappeared. And you don't feel anything?' His quizzical face froze pending an explanation.

'Right now, I don't.' Her eyes followed the charcoal lines of an abstract painting above his head; there was a sort of comfort in the non-figurative forms. He leant forward joining the tips of his fingers. 'So why are you here?'

'It seemed a good idea at the time.' She ground out a cigarette in a standing brass ash tray and let the residual smoke curl from her nostrils. She was floating, out of touch, in some absurd kind of existential trance; if anything it felt good. His unwavering eyes didn't faze her.

'Earlier, when you told me about your family situation I saw someone who was concerned. It was in your face and body language. Then you used cigarettes as a prop to give the impression of aloofness. It doesn't wash, Sal. Why not ask for help? From what you told me I think we may be dealing with some magical thinking here. You feel that asking for help is a weakness. Or that you might use up your quota of God's grace and have no further call on Him when the chips are really down. This kind of self-rationing is quite common among spiritual people.' He paused and looked intently at her. 'How do you feel about that?'

She thought for a while, looking down at the synthetic nylon glint in the pile of the beige carpet. He had touched a nerve. 'There's something in that, I suppose.' She had a desire to be honest. 'I don't like to ask for help, as you put it, too often. The boy who cried wolf … there seems to be merit in holding off in case a real need arises. I'm not sure we should presume on an infinite amount of divine grace …'

He waited, reading her face to see if she would go on. 'Don't you think you have a real need right now?' he prompted.

'It could get worse.' She immediately regretted it.

'How?'

She felt trapped. There was no answer, except losing her husband and her son, sinking into alcoholism. Did he really expect her to say that? Her heart quickened to a sickening refusal. 'One could think of … scenarios …'

'This isn't a debate, Sal,' he said gently. 'We're not scoring points. I said you were concerned earlier. Now I see fear. Control, yes. But fear too.'

'I'm not afraid. Worried maybe. That's to be expected.' How had he detected fear in her? It was just a try on.

He stroked that straggly beard and craned forward. 'Your defences are up again.' She didn't deny it but simply asked how she was supposed to respond.

'Get in touch with your feelings and you wouldn't have to ask that question,' he said.

'Everybody blocks from time to time,' she replied evenly. 'It's natural.'

He nodded his agreement but added, 'Do you know why? Hiding feelings usually means insecurity.'

She shrugged and pursed her lips, unimpressed by that snippet that could be gleaned from the blurb of any self-improvement paperback to be found in any corner drugstore along with true romances and motor mechanics.

'It's often the fear of rebuff,' he went on stolidly despite the disaffection which he felt coming from her. 'The fear that people may laugh at our deepest feelings. It's a vicious circle too. The more we repress, the more we fear revealing ourselves. Does that make sense to you?'

'Of course,' she said smoothly, feeling safe again. 'It's a very natural reaction. There always is that risk of rejection.'

He joined his hands in front of his face, hooking the thumbs under this chin. This wasn't going anywhere; she was side-tracking again. His partners called it the 'convention syndrome' because the patient joined in the discussion as if he or she were at a convention of shrinks instead of being in therapy. He wasn't sure to what extent Sal had slipped into this mode or had chosen it deliberately. He would have to turn her around or quit. 'How do you imagine your feelings would come out? Do you have a fantasy about that?' The question was oblique, not directed to the nature of her fear.

She loooked at her hands clasped in her lap. 'I suppose it would be maudlin ... unseemly.' Her father gave flowers to her mother on her forty-fifth birthday, carnations and dahlias. Unbelievably, her mother had turned aside and cried. The flowers were kept in a vase on the sideboard long after they were withered. Sal liked the gesture and the happiness it brought. But there was something pathetic about her mother's reaction. How could she allow herself to be bought for a bunch of flowers that had probably been selected by his secretary? Sal lit a cigarette, stating, in case he thought it had some deep significance, that she like to smoke.

'Sal, you sound as if you are talking about someone else. This session is for you. You. If you don't reach within yourself we're not going to progress.' He stopped to see if this was getting across. 'Now, could you elaborate on what you mean by unseemly?'

'I'm not sure. Demeaning, I suppose. Raw. Too raw ...'

'What do you associate with raw?'

'Naked.' She looked up in surprise and decided to go on. 'Shame ... outpouring. Loss of control ...' The white noise of the air conditioning suddenly intruded. Nausea swept over her. She was in some derelict tenement smelling of last week's garbage. His waiting was relentless. 'I wouldn't be able to stop ... Hysterical maybe. Like an animal ...' Her voice was getting louder, blaming him for this. 'Being seen as wild ... unladylike. Yes, out of control. There would be so much shame ... afterwards.' She rummaged in her purse. He pushed a box of kleenex towards her along the glass-topped coffee table. It seemed so crass and pre-meditated to have a lousy box of kleenex to hand.

'How do you feel right now?' His eyes were sympathetic but she knew he was a predator. She stopped sniffling and pulled herself together.

'I'm all right.' She looked into the middle distance, feeling ashamed and manipulated. He had orchestrated everything, right down to the tissues.

'You have strong feelings. You will have to let them out. They don't go away.'

'It's a little simplistic, isn't it? The idea that repressed feelings must erupt or cause cancer or something.' She made a dismissive gesture. 'There's nothing wrong with being guarded.'

'What about the panic attack you mentioned earlier?' He wasn't ready to give up just yet. 'Those attacks happen for a reason ...'

'I'd been playing tennis. It could have been physical.' She turned aside. 'It's all so trite.'

'So is the truth. Obvious and pedestrian. We're not very complex mechanisms when all is said and done. We want to be different of course. Enigmatic and interesting. But that is just a rationalisation for hiding ourselves. The real reason is, as you said, the fear of being rejected after we've put out to someone.' He chose his next words very carefully. 'It's not pride. It's despair.'

'That's ridiculous!' She fell back as if she'd been hit. Despair was the sin of the non-believer, the person who refused to put his trust in Christ. Dr Lanyi was being gratuitous in using these moral terms.

'Why is it ridiculous?' His steady gaze pinioned her. She felt real anger at being goaded by this shrink playing God. The slow-burning magma spread through her, deadening other senses, suffusing her mind. Distantly, like a faint echo, she heard him ask, 'What are you thinking about right now? Right now.' Close to the edge, perilously close with pressure building behind, forcing her over. 'My father ...' she rehearsed under her breath. But she couldn't. Not now. Not ever.

He looked at his watch and stood up. 'Think about it, Sal, before our next session.' Watching his departing back, she felt used and humiliated. Why in God's name had she come here? She felt battered, beaten to a pulp.

Her head swam as she drove home and tears of shame blurred her vision. By rote she drove into the Giant Foodstore parking lot to pick up some groceries. The refrigerated air helped to calm her as she wheeled the cart along the aisles, past the bathroom section and around by the seafood. She traversed several aisles before even thinking about her shopping list. Then it struck her that she had no one to shop for. She stopped by a tank of live lobsters and tried to collect herself, watching the feelers slowly waving in the aerated water.

It didn't take long to finish her rounds of the store and it was the first time she had ever qualified to exit through the express check-out – five items or less. The amazing shrinking family.

'Hi, Sal.' It was Geoff's mother, coming in to shop in her tennis outfit. Sal hadn't seen her for about five months and would have avoided her now if she'd had the chance. 'How's the family? Has Robbie decided about college?'

'Not yet.' Sal smoothed her eyes with a forefinger and forced a smile, relieved that the secret was safe. Clearly this neighbor had not seen or heard about the TV program. 'How's Geoff?'

'GWU. Engineering. Can you believe it? An engineer in the family. He'll be living at home too.'

'That's nice,' Sal said.

'You know,' the woman moved closer to share a confidence, 'we were very lucky. Geoff nearly got invoved in the Chaikha Rani – the cult that's in the news these days. Fortunately he showed us their promo literature and we talked him out of it. There but for the grace of God … You just can't be too careful nowadays …' She went on shooting the breeze while Sal bent forward over her almost empty cart trying to absorb the unintended blows that rained down on her.

'Are you all right, Sal?'

'I'm fine, thanks.'

'We're having a little celebration on Friday. Maybe you and Bob could drop by?'

'We'll see … I'll call you.'

'Sure thing. I must fly. I'm out of everything.' The tennis skirt flapped against her brown hamstrings as she headed towards the frozen foods.

Sal walked out of the store into the blistering heat and didn't give in to the hurt until she was safely inside her car. On the way home she stopped by the ABC liquor store.

Chapter 25

James checked the equipment, snapped the briefcase shut and stowed it in the trunk. Then he changed the tags on the car and nodded to indicate that he was ready. He sat behind the wheel, switched on the ignition and moved out into the traffic, driving carefully so as not to attract attention. It was ten-fifteen and there was no moon, a good night for what lay ahead.

There was no conversation; each man nursed his own thoughts. From time to time Art shifted position in the back seat to give relief to his stomach. Other than that and the muffled hum of the three-litre engine there was no sound.

It was about eleven when they reached Kilburn and turned into Priory Road. James switched off the engine and let the car cruise to a stop outside the house. The cul de sac was quiet and the nearest street light was safely distant. Frankie and James slipped balaclavas over their heads.

Using the hedge for cover the four men approached the front of the house, moving slowly so as not to crunch the gravel underfoot. To the left of the steps leading to the double oak doors was an annexe that looked like a conservatory. Inside, a brown-robed figure sat, reading in a dim light.

'Damn.' Frankie pulled James back into the shadows and signalled a retreat. Back in the car he said. 'How do we get past that look-out?'

'There might be a way,' James suggested. They agreed a plan of sorts. James went to the back of the car and got what he needed from the briefcase. Then he went back into the garden on his own, crouching as he went. He moved on to the grass and positioned himself behind a tree to the left of the conservatory.

They didn't see his arm rise but they heard the gravel rain down on the glass roof of the conservatory. The figure inside stirred, looked up and went back to his book.

'Again!' Bob said under his breath. The pattering sound reached them once more. They saw a torch being switched on. As the disc of light moved closer into the open they saw James circle round the tree, keeping cover. The torch beam swept the garden and the bushes, and then went out. The figure went back towards the conservatory.

James moved silently across the grass. There was a muffled cry as his arm went around the sentry's throat. Instantaneously his right hand did its work. He kept the pressure on until the chloroform took effect. He dragged the prone figure across the grass and left it on an incline behind a laurel hedge.

'Good work,' Bob whispered when James rejoined them. Just then a van turned into the cul de sac, its headlights on full beam.

'It's more of them,' Art groaned.

'Get down,' Frankie ordered. They crouched behind the car in the shadow. The van passed slowly then stopped. At the turning circle at the end of the cul de sac it went into reverse, the vicious revs shattering the silence. It passed them again, its lights raking the hedge behind them. Relieved, they watched it turn back into the main road.

'Jesus Christ.' Art passed a hand across his face.

'All right,' Frankie said. 'We should be able to get in through the conservatory now.'

'No,' James said. 'The annex is separate. I had a look. There's no adjoining door.'

'Are you sure?' Bob asked.

'Yes.'

'Then it's back to the original plan,' Frankie said. 'The front door.' He started to move forward.

'Wait,' Art had an idea. 'Maybe the guy in the bushes has a key on him.'

James checked this out but returned shaking his head. He and Frankie then went towards the steps leading to the main door. They worked quietly on the lock using an assortment of steel instruments in the light of a pencil torch. After about ten minutes they returned to the car.

'It's no use,' Frankie whispered. 'It's a Yale GX, tempered steel. We'd need Barney for a job like that. It's a fucking fortress.'

Bob looked at the door. One door separating him from Robbie. He knew suddenly he was in there. 'Blow it off,' he grated.

'No way, mate,' Frankie said. 'You're crazy. Let's try the back. James, you and Art keep an eye on the bloke in the bushes. Give him another whiff if you have to.'

Frankie and Bob crept round the side of the house and climbed over a wrought iron gate. The back garden was long and walled and had what looked like a mews at the far end. Staying close to the back of the house they peered into the downstairs windows. The first room was a large tiled kitchen in which two cult members were doing chores.

They had to get past that window to test the back door. They crawled under the level of the sill. The back door was locked, bolted on the inside. Judging by the sounds, someone was approaching it from the kitchen. They crawled away and lay face down as one of the orderlies came out with a plastic bin. With his face down in the grass Bob had no way of knowing whether the light from the door reached him or not. His heart hammered against the earth like a pile-driver. He heard the rattle of trash cans and finally the sound of the door being bolted again.

'It's OK,' Frankie whispered. 'Work your way over to the far wing.'

The main window here was lit but heavily curtained. Bob found a chink. It was a very large candle-lit room, almost full with kneeling or crouching figures; he sensed that some ritual was about to begin.

'How about the upstairs rooms?' Bob asked softly. Checking these out meant going further down the garden into the open. It was risky.

He followed an ivy-covered wall for as long as he could. Of the four upstairs windows only one was lit. He was just about to return when a figure came to the window and looked out. Bob stayed rooted to the spot hardly daring to breathe, pressing his face into the ivy. The light from the window was on him. There was no doubt about that. His only chance was not to move. But that meant staying unsighted. He was trapped. Obviously Frankie could see him but would he understand the predicament? He wanted desperately to turn his face but couldn't risk it. Fortunately, and to his enormous relief, he heard the sound of a window sash being lowered and bolted and drapes being drawn. Slowly he turned around. The danger had passed.

Back in the car they compared notes.

'There's no easy way in,' Frankie said. The kitchen was out of the question because it was occupied, the doors were impregnable and the upstairs windows seemed impossible to reach because, as James pointed out, the steeply pitched roof gave no hold for a grappling hook.

'Jesus Christ, we've been here for an hour already,' Bob said. 'And where have we got? I say we take our chance with the kitchen ...'

'Look, if we bust in we lose the element of surprise.' Frankie was adamant.

'Then we wait right here until morning and catch them coming out.' There was finality in his voice.

Frankie rounded on him. 'You're beginning to get up my nose, do you know that? This has to be covert. You can flit back to the States. But this is our patch. I'm not going to face a kidnapping rap for you or anyone else.' He pointed a finger at him. 'Now you do it our way or not at all.'

'He's got a point,' Art reasoned.

'I didn't come here to piss around,' Bob said in a strangled whisper. 'Just give me one of the pieces you're carrying and you can take off. Just get out of here ...'

'Right. If that's the way you want it. It's no fucking skin off my nose ...'

'Oh Christ, cut it out,' Art pleaded. 'Just calm down.' He was half hoping they'd call it off, at least for tonight. It wasn't his just stomach now; the pains had moved to his chest.

The four men sat in the car in silence. There was no way Art was going to let Bob go in there on his own and yet he knew deep down that they couldn't just walk away. There would be no second chances. For one thing the sentry would be discovered and the cult forewarned. They had to do it now. Somehow.

Chapter 26

The patio table was near the huge maple tree where Robbie used to have his tree house. Although the tree clogged the gutters with its leaves each fall, Bob refused to cut it down. Over by the double garage was a patch of burnt grass where home plate used to be and, fixed to the redwood deck that led from the kitchen, was a basketball hoop that had come a little loose. The yard which was sprinkled in summer and ministered by Lawndoctor in winter was full of memories.

Sal sat at the table feeling wretched. There was a time when she had worked well there, with Robbie in the tree house and Bob swaying in the hammock slung between two copper beeches, the *Washington Post* over his face.

Thinking it might be better to be active she started to clip the hedge beyond which the Cross family cavorted in their pool, but quickly moved to another hedge where there was less risk of being drawn into conversation. The routine of work calmed her and she tried to understand the anger that Dr Lanyi had provoked. And then bumping into Geoff's mother in the supermarket …

She had to keep something in reserve because there was always further to fall. Despite her rationality there was a corner of her mind that warned her not to tempt fate by aspiring to happiness. Several times in her life she had ignored that magical axiom by presuming upon good feelings – with disastrous consequences. She resolved never to take that risk again; instead she would pitch camp on a safe low ledge and leave the summit to the foolhardy.

Perhaps she took everything too seriously. Her mother used to rib her about having no light touch. When she was fifteen she worked hard to develop a light touch but it never came easily to her and eventually she gave up the attempt with the consoling thought that light touches were for lightweights. She sided with Socrates: the unexamined life wasn't worth living. Where did that leave Bob who muddled through without a care in the world?

For years she had experienced the quiet satisfaction that Robbie was deep-rooted and substantive, and would have a sound whole life on this planet, perhaps even make an impact. That was why the recent events hit her so badly. It was precisely because of his constancy that he had made a total commitment – but to an obscene lie. A light touch might have helped him to laugh at Paajit or ridicule him, as Bob would have done, instead of falling under his spell. Yes, Bob would have laughed the whole thing out of court, whereas Robbie, poor serious Robbie had walked right into it and given himself completely. It was galling. That innocence could be so misused.

In all of the New Testament there was not one reference to Christ making a joke or laughing …

'Galleys ready yet, Sal?' Father Molloy walked into the yard, bowing as he passed the elevated deck. Oddly, she was not glad to see him. Instinctively she replaced the sunglasses which had been pushed visor-like up into her hair.

'I'm afraid not. Maybe this evening.' She waved him to a cushioned wrought-iron chair, pulled off her gardening gloves and brought out some iced tea.

'Any news yet?' he asked meaningfully, setting his briefcase on a nearby chair. Because of the humid heat he wasn't wearing his collar and his neck had that sick hue of proud flesh.

'Not yet. Bob hasn't called.' She sat opposite him and poured tea into the frosting glasses.

'Well, hang in there. You should hear something soon.'

After some silent rehearsals she told him about her first and last experience of therapy. She left nothing out, seeing it as a sort of confession and hoping he would deem her anger to be justifiable. He listened intently, his faded blue eyes the colour of washed denim. He had nothing against therapy; he just couldn't see the point of it. For him the peace of Christ was all anyone needed. From long habit he repeated in his mind: Be still and know that I am Lord. Be still – it was such a wonderful injunction, carrying with it the confidence and concern of a real father, seeing the commotion in the heart of his child. Be still.

'We all have trouble with feelings,' he said gently. Sal was not going to get the endorsement she wanted. 'When I was a young curate in LA I preached for years about St John's concept of love. But I always called it "charity". I just couldn't say the word "love". We're all scared of it.'

'But despair ...' Sal began. 'I'm not sure of the connection. I thought I understood it but now ...' It was unusual for her to appear confused.

'I suppose what he meant was that if you're afraid to show feeling then it might suggest a lack of trust in God and His creation. But "despair" seems a bit strong.' He looked at her in the shade of the huge patio umbrella and wondered if he was helping. She sipped from her glass; the amber liquid flared in the sun.

'I'm just not sure why it bothered me so much. There seemed to be a moral implication.' She felt wretched, as if her mind now was blocking. The priest in his dusty black suit seemed to move out of focus in the heat haze.

As if reading her thoughts he moved his chair out of a sun patch. They were all lost, seeking shelter. 'I suppose hiding feelings could be a form of dishonesty,' he said. 'Imparting information is easy. But imparting yourself is something else. Christ did show anger in the Temple. I suppose we don't really communicate unless we put out to one another. And that's always a risk. Yes, I think I see what he was getting at. Complete honesty is risky.'

Sal was hurt. It almost seemed as if her long-standing mentor was in league with Dr Lanyi. She would have to think all this through later when she felt better. 'Maybe I'm not the Christian I thought I was.' The churlish inflexion of self-pity appalled her.

'Don't judge yourself, Sal,' Father Molloy said kindly. 'Some people are very … up front emotionally.' He winced inwardly at this jargon but reminded himself of St Paul's advice to use the idiom of the day. He waved a mosquito away with a vague limp hand. 'It's easy for people like that to share everything. You always know where you stand with them. Bob is a bit like that. You're different, more guarded. But who can say he's better than you? It just comes more naturally to him.'

She sat rigid, letting this new humiliation wash over her. Despite his attempted neutrality the priest really was implying that Bob, a worldly non-believer, was in some sense a better Christian. And she had worked so hard at it, gone by the book. So now she was the Pharisee, the whited sepulchre; it was a rough twist. The fourth step of her mother's Alanon program was to take fearless moral inventory. Now Sal's time had come to confront herself. Since Robbie took after her he must have inherited the same capacity for self-deception. Going by the book had failed them both. She was sickened by all the wasted effort.

The priest watched her stroke her temples and close her eyes behind the sunglasses. He was drawn to this deep-thinking woman who tried so hard to reason her way to goodness. She was inner-directed, strong and yet helpless, as if her strength recoiled on her, catching her unawares; it was so unfair … to her. The conflict made her brittle; it vied in her face. She was the kind of woman he would have chosen if that had been his vocation. He remembered when he reached that dangerous age for priests, mid-thirties, the final cross-roads, he had agonised alone in his room and decided to go on. If he'd met Sal then …

He had an urge to put his arm around her and say: Sal, you are a wonder. Lighten up old girl. Take off those glasses and look at the sun. The breathless sky. Look around you. It really isn't so hard to live. Instead he patted the back of her hand and said, 'We're all restless. Remember Augustine: "My soul will never rest until it rests with Thee, O Lord." Sometimes,' he squinted into the sun, 'I think we have no tolerance anymore. We want instant gratification. We should accept whatever comes, offer it up. Surrender.'

She looked up. Something was coming together in her mind. 'That might be it. I haven't really surrendered.' She though of that startling Easter rite where the celebrant prostrates himself on the altar in complete surrender. She had seen Father Molloy perform this liturgy of the cross. It had always fascinated her, not least because it was so abject. God gave the gift of free will and you freely gave it back, to be guided by Him in everything even unto death, yielding up the instinct for survival itself. If one could do that in faith there could be no fear, no despair. She prayed silently for a stronger faith, realising that she had slipped. Maybe because the Chaikha Rani had shown the mutation of blind acceptance, the obscenity of faith in the abstract, which could, directed to a sinister purpose, engender passionate belief even in the Anti-Christ. Tears came to her eyes when the priest put his hand on her head and prayed over her, 'Blessed are those who believe and have not seen ...'

Full of self-loathing she dredged that lurking question from the depths of her misery, 'Could faith be ... conditioning?'

'It could be,' he answered gently. 'But not when you know the Lord.' The sun declined behind the maple tree and evening was ushered in by cicadas and the glimmer of early fireflies.

'Do you know ... Him?' Her voice was hoarse, and faltered with the admission of her own lack of faith.

'Yes,' He nodded slowly and added in a quiet understanding voice, 'I'm not brainwashed, Sal.' She wept openly then.

He blessed her and said, 'God will strengthen your faith. Be open to Him. Peace be with you, Sal.'

Chapter 27

Despite his keen desire to put a thousand miles between himself and that dark, sinister house, Art knew they would have to do the job that night. He had done what he could to heal the growing rift between Bob and Frankie and had just now made a practical suggestion which, judging by the silence, Frankie was still turning over in his mind.

'I could do it,' Bob said.

Frankie ignored him and consulted James who said, 'It depends on how well secured it is. It's worth a try, I guess.'

'All right. Take what you need. If you get inside you know what to do.'

'Sure.' James hooked a jemmy and diamond cutter to his belt and made for the house in a crouching walk.

From the car they watched him test the strength of the old metal down-pipe. He began to climb slowly, planting his feet against the brickwork. Chunks of rusted metal, dislodged by his gloved hands, fell to the ground as he rose. Half way up a metal bracket gave way and the pipe started to come loose from the wall. He paused to take stock.

'He's not going to make it.' Frankie reached for the torch to signal him to come down.

'Give him a minute,' Bob urged. 'Let him decide.' The pipe was still connected at the top of the building but it looped outwards so that James could no longer reach the wall with his feet. He crossed his ankles around the pipe and began to shin up, painfully, inch by inch. There was one more retaining bracket between the window and the roof; it all depended on whether that one would hold. A chunk of mortar fell to the ground.

'Christ, it's going to give way,' Art groaned. Just then James swung sideways and grabbed the window sill with one hand, taking some of the strain off the pipe. He eased himself up another few inches until he had both hands on the sill. He found a toehold in the old brickwork and climbed the rest of the way until he was kneeling on the window ledge. He started to work on the middle pane. They heard the faint sound of the glass cutter and the snap of a latch. James slowly pushed up the lower half of the window and eased himself through, feet first.

He dropped quietly to the floor behind the heavy drapes and peered into the room. It was a kind of dormitory. In the gloom he made out bunk beds and sleeping bags on the floor. He waiting for a while until his eyes grew more accustomed to the dark. But even then he couldn't be sure that the room was empty. With the Browning in his right hand he cautiously edged forward into the dark, airless interior. The smell of incense and sweat made him want to gag.

Picking his steps between the empty sleeping bags he reached the bedroom door and gently turned the knob. The door opened on to a large landing which was partially lit. He could see the staircase. If anything went wrong he could vault over the banister and get to the front door before they got to him. Maybe. Just then a robed figure came up the stairs and knocked at another door further down the corridor.

'The Ranitka is starting in two minutes.'

'Be right there,' a voice answered.

The figure moved across the landing in James's direction. James gently closed the door and pressed back against the wall listening to the footsteps coming closer. A knock sounded on the door. 'Come down. Two minutes to Ranitka.' James raised the gun over his head, holding it like a club.

'Did you hear me? Is anybody there?' The door began to open.

'Be right there,' James said.

'Good. See you later.' The footsteps receded. James took a deep breath and waited a couple of minutes for the ceremony or whatever it was to start. He heard two other members going downstairs and reckoned that by now the top floor was deserted.

He crossed the landing and edged down the stairs, staying close to the wall where there was more cover and less creaking. As he approached the last flight of steps he stopped dead and flattened himself against the wall. Paajit, dressed in white and flanked by six acolytes, passed along the ground-floor corridor in procession. James stayed put until they'd gone into the room where the ceremony was to take place. He heard the gilt doors close after them and he waited for another while until he heard the chant begin. It seemed almost certain that all the inmates were now assembled in that room. A quick search of the ground floor seemed to confirm it.

He moved cautiously past the entrance to the temple, went down the corridor to the front door and unlocked it.

'Anybody see you?' Frankie whispered. James shook his head. The four men entered the house and found themselves in the long dark hall which smelled of incense and tuolene. With James leading they followed the sounds of chanting which came from behind the ornate door recessed in an alcove towards the back of the house. The walls of the corridor were panelled in dark wood up to about shoulder height. At this level a shelf extended along the wall and held, about every five feet or so, a small altar dressed with flowers, night lights and smoldering joss sticks. Above each station – the resemblance to the Stations of the Cross was striking – there was a gilt-framed picture of a temple leader. Bob scanned the pictures until he found the one of Paajit. He noticed the prayer mats that lay carefully folded beneath it.

The temple door was not locked. Frankie drew his Browning automatic from its holster and with his free hand eased the door open half an inch. He gestured to Bob who peered into the chamber. At the far end of the room he could make out several statues on an altar dimly lit by candles. The statue in the center was in the form of a satyr playing a flute; it was white and stood out from the rest. Surrounding the altar were six pillars, five in white, and one in black.

His eyes gradually became accustomed to the darkness in front of the altar. He could see Paajit sitting cross-legged in the middle of the room on a flower-covered dais about one foot high, surrounded by some thirty brown-robed disciples. They swayed slightly to the chant. He couldn't distinguish any other form or face; Robbie could be there but he had no way of knowing. At a command from Paajit the chanting grew louder.

'Now!' Bob whispered urgently.

'No. Wait.' Frankie grabbed his arm.

The chanting grew in volume and became more frenzied, sometimes in harmony and sometimes dominated by one voice as if the spirit moved in a single soul. Then the chorus receded and the chosen voice came through, strident and triumphant. At regular intervals a figure rose and approached the altar with bowed head, placing flowers, fruit and money at the feet of the all-presiding statue. As they passed Paajit they bowed to him and he put his hand on their heads. They returned from the altar backwards and sank down on to the prayer mats. All the time the chant was building again to a crescendo of desperate pleading.

'My God,' Art groaned, scanning the moronic confraternity.

Paajit suddenly stood up and blew a conch shell. There was immediate silence. The kneeling figures stopped writhing and bent forward touching their heads to the floor, arms extended in supplication.

'The Lord Rani has descended,' Paajit announced, approaching the altar with outstretched arms. He mounted three steps and bent to kiss a black stone on the altar table in front of the statue. Then he turned and addressed them. 'We wait for Him to speak through me, His servant ...'

'Now!' Frankie gave the command. The four men crashed through the door.

'Stay down!' James shouted. He dropped to one knee holding the gun with both hands. The shocked silence was broken by screams which gradually subsided to a continuous wail with an echo of incantation in it.

'Who are you?' Paajit demanded. He shaded his eyes with his hand. 'How dare you disrupt the sacred Ranitka?'

Bob scanned the room desperately for Robbie while the others took up strategic positions. He shone a torch in the scared yet disassociated faces one at a time. They all looked the same, flinching from the light. He could hardly tell the sexes apart. In a moment of terror it came to him that Robbie had blended completely into the cult and become indistinguishable in mind and appearance. What if he was here but he couldn't recognise him?

'Where's Robbie? Where's my son?' he shouted.

Paajit made the connection. 'It's you. Don't you ever learn?' In his white robe he stood on the top step of the altar, unmoved by it all.

'Where's Robbie?' Bob demanded again, his fear compounded by Paajit's composure.

'He's everywhere and nowhere,' Paajit intoned. 'Part of the shared soul of Rani. Now, enough of this! Sondal, call the police.'

A girl wearing a hejab got unsteadily to her feet and went towards the door.

'You're not leaving this room, Honey.' From his kneeling position James drew a bead on her.

'Be a good kid,' Art said nervously, 'and sit down.'

'Go!' Paajit insisted. He freed a bare arm from the folds of the robe and pointed to the door; his denatured face flickered briefly at the force of the command.

The girl edged in that direction. Bob grabbed the other gun from Frankie and put it to the side of Paajit's head, his other arm around his throat. 'Take another step and your leader is a dead man. This time he won't have a prayer.'

She stopped in her tracks, crumpled to the floor and began to moan.

'Obey me,' Paajit commanded her. 'They can't hurt us. We are the Divine Within and they are but Euchites of the outside world. They have no dominion over us. Remember the teachings ...'

Bob cocked the gun and pressed it to his head. 'Do you think he has the power to survive a forty-five calibre slug? It would rip out what's left of his fucking brain.'

'Do not fear the Evil One,' Paajit said imperiously. 'It is nothing but a tribal dance of intimidation, a false show that cannot prevail over our reality. Rani has sent them to test your belief. Sondal, go. You have nothing to fear. Rani is with us.'

She got to her feet again. Bob felt a new concern. Were they all so mad that they had no sense of fear? Paajit didn't seem to be fazed by the gun pressed to his head; he was in control and offered no resistance. Did he really have the power to loose and bind ...? On an impulse he knocked Paajit to the floor, whirled round and smashed the gun barrel into the white statue which shattered into a thousand pieces. Frankie took his cue, kicked over trays of offerings and set about destroying the other statues. He picked up the black stone from the altar table and smashed it against one of the pillars. The sounds of destruction were followed by an unearthly silence.

'Where's the power of Rani now?' Bob demanded. 'See, there's nothing left to save you or your precious leader. You poor deluded bastards.' He kept a strangle-hold on Paajit's neck to prevent him from speaking. He turned to the girl who was on the verge of hysteria. 'I'll ask you one more time. Where's Robbie? Tell me or your leader's head's going to come off just like that junk statue.' There was desperation in his voice. It was his last play. Paajit tried to speak but Bob increased the pressure on his throat. He would kill him if he had to.

'Sleeping upstairs ...' she moaned.

'Get him. Frankie, you go with her.' It was working. At last. He released the pressure on Paajit who said with a deathly smile, 'Take your pick. We're all the same. Our souls are bonded. Uniqueness is a western invention. It makes no difference who you take, no difference at all.' He started to laugh. 'Do you see? The battle must be won. There is no escape from that. So whoever you take, Rani goes with them and his vengeance is boundless ...'

'You're full of shit.' Bob said it almost as an aside; his attention was now focussed on the doorway. They waited in a strange motionless state.

Art surveyed the prone figures and murmured sadly and in bewilderment, 'What do you kids get out of this? God in heaven, you poor bastards. Conned right up the yin yang. Do yourselves a favor and get out of here.' He rubbed his abdomen which was giving him hell.

Sondal returned first and fell trembling to her knees. Frankie followed, carrying a gaunt figure in his arms. 'Is this him?'

Bob looked at the taut drawn face and nodded. But the relief of having found him, of being able to identify him, vanished as he took in the weakened condition of his son. Robbie tried to speak coming out of sleep, 'Is ... it time ... already?'

'It's time to go home.' Bob's voice shook.

'I ... belong ... here.' Some dim awareness showed in Robbie's half-closed eyes.

'Yes, you belong here,' Paajit said. 'You are being taken by force, by Lakhryon, your father. You go to Maya, alienation from the deities but you have surrendered your will to us. The struggle must continue or you will never know freedom or inner peace ...'

'Shut your mouth!' With a short powerful jab Bob knocked him to the floor. He stood over him, the pistol poised above the shaven head ...

'No!' Art bellowed. 'Leave him. It's over.' In three strides he reached Bob who handed the gun to him as if he couldn't trust himself with it.

Frankie carried Robbie out to the car. Paajit got to his feet and called after them, 'He'll never be yours again. He never was yours. Robbie, remember what you've been taught and you will overcome. Your will is here with us.' He stretched out his hand palm upwards and closed it into a fist.

'Up your ass,' Art said, 'you mad goombah.' He and Bob left. James waited for a while, ordering them to stay on the floor face down. Then he retreated quickly, ripping out the phone as he went down the hall.

They put Robbie in the back seat and took off at speed, leaving the dimly lit doorway of fifty-six Priory Road, hopefully for ever.

'We made it,' Bob said in disbelief. His hands trembled from delayed shock; he was running on empty.

'It was touch and go there for a while,' Frankie said. He removed the balaclava and used it to wipe his sweating face.

'We made it,' Bob repeated vacantly.

As arranged, Frankie took a syringe from a case and filled it from a small bottle.

'Are you sure about this?' Bob asked uneasily.

Frankie jabbed the needle into Robbie's arm and shot the plunger home. He was out cold within ten seconds and breathing normally. They took off his robe and put new clothes on him, slacks and a pullover. Bob had a bad moment looking at the emaciated body. He started to say something but his voice broke off.

'Take it easy,' Art said. 'He'll recover. Give him time.'

Bob nodded. His mind was blitzed by conflicting thoughts which came and went too quickly to be dealt with. They had done it. He had rescued Robbie. But he looked so sick and weak. What had they really done to him? What was it that Paajit said, or was it Sal? Had they committed an outrage, flown in the face of God? He started to shake again and fought to control himself and those racing thoughts.

As if reading his mind Art said to nobody in particular, 'That place really spooked me.'

They passed through the lobby of the hotel, supporting Robbie between them, pretending they were all a little drunk. They put him to bed in Bob's room.

'He'll be out for the night,' Frankie said. He straightened up. 'Well, that's it I suppose. Mission accomplished.'

Bob paid him the balance of the money and thanked him for his help. He turned to James and said, 'We couldn't have done it without you. I won't forget what you did.'

'That's OK.' James smiled for the first time; he could have been a different person. It came to Bob that he didn't know these men at all and never would. They just did a job, got paid and left.

'I'm sorry I dumped on you earlier.'

'No hard feelings, mate.' Frankie extended his hand. 'Maybe we'll work together again sometime. Give Aldo our best.'

After they'd left Art asked Bob if he was all right.

'A bit shaky, I guess.'

'Get a good night's sleep,' Art advised. 'We can get an early flight to Kennedy tomorrow. If you need me just holler.'

'Thanks.'

Art went through the connecting door to his own room.

Bob lay on the bed next to Robbie's. He was too wound up to sleep. Besides, he couldn't take the chance in case Robbie woke up. His mind raked over the day's events. Despite several near misses it had worked out well in the end. Maybe even Paajit had been discredited in front of his disciples. That would be a nice bonus; better than making a martyr of him. But there was still a doubt in his mind that he couldn't get to grips with. He displaced it with the incredible thought that here he was with Robbie at last, as close as that time they'd gone camping in West Virginia and slept side by side on the ground-sheet. As if to confirm the fact he got up several times and sat on the edge of Robbie's bed, looking at the thin face, tense and twitching even in drugged sleep.

'Whatever it takes to make you well ...' he swore under his breath. 'However long it takes.'

He lay on his bed, leaving the ceiling light on to prevent himself from sleeping.

Chapter 28

It was morning already. Bob knew that he must have dozed off. He struggled for awareness, trying to cope with the unfamiliar surroundings. He focussed his exhausted mind first on the small chandelier that hung from a plaster rose in the high ceiling. Suddenly it all came back to him: Robbie! The other bed was empty! His eyes burned, searching every corner of the room. They'd come for him in the night. Maybe the rescue had been a dream. Jesus, God, give sense to this!

Then he saw, through the white muslin drapes, Robbie's shadow on the balcony ten floors up. He saw the figure move slowly toward the balustrade and mount it. Bob was rigid with terror. There was nothing he could do. He watched Robbie move to the edge of the balustrade. A roar of grief died in his throat as Robbie hurled himself over the edge. He fell freely, gloriously, his robes billowing, his arms outstretched to sudden death ...

The scene repeated itself over and over, searing his mind even when he was fully awake and had double checked that Robbie was still sleeping.

'What's up?' Art rushed in, rubbing his eyes. 'I heard a shout.'

Bob couldn't answer. He tried to stand but his legs gave way.

'Must've been some dream.' Art went to the fridge and poured two miniatures of London gin into a tumbler. 'Here, get this down.' He helped him sit up, putting his arm around his shoulders.

'It was ... awful ...'

'Don't talk. Drink.' Art kept the tumbler to his lips until he had drained it.

'I think ... I'm losing it, Art,' he said helplessly.

'No, you're not. It's just a natural reaction to yesterday. For us it was just a job. But for you ... well, it's different. Look, we're all here. We made it.'

Bob nodded slowly; with the sun coming up and the reassuring sounds of traffic, normality returned. A small bird perched on the balcony and flew off, chirping, in the direction of Marble Arch and the trees beyond.

'You're soaked to the skin,' Art observed. 'Go and shower down.' He was like a coach fussing over his star player. Bob obeyed meekly, strength returning to his legs. Art followed him solicitously into the bathroom in his striped baggy pyjamas, handing him soap and wash cloth and getting the towels ready.

'I feel such a jerk.'

'Listen, you can't be a tough guy all the time. The mind can only take so much.'

'Christ, why did you have to say that?'

'What I mean is feelings,' Art corrected himself quickly. 'Feelings have to come out somehow. Dreams aren't the worst way. I've seen worse.'

Robbie was still comatose on the way to Heathrow. Frankie had given them librium to keep him sedated. They put him in a wheelchair and boarded the plane first, seating him by the window. Bob asked the stewardess for a pillow and blanket and made him as comfortable as possible. 'So far so good,' he said. 'But what about food? He's wasting away.' It was pitiful to see his gaunt aging face. He remembered how Robbie had enjoyed his very first flight, to Great Falls, Montana. There had been rapture in his face, looking out at the sunlit crumbly clouds, the patchwork quilt of the Mid-West with its squares and circles of green and fallow land, the swirling contours of the Rockies. The old question returned. What in God's name had gone wrong since those cloudless days?

'He'll survive till we get home,' Art said. 'Remember, at that age they just bounce right back. Maybe he should go on a drip. Aldo knows a clinic. So don't worry about it now. Get some sleep. I'll keep an eye on him.' He picked up the in-flight magazine and began to read; it was the first time he'd ever faced a take-off cold sober. Fear, he guessed, was relative. The chest pains had bothered him but they were gone now. Probably wind. With any luck he wouldn't stroke out. There was nothing much in the magazine apart from tourist ads and short stories written by women, so he called the stewardess and got a copy of *Newsweek.* He read an interesting piece about the preparations for the launch of the next space shuttle, *Challenger.* Now, that was something Americans could be proud of. That was what they should be doing instead of farting around with Latinos and Arabs. Every little fly-speck of a country nowadays seemed to get its rocks off by taking pot-shots at Uncle Sam.

Bob woke three hours later. 'Everything all right?' He rubbed his eyes which felt sore, and readjusted the pillow behind Robbie's head.

'No problem.' Art had done as much of the crossword as he could and he put the magazine in the seat pocket. 'Want to talk?'

'Sure.' Bob brought his seat to the upright position.

'You came close to shooting Paajit,' Art remarked. 'There wasn't a whisker in it, I'd say.' There was no censure in his tone; he was simply making an observation.

'Yeah, but I'm glad you stopped me. I had him figured for a real monster but now I just don't know. The way he stood up to it all ... He didn't seem to care. Maybe he really believes all that stuff ... I could smell the madness in that house.' He lit a cigarette and was careful to blow the smoke away from Robbie's face.

'Me too,' Art agreed. 'Well, it's all over now and there's no point in ruminating on it.' Art gave him a quizzical look. 'Do you still blame yourself?'

'I guess so. What you said about feelings ... Maybe I never let Robbie know how much I ...' He faltered and looked into the middle distance. 'But I always thought he knew. He must have known ...'

'You still can't say it, can you?' Art shook his head and gave a woebegone smile. 'You travel halfway round the world risking everything. You'd go to hell in a handbasket for him and you still can't say it. And you know something? Neither can I. Funny isn't it? I guess it's not the system after all. It's us.'

After that the conversation became strained and desultory as if they both wanted to pull back from the edge. Or maybe it was that everything that should have been said between them had been said. Anyway there were practical matters to be taken care of, getting through immigration and customs at Kennedy – Art held his head high following the sign that said 'Citizens of the United States' – driving across town to La Guardia for the shuttle, and finally taking a cab from National Airport to Langley. On that last leg, the cab-driver, intrigued by the address, took them for CIA agents guarding a Russian dissident who'd had a hard time in a Gulag.

Bob hardly spoke at all after landing at Kennedy; logistics as usual absorbed all his time and energy. It felt more comfortable that way. But when they got out of the cab at Langley he said again, 'We made it.' It was becoming a refrain.

It was mid-afternoon local time when they brought him into the house. Sal's incredulous delight turned to concern when she took stock of Robbie's condition as he lay on the settee in the lounge. She fussed over him, feeling his forehead, taking his pulse. She made chicken broth and tried spoon-feeding it to him, but he gagged and retched weakly.

'It's probably a reaction to the librium,' Bob said. He and Art stood helplessly looking on.

'Librium?' she repeated. 'You've been doping him?' This was her own soma too but she got it on prescription.

'How else … could we …' Bob's arms fell helplessly to his sides.

'He could asphyxiate …' Her blood ran cold. Numbness in her extremities signalled a panic attack. But she couldn't afford to drink. Not now.

They agreed to call the clinic Art had recommended. Bob got the car out. Within the hour Robbie was put on a drip-feed. The doctor said he would be comatose for another twenty-four hours at least. There was no point in waiting. He assured them that Robbie would get his strength back in a week or so.

Art insisted on driving them home from the clinic. Bob passed out in the back seat from sheer exhaustion mumbling, 'Safe … he's safe …'

'Bob's been through a lot,' Art said.

'I know,' she replied. 'I want to thank you too.'

'That's OK.' He felt embarrassed, since it had been a business deal. 'Bob is strong. But there are limits.' He threw her a sidelong look.

'Yes, limits.' She wondered what lay ahead. Her husband and son unconscious. Dear God, had she the strength to help them, to fight her addiction which gave its own form of oblivion? She felt in her purse for the bottle of Dalmane. The trees along the Parkway had begun to shed their leaves. Through the spiny branches the moon threw lozenges of cold light on the water of the Potomac.

PART III

Chapter 29

'Move house?' Sal's reaction was predictable enough. She looked startled and laid her book aside without inserting a book mark.

'What choice do we have?' Bob wiped his hands on a towel. He had just serviced the lawn mower and put it up for the winter. 'Robbie's safe enough now in the clinic. But when he comes out, what then? Do you want those creeps surrounding the house again?'

'They're hardly going to come over from London on the off-chance ...' She lapsed into silence, conscious of how she always seemed to debunk him and his ideas. The thought of moving house certainly did not appeal to her but it seemed as if he intended to move with them. She wondered how his relationship with Linda stood but didn't want to ask.

'I wouldn't count on it,' he said. 'Paajit is a fanatic. Anyway, the Chaikha Rani have a few places in New York now. We can't afford to lose Robbie again. Or be sued for kidnapping for that matter.' He washed his hands in the kitchen sink, a little surreptitiously for she never approved of that.

She looked out the bow window at the thinning junipers and dogwood, at the red and ochre leaves Bob had just raked into piles at the curb where the van had been parked that night several months ago. She looked at her watch and started to wind it; if she lost track of time and dates there would be no order left. Already the disciplines of her life were crumbling and she woke each morning with a leaden feeling that made the prospect of a new day frightening. Deep down she knew that he was right about moving but she dreaded the effort involved. She sighed in a way that put the onus on him.

He took it as assent and called the realtors and movers. His dwindling finances and the hasty nature of the move, which put him in a weak bargaining position, gave him no option but to trade down. The much-vaunted market mechanism showed little sympathy for their plight.

They settled finally on a modest apartment in a security building near Potomac in Maryland. It came with drapes and carpeting which clashed with Sal's furnishings. She tried to mould the new place in the manner of the old but it was not possible. Bob felt sorry for her as she tried different configurations of furniture, none of which quite worked. In the end they had to sell off a lot of their stuff. The biggest wrench, however, was leaving her old parish, even though Father Molloy assured her that she would continue as co-editor of the magazine.

They had taken the new apartment under an assumed name and had left no forwarding address. With the exception of Father Molloy, they had cut all their ties. It was an odd twist. First, Robbie had gone missing and now that he was back they had all disappeared off the face of the map. Sal wondered where it would all end.

The move, which was accomplished between visits to Robbie, meant little to Bob though he did regret losing the house in Langley that had been the culmination of many years of hard work and dreams. But it just wasn't a priority now and he never went in much for home comforts. He had spent most of his young life in a bunk house and many nights sleeping under the stars. His first decent house in Falls Church had amazed him with its plant room, air conditioning, humidifier, heating unit and sump pump. It was like living inside a machine. The house was constantly humming, its different engines idling, creating an enclave that mellowed the rigors of climate.

He helped Sal as best he could with the new place. His first task was to put unbreakable plexiglass in what was to be Robbie's room.

On their next visit to the clinic Robbie looked better. He was accepting some solid foods but 'sacrificing' them himself. Some color had returned to his face and the shadows had faded from around his eyes. His hair had grown about a quarter inch but it was patchy and flecked with grey as if singed. He was still very withdrawn.

The hospital atmosphere somehow made Bob and Sal feel more secure. It imparted a sense of normality, of regular illnesses like varicose veins and hernias, of tried and tested cures administered by starched nurses and competent doctors. Bob put the flowers and grapes on the bedside locker, fighting off the sudden recollection of offerings being laid on the altar of Rani.

'How are you feeling today?' Sal inquired in soft tones. 'We moved house,' she added to fill the silence.

'Why?' he asked without any expression in his face.

'Oh, it's more convenient for work,' Bob said uneasily. It wasn't exactly a lie; he had changed his job. The manager of the shoe store at Tyson's Corner had told him he wasn't a consultant who could drop in when it suited him. Bob couldn't argue with that, so, through a contact, he found himself a new job in a furniture store in Maryland. It wasn't as well-paying and he had to start again on the ground floor, but at least he didn't have to deal with feet anymore. He sat on a chair beside the bed, conscious of Robbie's eyes on him.

'What is it?' Bob asked.

Robbie raised himself up on the pillows. 'Why ... desecrate the ... temple?' He fell back and began to weep, strangely, without the chrism of tears.

Bob was taken aback. 'We were scared, Robbie ... scared they wouldn't tell us where you were. We had to do something.'

'You didn't have to do that.' He turned his face aside and started to chant; it was muffled by the pillows.

'Talk to us,' Sal pleaded. 'Don't shut us out. We love you.'

He gave her a withering, imperious glance that made her lapse sadly into silence. But at least it was an expression.

'Is Calvin here?' he asked.

'No, darling. We don't need him anymore.'

'I'm tired now,' Robbie said, closing his eyes. 'I'd like to sleep.'

'Of course. We'll come by tomorrow.' She stood up, bent forward as if to kiss him and tucked in the sheet instead. Though he was still very distant, there was a coherence in what he said.

On the way home Bob looked on the bright side. 'We'll be able to take him home in a few days.'

'Yes,' she said uncertainly, wondering what the next stage would be. Projecting made her uneasy and she changed the subject. 'What did he mean about desecrating the temple?'

He took his eyes off the road and looked at her briefly. 'We had to throw a scare into Paajit. He wouldn't tell us where Robbie was.' It sounded so bland but how could he describe the panic that had risen in him when, sharing the madness, he thought that Robbie had blended completely with those other souls and become truly lost?

'So?'

'We smashed a few dumb statues ...' He hesitated then decided to come clean. 'And we ... I roughed up Paajit a little bit. For effect.'

'For effect?' She didn't mean to carp but it had clearly upset Robbie.

'We rescued him, that's the main thing. He's home where he belongs.' He could still hardly believe how successful the mission had been. He recalled the quiet heroism of James and the way Art had rallied despite his fears. His thoughts were interrupted by a knocking sound coming from the engine of the old Buick. It probably needed a re-bore. Where the hell was he going to get the cash for that?

'I suppose so,' she said noncommittally. She must not vent her guilt on him. He had done his bit. But she had experienced her own form of desecration while he'd been away.

'He's getting stronger,' Bob remarked. 'I reckon it's only a matter of time before he gets back to normal. It may be a longish time but that doesn't matter. We're safe now in Maryland. No one can bother us. You know,' he looked at her with a sidelong smile, 'I feel kind of good.'

'I'm glad.' She tried to empty her mind of reservations by looking at the colored landscape speeding by. If Bob had no doubts she should hold her peace and accept his unquestioning attitude. He was entitled to his hope even if she wasn't quite able to share that grace-giving virtue.

Chapter 30

The new job at the Furniture Discount Warehouse wasn't the most exciting one around but it gave Bob something to do and he did need the money. He would stand near the entrance, greeting shoppers, 'How're you folks today?'

'Just browsing, thanks,' was the usual reply.

'All righty.' Bob would give them his card, adding, 'If you need any help just holler.'

He would follow them around the store anyway, clipboard at the ready, to help them interpret a price tag or point out a subtlety of interior sprung mattresses. Though he tried his best he couldn't quite recapture the relish for selling he once had. The match of will and wit that used to appeal to him now seemed tacky. He preferred to let people make up their own minds – the significance of that was not lost on him – and confined his efforts to explaining technical details and comparative prices as best he could. He hadn't lost his balls, as his former boss had put it, but he had taken that first unsettling step back from himself and his job, and the new perspective was shattering. He began to understand how Sal had been immobilised by conscience.

Linda was often in his thoughts; he felt grateful to her for speaking to Aldo on his behalf. Without that help he could not have mounted the rescue attempt. He saw Linda as often as he could but it wasn't often enough. They consoled themselves with the thought that when Robbie was well they would continue with their longterm plans as if nothing had happened.

Robbie was now home from the clinic and seemed to be growing stronger as the days went by. Bob watched his progress carefully but equally carefully he tried not to intrude. He was generally pleased with how he was shaping up. There were, of course, some bad moments, like the time he locked himself in the bathroom and Bob broke the door down only to find him dozing in the bath. Robbie had become more outgoing, had begun to paint again and was getting back to reality. His face had filled out and his hair was almost long enough to part. Soon they would have to see about getting that idiotic mark off his forehead.

Bob had been worried that Paajit might have put the fix in good after he got him back the first time. So, he was half expecting Robbie to be even more spaced out this time around. To his surprise and relief this was not the case. Maybe Calvin had put in the right circuit-breakers and helped him to withstand Paajit. Or maybe it was simply the opportunity they had on this occasion to restore Robbie's physical health that had done the trick. He was certainly eating and sleeping well.

One evening they watched some of the old home movies together. They came to a piece of footage that showed Robbie as an eight-year-old talking on the phone to a school pal. The trim little figure paced up and down, posturing a little bit, trying to hold the receiver between shoulder and chin like detectives on TV, except that he got the cord wrapped around his neck. His eyes were full of excitement, talking to his friend about a slumber party they were planning.

'You were eight then, Robbie,' Sal said. 'You didn't know Dad was filming you. Did you enjoy the movie?'

'Yes.' He nodded. 'But I feel as if you're watching me all the time ... for reactions or something.'

'Well, maybe just a little,' she admitted with a smile.

'But we don't want to crowd you,' Bob put in. 'We made that mistake the last time, with Calvin and everything. You just hang in there and go at your own speed. We have all the time in the world. But I think you're making real progress as it is. How do you feel about it?'

Robbie thought for a while, looking down at his hands. 'I think the haze is beginning to clear. It's like ... coming out of a tunnel or something. The light gets brighter and brighter. You want to reach it but it's a little scary too ... because you're not really sure what's waiting out there.' His eyes were wide; he had almost lost the thousand-mile stare. Sal put her arm around his shoulders and he didn't resist.

'Do you still feel bad about ... what happened in the temple that night?' Bob had to ask, but he hoped it wasn't forcing the pace.

To his relief Robbie answered, 'No, I'm over that. I still feel a certain pull from time to time. But it seems to be getting less ... especially since I stopped chanting.'

'That's great.' Bob lit a cigarette and immediately stubbed it out, remembering how Robbie used to dump on him about smoking. He would quit again; all it needed was willpower and he now had some sense of the wonder of being able to choose.

Sal gestured to the walls of the cramped apartment. 'The change of scene probably doesn't help but it's the best we could do.'

'Why exactly did you move? I don't think you told me.'

Bob looked to Sal for guidance; he didn't want to lie. 'We thought it would be for the best,' he said neutrally.

'But why?' He nodded to Sal who re-filled his coffee cup and cut him another wedge of pecan pie.

'In case they came for you again.'

'You gave up the house in Langley? You didn't have to do that.'

'We couldn't afford to take the risk.' Bob paused for a while and went on with some hesitation, 'Robbie, that first time Paajit came for you ... What I mean to say is, did they force you to go with them ... or did you agree to go?'

Robbie stirred his coffee and watched the cream swirling into the brown. 'I can't really remember. I suppose I co-operated up to a point.' He hung his head; the admission must have cost him a lot.

He turned in early and Bob lent a hand in the kitchen. 'What do you think, Sal?'

'You know me. Always afraid to look on the bright side.' She smiled wanly as if embarrassed about sharing this with him. It was in fact a rare enough moment. 'No, I think we have a good chance. You may have been right all along.' She paused; almost inevitably another guilt feeling rose up in her. 'To think I almost gave up on him ...'

'No, you didn't,' Bob said adamantly. 'You were just feeling down, that's all. Robbie really relates to you. It's nice to watch you two guys together.' He stacked some plates in a kitchen press; they still felt warm from the dishwasher.

'I could say the same about you two,' she said.

The following Saturday afternoon Bob and Robbie were in the back yard tossing a baseball to each other. Red crab apples lay crushed in the dormant grass; sycamore seeds spiralled downwards in the light breeze and a profusion of chestnuts lay open on the ground, the shiny brown nuts sheathed in marshmallow flesh. The raging heat was over and the fall was welcome in its own right. From the kitchen Sal could hear the snap of the ball against the leather mitt and she looked out at them from time to time.

Bob suggested time out; there was something he wanted to get off his chest and this was as good an opportunity as any. They sat on the grass together.

'Remember that Little League game, the Green Machine All Stars? You were about nine or thereabouts ...?' Robbie nodded. 'And I dumped on you for crying? You don't know how much I've regretted that ... and other things. I was too hard on you. I know that now ... If only we had the time over.' He clasped his hands between his knees, his chest tight from unexpressed feelings. 'My old man was tough ...' He decided to change tack. 'That's water under the bridge. There was no awareness back then about relationships and all that. It's hard to change, Robbie, or break away from your background. I guess what I'm trying to say is that ... I care a lot about you. Always have. You know what I'm saying?' He shredded a maple leaf that fell to dust in his hands, leaving a delicate herringbone spine.

Robbie gave a slight smile. 'I love you too, Dad.'

Relief, first, and then elation swept over Bob; this was more than he had dared hope for. 'Play ball!' he shouted but immediately realised that he was still trying to avoid that mysteriously delicate issue. So he took off his well-oiled mitt, put his hand on Robbie's shoulder and said, 'You don't know what it means to me to hear you say that. You should tell Mom too.'

'I will,' Robbie said.

The first snow came early that fall. Robbie looked on as Bob put snow tires on the Honda Accord.

'I'd like to drive, Dad.'

'Do you remember how?' Bob looked up from his kneeling position in the driveway.

'Sure I do.' He seemed a little miffed by the question. His nose was glowing under the red ski cap; he looked almost like a kid again. The mark on his forehead had been surgically removed earlier that week and the scar was healing well in the crisp air.

'OK, let's try it.' Bob sat in the passenger seat and let Robbie drive around the block. It was good to see him do something so normal and mundane, involving simple skills. His co-ordination and reflexes were fine. Another dose of reality, the best therapy.

Sal was less enthusiastic. 'Do you really think he's ready?' A flicker of concern passed over her face.

'He drives as well as I do.' Bob championed the cause as best he could.

'But to let him out alone in the car ...?'

'Not alone, not at first. But he's got friends in Virginia he could call on. It's just twenty minutes on the Beltway. It would be good for him. I'm sure of it. We've got to show that we trust him. If we keep him cooped up here he's going to get the wrong impression.' He paused, waiting for her judgment.

'Maybe.' She was encouraged by the pace of Robbie's recovery; he had even told her out of the blue that he loved her. But it was difficult to shake off her innate pessimism.

With a convert's zeal Bob set about rebuilding his relationship with Robbie. Initially he was motivated by gratitude – for being given a second chance – and by a sense of duty, but as time passed he began to realise how completely natural and unembarrassing this kind of closeness could be. He enjoyed Robbie's company; their time together was more deeply rewarding than he ever could have imagined. This was a revelation because, being something of an achiever, he had always believed that satisfaction had to be bought by effort. He started to live in the now.

They went to ball games, to movies and Smithsonian exhibitions and sometimes they just hung out together. Bob worried about not being able to see Linda more often. He tried to make up by calling her from work as often as he could when she was alone in her apartment during the day; he knew that was the worst time for her. She seemed to understand his predicament which he once described as 'juggling a dozen Indian clubs at the same time', but he was sensitive enough to realise that understanding could be stretched too far.

Recently when he called to the club, leaving Robbie outside in the car, Linda had seemed upset by the fleeting nature of the visit and had inquired not just about Robbie but about Sal as well. He wondered about the significance of that; it scanned only one way and it unnerved him. His other reservation during this time was that he might give the impression of being a sort of chaperone for Robbie. But he needn't have worried. Robbie didn't give any indication that he wanted to be on his own; indeed, he didn't seem all that keen on renewing his old acquaintances in Langley and McLean. Coming home from the Pizza Hut one evening Bob asked him why.

'Oh, I don't know,' Robbie said. 'Does there have to be a reason? Maybe I'm just enjoying your company for a change.'

Bob returned the smile. 'I know I'm great fun to be with. But maybe you should look up your old pals. I know there were problems with Geoff and Jenny. But there were others, weren't there?'

'Yes, a few.' He grimaced slightly. 'Would you go rushing back to your friends right after you'd made a complete asshole of yourself?'

Bob laughed. 'Now that you mention it ...'

'Anyway,' Robbie went on, 'I want to catch up on some reading. I want to be sure that when I go to college next term I'll know exactly what I want to do.'

'Great,' Bob said. 'Way to go.'

A light drizzle fell. Robbie, who was driving, switched on the wipers and used his hand to clean off condensation that had formed on the inside of the windscreen. 'Any chance of getting tickets for the Redskins game in Baltimore next weekend?'

'Gee, I don't think so. I heard they sold out.' A colleague at work had said they were as scarce as hens' teeth covered in rocking-horse shit.

'That's a pity,' Robbie said. 'I'd like to have seen that game. Theisman is really primed for it.'

'I'll get the tickets,' Bob said.

'And, Dad.'

'What?'

'Thanks. For everything.'

They turned into the forecourt of the apartment block. This was reality and Bob wanted years of it.

Chapter 31

It wasn't totally unexpected when Art called to say Aldo had a job for them.

'He wants us to leave tonight?' Bob asked in surprise and with some annoyance for he had planned on spending the evening with Linda.

'Yep. We have to get to Miami Airport by midday on Saturday and back the next morning. That's why I need an extra driver.' He sat down heavily in his crumpled demob suit.

'Art, I have to ask you.' Bob feared the worst. 'What are we collecting at the airport?'

'Don't worry. It's just dough. Aldo's got a big connection in El Salvador who has to get his capital out before the currency is devalued. It's nothing heavy.'

'Are you sure?'

'Of course I'm sure. I wouldn't snow you, Bob.' He delved into a cavernous pocket and produced a handkerchief the size of a shirt. He blew his nose with great deliverance and wiped off his mouth for residuals.

'Don't say "snow" for God's sake.' Bob felt relieved.

'Sorry.' Art laughed briefly. 'No, seriously, it's no big deal. Nothing ... immoral. OK?'

Bob was reassured. Maybe he hadn't sold his soul after all. An idea occurred to him. 'Why don't we take Robbie along for the ride? It'll do him good.'

'Gee, I dunno.' Art rubbed the back of his neck and exercised his slack facial muscles.

'Come on. He's fine now.'

'OK. It should be a straightforward run.' He did a quick tour of the new apartment which in his opinion was just the ticket. Now that his youngest two were ready to fly the coop he wanted to move into an apartment as well, to be shut of crab grass, clogged gutters and rising damp. He said hello to Sal, threw back a glass of iced tea in one gulp and left.

Bob called Linda to cancel the date. She listened to the explanation in silence, then said, 'So now it's Aldo's fault.'

'I'm sorry, Linda,' was all Bob could say.

'I'm sorry too.'

Art came back at seven that evening in a Ford Ranch Wagon which had a sleeping bag in the back. They met him in the forecourt.

'Hi, Robbie. You probably don't recognise me.' Art smiled as if he were posing for a photograph.

'Yes, I do,' Robbie said. 'Thanks for all your help.'

'Oh, I didn't do much.' Art shrugged off the gratitude. 'It was your Dad who did it all. It's good to see you looking so well. All aboard that's goin' aboard.' He switched on the ignition and put the seven-litre V8 engine into gear.

At Rock Creek Park they merged on to the outer loop of the Beltway and filtered, or rather barged, through the traffic until they got into the fast lane. Art wasn't the greatest driver in the world – even his reflexes were laid back – and since Bob always preferred to be at the controls, he wasn't the best passenger. Still, once they made the four-lane highway it was simply a question of pointing the car in the right direction. With the power steering in this wagon all that was required was an intermittent touch of a finger on the wheel.

'Who do you fancy next Saturday?' Art asked.

'The 'Skins naturally,' Bob said. He was navigating from a Triple A triptych which rested on his knee.

'Me too,' Robbie chipped in from the back. 'Riggins is on form. He's going to carve his initials on the Dolphins' defense. The 'Skins are peaking at the right time and nothing's going to stop them making the Super Bowl this season. I'm really looking forward to the game.'

'You got tickets? How did you manage that?'

'Contacts.' Bob tapped the side of his nose. 'When you're hot, you're hot.'

'Jeez, I couldn't get any.' Art looked inconsolable. He had hunted high and low for tickets and not even his regular scalp could oblige. The thought of watching the game on TV with Merna shoving the hoover under his feet and wanting to switch over to some goddamn daytime soap was cold comfort compared to being there in Baltimore with the cheering crowds, the hot dogs and pretzels and cold beer ...

Bob turned round and winked at Robbie who took his cue, produced two tickets and put them under Art's nose. 'Dadaaah! How about these beauties?'

'Fantastic,' Art said, grinning hugely. 'My blessings upon you.'

'Bring Art Junior and we'll make up a foursome,' Bob suggested. 'Two young Turks and two Mastoras. What do you say?'

'That's the best suggestion I've heard in a long time. Hey, thanks a lot.' He squirreled the tickets away into his inside pocket. They meant more to him than the two and a half million monopoly money he was going to pick up in Miami. He patted the cavernous pocket that held the tickets.

By the time they'd picked up Route 95 the sun appeared wanly. Art switched off the heater; they probably wouldn't need it any more. Indeed, after another few hundred miles they would have to switch on the air-conditioner. Checking on the silence in the back, Bob noticed that Robbie had nodded off.

'There's loose change in the glove compartment,' Art said. 'We'll hit a toll plaza south of Richmond.' He had obviously done this run before. 'So you thought we were going to pick up ganja, huh?'

'It did cross my mind,' Bob admitted.

'No way.' Art made a chopping motion with his hand, definite and clear cut. 'Goddamnit I used to work with the narcs.' A smile of fond recollection creased his face. 'Did I ever tell you about Billy, the coke-user?'

'No. But I've a feeling you're going to.'

'Well, he wasn't such a bad kid. But he had a very expensive habit. Coke doesn't come cheap on Fourteenth Street and he was up to several shots a day.'

'How did he get the bread?' Bob was interested, relaxed and receptive; he had recovered his sense of enjoyment and he even felt excitement at the modest mission they were embarked on.

'Shoplifting,' Art explained. 'He was a master. He lifted everything from typewriters to jewelry, clothes even. Didn't get caught for years. Know how he was finally busted?'

'Tell me.'

'He was trying to get out of Woodies with a huge cuckoo clock. He had his jacket thrown over it. The floor walker passed by without noticing anything. But it was midday ...'

'Oh, no.' Bob laughed in anticipation. Grooves spread out from the corners of his mouth like ripples in a pond.

'You got it. The goddamn cuckoo started to pop in and out, croaking and honking. Billy got flustered and tried to push the cuckoo back into the hole. He got sent down of course. State Pen. But he got into a recovery program and I believe he's doing all right now.'

'Sandlapper country,' Art remarked as they crossed into North Carolina.

'Tar heels,' Bob corrected him. 'We're making good time.'

'Robbie looks good.' Art checked the mirror to see if he was asleep. 'How's his mind?'

'We're making it. Slow but sure.' He paused to gather his thoughts. 'I'm a lucky SOB to be given a second chance with him. That's all I wanted. I'm not going to blow it this time.'

Art gave him a sidelong glance. 'How about Linda?'

'She's fine too,' Bob answered noncommittally.

'That's not what I meant.' Art wasn't going to let him off that easily. 'You're going to hafta decide, you know.'

'I know.' Bob shifted in his seat. 'It'll all work out in time.' Art could be so nosey at times, and get away with it because he meant well.

'Actually,' Art went on in that phoney lugubrious tone of voice, 'I'm not so sure you are lucky after all.'

'What do you mean by that?'

'It's a tough choice. Sal is a fine person too. She may be better for you in many ways. Difficult stuff all this. My life is more straightforward and though I hate to admit it, I think I prefer it that way. Past it, I suppose. Just waiting for the call now, the grim reaper ... I wonder what the hereafter will be like?' Art mused dolefully. 'With my luck they'll make me a bouncer at the pearly gates.'

'Suppose it's the other place?'

'They don't need bouncers there.' They laughed. 'Mind you,' Art continued, 'it's not so funny. I thought I was getting a stroke over there in London. But it was only wind. I don't know what I did to deserve this stomach.' He patted it fondly.

'Talking about London,' Robbie said having just woken up, 'you never did tell me how you got into the temple. We used to post a look-out, as I recall.'

Bob nodded to Art, who wasn't sure how forthcoming he should be. 'Well, we had professional help,' Art said. 'One of the guys was ex Green Beret. He took out the sentry with the help of a little chloroform ...' He went on to relate more of the happenings of that quiet moonless night, as he drove nonchalantly with nothing more than a pinkie guiding the powerful car. Bob listened in silence to the slightly embellished account. Oddly enough it was he, and not Art, who lacked the stomach for re-living those events.

'I'm impressed,' Robbie said at length.

'It was no joke at the time,' Art confessed. 'There were some bad moments.'

'Paajit must have been furious,' Robbie said with a chuckle. 'I can just imagine the look of righteous indignation on his face.'

'You don't hold a grudge for what he tried to do to you?' Art seemed surprised.

'What's the point? It's over. What can I do except put it down to experience?'

'I suppose it is kind of funny now that it's all behind you.' Art looked around at him. 'Tell me, did Paajit believe all that stuff he was feeding you?'

Robbie thought for a while. 'I honestly don't know. Maybe he believed just enough to make it plausible. I think he probably always had a screw loose.'

'But what do they get out of it?' Art persisted.

'Money, for a start. In that one temple I reckon we pulled in two to three thousand dollars a day. Then there were inheritances and donations on top of that. All tax free of course.'

Art whistled softly. 'Not bad for a bald deadbeat. But it couldn't just be about money. I mean there are simpler ways of making that kind of dough.' He caught Robbie's eye in the rear-view mirror.

'I think you're right. It's mainly power, having control over other people. That's a huge turn-on for these no-hopers who can't make it at anything else. It's their cry for significance.' Robbie spoke calmly without any trace of resentment. Bob was delighted at the way he had detached from the cult and from what must have been a dreadful experience. Indeed there was a maturity about him that he had not seen before. Was it conceivable that he had benefitted from exposure to those weirdos? What was it Sal used to say about real growth being painful?

'It's some trip all right,' Art said. 'I guess for them it's better than taking hostages. They hate the West, so imagine the mileage they get out of enslaving American kids. It's perfect in its own way. Sick, but perfect.'

Art wondered where it would all end. The so-called American Dream promised a lot but it made the youth soft and pampered, easy pickings for terrorists who were driven to vent their savage indignation on the West.

The sun was stronger now, though declining. It reminded Bob of the summer just past when it wasn't merely the heat that drained his spirit. Thank Christ it was over. There was one question he still wanted to put to Robbie and now seemed as good a time as any.

'What about the Iranian connection?' he asked. 'We heard that the Chaikha Rani were linked in with that fundamentalist business over there.'

'I was never sure about that, myself,' Robbie said. 'Islam was part of it, but only part. Sometimes we were lectured about the Sharia and Al Jihad and the danger of Western values. But I'm not sure how far they took it. Paajit and some of the more senior guys were into it more than we were. But I don't think they were activists. I think they saw themselves more as the thinkers behind the revolution.'

'Like armchair socialists?'

'Exactly.' Even though it made no difference to Bob what the Chaikha Rani did or didn't do, since he was now completely free of them, the answer, surprisingly, eased his mind.

They drove through the night at a steady seventy miles an hour, a safe margin of tolerance over the speed limit. Bob liked night driving, cutting through the darkness, the headlights sweeping ahead, giving a sense of blazing a trail into the unknown. Robbie was taking his turn in the sleeping bag and was snoring peacefully.

Like a terrier with a bone Art returned to the complex question of Bob's love life. 'Now that Robbie is back to normal you're going to have to make a choice,' he said.

'I know that. What are you, a Dutch uncle or something?'

'I'm only saying ...'

'I know what you're saying.' Bob reached for a cigarette but, instead, threw the pack out the window.

'Good move.' Art was silent for a while; then he asked out of the blue, 'Do you know how they trap monkeys in Africa?'

'How do they trap monkeys in Africa?' Bob acted the straight man.

'They put a box in the jungle. It's got nuts inside. There's a hole in one side of the box. The monkey puts his hand in the hole and grabs the nuts.' He demonstrated by taking his right hand off the steering wheel and making a fist.

'So, how does that trap him?' Bob couldn't tell whether this was a joke or a homily; he suspected the latter.

'He can't get his hand out again unless he drops the nuts. That he won't do. He wants the best of both worlds. But he's trapped, see? He has to make a choice.' He looked across to see if the point was taken.

'Art?'

'What?' He swerved to avoid a small racoon.

'Drive.' But he couldn't deny that Art had a point. For some reason the divorce seemed to have slipped down the agenda. Not even Robbie had mentioned it.

When they crossed the State border into South Carolina Art pulled over to the hard shoulder and Bob took the wheel.

'I'll drive if you like,' Robbie offered; he had just woken up.

'No, that's OK. But climb into the front and let Art stretch out.'

Art clambered into the back and wrestled himself into the newly-vacated sleeping bag. 'Wake me early,' he said. 'And I mean at the first crack of a sparrow's fart. It takes me a while to come to.'

Bob took hold of the gear shift which was mounted on the steering column and put the car into drive. As they set off again he could feel the power of the engine which was obviously souped up.

'Is this moonlighting, by the way?' Robbie asked, fastening his seat belt.

'Sort of.' Bob didn't really want to explain the deal with Aldo. 'I owe some favors,' he added so as not to appear too evasive. He owed a lot of money too, but the whole country lived on credit, so who cared?

'On my account?' Robbie pressed, looking straight ahead through the windscreen.

'In a way, I guess. But it's a small price to pay.' He liked the idea of Robbie sitting up front with him as they hurtled through the night. 'Watch the road. I want to make up some time.' He passed the map to Robbie and gunned the car to eighty. The risk of encountering a speed trap at that time of night was negligible.

'I'll make it up to you,' Robbie said quietly.

'You have already. Believe me. These last few months have been just great.'

'But ...'

'No "buts", Robbie.' He hesitated, then decided to take the plunge. 'You've given me a new lease on life ... I can't really explain it. When you left it was a nightmare. All that waiting nearly made me believe in purgatory. It was bad but it sort of opened my eyes about what's important and what isn't. It's taken me a long time to grow up, to separate the bullshit from the buckwheat. Can you believe I hit the forty mark and was still wet behind the ears? Oh, I was street smart all right but I still didn't know which side was up. See those headlights out there, the way they're leading ahead of us? That's where I wanted to be, way out in front, peering around the next corner instead of being here with you, taking each moment as it comes, just hanging out together. I needed that kick in the pants all right.' He paused and drew a deep breath. 'At least you're going to grow up a lot faster than I did. I can see it in you already. You won't suffer from "arrested puberty" as your Mom might put it. Am I making any sense?'

'Yes,' Robbie answered quietly, looking out at the yellow beams forging ahead through the darkness. 'I understand.'

The dawn came up in Georgia, seeping into the darkness. Bob took route 295 around Jacksonville and took a hack time. They were ahead of schedule. Around Daytona he had to cope with hordes of bike riders, aging hippies still clinging to a laid-back style. Route 295 petered out just south of Fort Pierce and Bob picked up the Florida turnpike. Robbie fed him cash for the toll gates.

By noon they reached the outskirts of Miami and Art woke up groaning and grumpy like a bag of cats. He noticed the progress they'd made. 'Boy, you must have had the pedal to the metal,' he complained. 'No wonder I feel shook up. Why didn't you wake me earlier?'

'The sound of your snores was music to my ears.' Bob winked at Robbie. Art's snores had not been the normal staccato ones, but were long drawn out, reverberating around his rubbery lips.

'Put on the air conditioning for God's sake,' Art grumbled. 'I'm sweltering back here. Goddamn swampy dagoland. Motor bikes, rockets and oranges. What a mess.' The process of waking up was clearly a difficult and painful experience for him. 'Pink flamingoes too. Miami Vice. Shit!'

'Do we have time for Disneyworld?' Bob asked with a grin.

They reached the airport before midday. Bob and Robbie stayed in the car in a satellite car park. They kept the engine running and the air conditioning on. Art went to the Viasa terminal and waited impatiently near the customs area. After a while he saw his contact being whisked through customs on his diplomatic passport. That should have been the hard part, Art knew, but diplomats were never even questioned, let alone searched. It was an extraordinary loophole and one which several Latin American countries made full use of. Art went straight to the men's room and waited by the hand basins.

Some minutes later his contact, Signor Aquilar Legarda, came in dressed in an immaculate linen suit and shook him by the hand.

'Good to see you again, Art. Let us go to more pleasant surroundings.' He brought him to a member-only airline club and sat him down at one of the desks reserved for hard-pressed executives between flights. He placed his attaché case on the desk and opened the combination lock. Art counted the neat stacks of high denomination currency and, using a wafer-thin calculator, converted it at the pre-agreed exchange rate. It came to two and a half million dollars right on the button. He handed over the receipt which was countersigned by Aldo, and took the briefcase. 'It may be the thought that counts but it's money that adds up,' Art said.

'You'll be able to deliver it tomorrow?' Signor Legarda ignored the quip. 'It is very important that we close the deal before tomorrow evening.'

'We're going straight back,' Art said. 'No problem.'

'Good. Thank you, Art. Please give my kindest regards to Aldo.'

'Will do.'

When Art got back to the car he concealed the case in a trap door set into the floor and joined the others in the bench seat in front. 'Simple as pie,' he said. 'If this keeps up the US will soon be owned by Third World politicos.'

'I heard that Marcos and Baby Doc own a good chunk of Manhattan,' Bob said.

'That's just the tip of the iceberg.' Art paid the parking ticket at the check-out and waited for the barrier to be raised. 'It's amazing that the State Department doesn't crack down on it. I suppose they have to keep cosy with those countries to stop 'em going over to the Russians. I sometimes wish we could get out from under all that. Space, now that's the ticket. Star Wars too. That'll soften up the Rooskies, wait and see ... It's a pity we don't have more time. We could've popped down to Cape Kennedy to see how the preparations for the *Challenger* launch are going.'

'That is a pity,' Robbie said.

Bob slept fitfully until they came to the environs of Savannah. He became fully awake when Art pulled off the highway for gas. They all went to the bathroom. Robbie volunteered to go to the nearby grocery store for coffee and sandwiches. Bob gave him a twenty dollar bill.

'Where's that kid of yours?' Art asked, buttoning his flies. 'We've got to make tracks.'

'I don't know what's keeping him,' Bob said. 'Let me go check.'

As they resumed the journey Bob ruminated on what he'd seen, tried to dismiss it from his mind but couldn't. He finally asked, 'Who were you calling on the pay phone?'

'What?' Robbie looked startled.

'The phone in the grocery store. Who were you calling?'

'The police.' Robbie said it quietly almost as an aside.

Art braked, swerved, put two wheels on the hard shoulder and tried to recover. 'What?' he demanded.

'It's for the best,' Robbie said vacantly.

'Jesus Christ!' Art pulled off at the next exit and switched on the CB radio. Within minutes he heard about police activity in the vicinity, County Mounties up ahead. He drove into the car park of an Economotel, parked behind the main building and sat over the wheel trying to concentrate.

'We'll have to abandon the car,' he said.

'Did you give a description of the car?' Bob asked Robbie sharply. His head swam; he couldn't make any sense of it.

'No,' Robbie said.

'Then it's OK,' Bob suggested. 'We can keep going.'

'Look,' Art replied bitterly. 'Don't take this the wrong way, but we can't be sure. I'm not taking any chances.' He was still badly shaken. Bob felt resentful but knew he had a point.

'If you ditch the car it may be traced back to Aldo.'

'No. That part is OK,' Art said. 'We don't take those kinds of risks.' He looked at his watch, jaw muscles working as he ground his teeth. 'I just hope I make it back to Washington on time.' He retrieved the attaché case and went into the reception area of the motel. He phoned Amtrak, but the times didn't work out. Finally he decided on a flight from Atlanta. Bob insisted on using his credit card to pay for the ticket.

'I'm sorry ... about this,' Bob said thickly as Art sat into the taxi, settling the case on his knees. 'I owe you one.'

'Forget it.'

'What were you trying to do to us?' Bob asked darkly. He was chafed and anxious at the same time. 'Don't you know what Art did for you? What more do you expect?' He gripped the back of the seat in front, trying to control his anger and disappointment.

Robbie's eyes filmed over. 'I'm sorry, Dad ... I don't know what came over me.'

After a suitable interval Bob and Robbie took a cab to the bus station and boarded a Greyhound for Washington. They took their seats and rode the first fifty miles in silence.

'Why did you do it?' Bob's face was like a bronze mask in the simulated sunshine coming from the orange perspex skylights of the coach.

'I thought it was ... drugs. I heard you talking ... about someone called Billy ...'

'Art helped him,' Bob put in sharply.

'I was half asleep when you were talking ... dreaming a bit. I got it all mixed up ...'

'I'm no saint but I wouldn't sell dope to kids. Neither would Art.'

'I know, Dad. I sort of flipped. It was all a haze ... as if someone else was making the phone call.' He shuddered at the recollection.

Bob looked at him for the first time since they'd boarded the bus and saw the regret etched in his thin face. He relented.

'These slips ... How often do they happen?'

'They were frequent at first. Then they lengthened out. Maybe this is the last one?'

'Let's hope so.' Bob felt the tension beginning to ebb from him and only then realised it had been caused by fear rather than anger.

A squad car passed by travelling at speed. For one awful moment Bob thought the police were going to flag down the bus. With relief he watched the flashing light disappear into the distance. Growth is painful, he reminded himself.

Chapter 32

The Christmas season was made official by the lighting of the tree on the Ellipse in front of the White House. Bob had mixed feelings about the coming festivities. On the one hand he had some leave coming so he would be able to spend more time with Robbie. On the other hand Sal would probably, as in former years, harp on the real meaning of the occasion and debunk all the commercial brouhaha that went with it. Also Linda would go to new York for two weeks to spend the festive season with stateside relatives.

On Christmas Eve his colleagues at the Furniture Warehouse invited him to a 'pig out' – salesmen together liked not having to use euphemisms – but Bob declined. He drove home, cleaving through the falling snow which floated almost horizontally in a blinding vector towards the headlamps. It was like driving into eternity, one's life parading by in a lost flurry of remembered details.

He thought of previous winters when he'd gone sledding, with Robbie sitting between his knees, steering with his feet, exhilarated by ice-cold tingling in the lungs, the sled hurtling down the hill at ungovernable speed, finally coming to rest in the crunching softer snow of the valley. Once they had both lain back on the sled, looking up at the pewter-colored sky criss-crossed with branches as intricate as hieroglyphics, as delicately stunning as a Chinese silk screen.

'This is neat, Dad,' Robbie had said, his excited breath sending out white smoke signals into the frosty air. Bob should have said something to match the moment but instead he consulted his watch – which he kept half an hour fast in those days – and raced off to deal with some problem which would in all probability have solved itself without the benefit of his ham-handed intervention. Thank God he now had a chance to mend his fences. He would never fight the clock again or plan the next step without having lived the present one. No more punching the fast-forward button.

This was a good Christmas Eve. Since Sal was a traditionalist, the apartment was well strewn with holly wreaths and glowing candles. While Bob arranged presents at the foot of the dressed spruce tree, they heard the sounds of carol-singing in the street below.

Sal had an idea. 'Robbie, why don't you get your guitar?'

'On your heads be it,' he warned, going upstairs to fetch the instrument, an old Mexican one well scored on the inlaid body and with the frets worn down. It was Bob's originally, one of his few mementos of Montana, but he had never mastered it. How he had acquired it he couldn't remember; it was unlikely that it had been a present.

Perched on the arm of a chair Robbie tuned it and sang 'Silent Night' to a simple chord accompaniment. His voice was light and carried a slight vibrato;

he made a moue every time he fluffed a word or a note. At the choruses Sal and Bob joined in. He placed his arm on her shoulders, surprised at how narrow they felt. Was it lack of familiarity or had she lost weight? He couldn't tell.

'That's great,' Bob said afterwards, applauding. 'You always could carry a tune.'

'Thanks, but no thanks,' Robbie laughed. 'I think you must be tone deaf.'

'Do you remember that Christmas play at school years ago?' Sal asked with a smile. She hadn't had a drink all day and felt reasonably steady.

'I was one of the Three Wise Men, wasn't I?' Robbie put the guitar aside and eased himself into the armchair.

'That's right. Can you remember what your big line was?'

Robbie thought for a while. 'Yes. It was something like, "We offer You gold, frankincense and myrrh." Didn't I fluff it or something?'

'No, it was fine on the night,' Sal said. 'But you really had us worried because at rehearsals you kept saying "Frankenstein" instead of "frankincense".'

'I remember that,' Bob rowed in with a laugh. 'On the big night we were scared stiff you were going to get it wrong, but you didn't. There was a long pause after "gold". And we sat in the front row hardly daring to breathe. Then out came the "frankincense" in a kind of shout and I think the "myrrh" sort of tailed off. It was hilarious. But you got it right OK.' The other thing he remembered about that night was that the other two Wise Men were played by black kids, probably the only parts that were open to them.

'Well, I guess that was the beginning and the end of my acting career,' Robbie said.

Sal stood up, smoothing her skirt as she rose from the pouffe on which she'd been sitting with her legs curled under her. 'How about midnight Mass?' For her this had always been the high point of the celebration of Christmas. Now it was her way of going back to better times. She had a keen recollection of going to midnight Mass when she was a girl. The glow of the church door in the distance, the sound of crunching snow underfoot, the crib inside with its own guiding star; these were simple yet powerful images that held for her the feeling of salvation, of being included in the Covenant. Now more than ever she needed to test that sense of hope and renewal.

'Sounds good to me,' Robbie said.

'We can drive down the Beltway to Langley,' Sal suggested. 'To our old parish.'

'I suppose Father Molloy will be the emcee,' Bob said ruefully but without any real malice.

'Celebrant,' she corrected him with a smile. She clapped her hands. 'Now come on you two. Go and change. I can't have you embarrassing me in those jeans. And, Robbie, you could do with a shave.' She rushed to the bathroom to do her face.

'I haven't seen Mom so up in a long time,' Robbie remarked.

'Yeah, it's good to see her like this,' Bob said. 'Christmas always meant a lot to her. I must admit it kind of rubs off on me too.'

'I know what you mean,' Robbie said solemnly. Then his face broke into a grin. 'But do we really have to change?'

Bob punched him on the shoulder. 'Let's go and beautify ourselves.'

Outside the church in Langley they met some of their old neighbors and took some ribbing about their mysterious move to Maryland. Had they become snobs or recluses or worse ...? Few of the neighbors knew the real story and simply took Robbie's presence for granted. This enhanced Sal's sense of normality; it was as if the last five months had not happened. Seasonal greetings were exchanged and the groups gradually disappeared into the church. Whenever anyone greeted Sal with a 'Merry Christmas' she responded with a 'Happy Christmas', emphasising the difference. Bob could never fully understand the message she tried to convey by this, since she herself could hardly manage simple contentment.

The church was octagonal, the altar in the middle, like theater in the round. Papal and American flags confronted each other across the gilded rafters. Bob led them to a pew half way down the aisle towards the altar. Sal tugged him by the sleeve of his jacket, whispering, 'Let's go nearer.'

When they'd settled in the very front pew she began to pray, her face in her hands. Maybe she had come close to despair but now she felt the first stirrings of renewal. Bob knelt too, but not exactly in an upright position; he rested his behind on the edge of the seat. Subconsciously he did not want to appear too devout since he was really there on sufferance; a sort of associate member. Nevertheless he did like the atmosphere which was calm and reflective and, above all, sane. Robbie sat between them, giving his shy smile whenever Bob exchanged a glance with him.

One of their old neighbors read the lesson, after which Father Molloy commenced Mass. 'Celebration of a sacrifice,' Bob mused; it was a contradiction in terms which he would never understand. After the Offertory, Father Molloy gave, or rather delivered himself of, the sermon. It was an imaginative homily dealing with how the innkeeper must have felt when he realised who it was he had turned away on that night, almost two thousand years ago. He was a symbol of the self-serving and the apathetic and yet the child was born to die for him. The priest's face was intense and furrowed. Yet somehow he seemed uplifted. It was, after all, a high point of the liturgical calendar. He looked towards where Robbie was sitting and spoke, in a voice full of special meaning, about the return of the Prodigal Son. With a tremor in his voice he went on to explain what repentance meant: *repenser*, to think again, to take stock of one's life in and through Christ. Sal remembered Calvin's attempts to get Robbie thinking again, for himself; in substance it was the same idea. Her face was radiant and Bob could not deny a certain constriction in his throat. The priest moved up a notch in his estimation.

When Sal returned from Holy Communion she whispered to Bob, 'Why don't you and Robbie go to receive?' Bob hesitated, mainly on his own account. As a non-believer he didn't feel it was right. In fact, he had received Communion only once before and that was at their wedding mass. And now, if he understood it correctly, he was not in the state of grace and could even be in a state of mortal sin because of his affair with Linda; something he was not prepared to rethink. Sal seemed to have forgotten all that, or else chose to ignore it, for she prodded him in the ribs.

He ushered Robbie down the aisle towards the communion rail, walking behind him in the slow-moving line. The choir of children and adults sang gentle hymns appropriate to the Communion rite. When they reached the altar rail Father Molloy put his hand on Robbie's inclined head and gave him a special blessing; anointing him with holy oil, he made the sign of the cross on his forehead where the mark used to be. Watching from the body of the church Sal was moved to tears; this was the moment she had longed for and prayed for.

Father Molloy then took a host from the ciborium and, smiling, held it aloft. 'Body of Christ,' he intoned softly. Robbie made no answer.

'Say "Amen", Robbie,' the priest whispered, extending the host towards his lips. 'Amen,' he prompted again, offering the bread, this time towards his hands.

Bob touched Robbie's elbow from behind. 'Put out your hands,' he urged.

Robbie made a sudden convulsive movement and stared wild-eyed at the priest. 'No!' he cried. 'The Anti-Christ is the Euchite of Lakhryon! Flesh-eaters of the nether world have set this trap. The Beasts of Revelation are abroad. Lord Rani, spare me this contamination!'

The choir stopped abruptly. The congregation looked on in disbelief. Father Molloy went pale and put the host back in the ciborium.

'... Rani Swamithan, Chandavarkar Nihad Rani ...'

Bob grabbed him by the shoulders to lead him away, but he broke from his grasp. He lurched forward, knocking the ciborium from the priest's hands. The hosts scattered all over the marble steps. Robbie fled up the aisle and out of the church, crashing through the heavy swing doors. Bob rushed after him. Sal was too stunned to move. But after a while, and in an agony of shame, she too left the church as Father Molloy got to his knees to gather up the sacred hosts.

Bob caught him half way down the hill towards Linway Terrace. 'Get in the car,' he grated. He was lost, bewildered by what had happened; his breath came in bursts.

The burning silence on the way home was broken only by Sal's tearful, fragmented prayers, 'Dear God, protect us ... *Suscipe Domine sacrificium de manibus tuis ... Ad laudum, ad Gloriam* ... Put on the armour of Christ ... For whatever I have done, forgive me now and always ...' Her hands fluttered from her throat to her eyes as if trying to obliterate memory and shame.

The car jumped into overdrive as Bob shouted, 'You've humiliated your mother! Is that what you want?'

Robbie wrung his hands. 'I didn't expect ... didn't mean ...' He looked wretched, pale as death, the death he thought was imminent when he was trapped at the altar rail.

'Don't give me that,' Bob snapped. His chest hurt from the hammering of his heart. 'It's not the first time you've ... sabotaged us.'

'What are you ... saying?' Sal asked vacantly, trying to stem the tears with the palm of her hand.

'Nothing.' Bob didn't want to go into the Miami incident. He turned to Robbie, the car swerving. 'Do you hate us?'

'Hate? I don't hate any living thing. I love you.' *I survived the Anti-Christ but now the Adversary knows too much. Heavenly deception has failed me. The walls of the outer world are closing in. Rani, give me strength to overcome this enemy, his power is great.* He looked woebegone and wept quietly but there was in his face a wistful, defeated expression which Bob couldn't fathom.

After they got him to bed Bob and Sal tried to talk, but the shock had affected them differently and there was little common ground. He tried desperately to salvage something from the wreckage. 'Maybe we pushed him ... Maybe he wasn't ready for that after all the junk they put in his head about the Anti-Christ or whatever. Father Molloy will understand in time,' he added lamely.

'I don't care about that,' she sobbed. 'I don't need your rationalisations.' Her mouth was big with tears, ugly and moist. She clasped her hands and twisted the wedding band that was embedded in her finger. 'It's not humiliation,' she spat out. 'Do you think I care what the congregation thought? No.' She looked at him out of red-rimmed eyes and said flatly, 'He hates us. When he says he loves me my skin crawls ...' The force of the admission made her stop.

'Don't say that. I don't want to hear it.' There was a plaintive note in his voice as though he, too, could almost admit that possibility.

'He's out of his mind,' she said with a finality that unnerved him. Reaching into her purse she scavenged for her cigarettes and tore the pack trying to get one out.

'It's just a slip,' he insisted. 'They happen from time to time. We have to take a long view. Tonight was just too much for him, what with the Communion and everything.' He adjusted the cuffs of his shirt as a brawler does after a fight, trying at the same time to stop the pounding in his blood and the fear that the fight might not really be over.

'You still don't understand, do you?' She viciously stubbed out the barely lit cigarette, getting ash all over her restless fingers.

'I don't want to understand if it means giving up. And I'm not giving up. Dammit, it's just started. What do you want, a miracle?'

It was a slur but it didn't bother her. His eternal hope was no longer a virtue which she couldn't share but a form of crass stupidity which she wanted no part of.

After he had gone to his room she opened her Christmas present to him, a bottle of twelve-year-old Black Bush; it would potentiate the librium she'd just taken. Before the comforting numbness set in, in her safe retreat of Maryland where nobody knew her and where the phone or doorbell would not ring, she wondered whether it was the genes of intelligence or stupidity that had made Robbie almost willingly forfeit his mind. She drank with a vengeance. Gone was the ladylike restraint, the fear of addiction. There were worse fears.

Chapter 33

Robbie spent a lot of time in his room where the unbreakable plexiglass window was just another reminder of how trapped he was. He had not been cunning enough and he knew now that they saw through the deception when he told them he loved them. The power of evil was slowly overcoming him; he could feel the shadow of doom fall across him, the mark of innumerable black suns.

He glanced at the books that lined the walls. Fiction. All sham, the work of Lakhryon, taking one away from the source, the fountainhead. His earthly father had given him *Coral Island* one Christmas; it was there on the middle shelf near the window, a children's classic of the nether world which described in lingering detail canoes drawn over bodies on the beach, keels severing the screaming forms, blood spurting, fearful cries of death from unrealised savages. That was in store for him.

Why had Lord Rani not helped him; had not Paajit interceded on his behalf? The answer was clear. He had not been guileful enough. He had given in to emotion and revealed his hand. Paajit had warned him of this danger and the need for eternal vigilance in the outside world. Now there was only one option left. He had to fight. It was no longer enough to try to survive the power of Lakhryon by deception. He had to bring him down, hurl him into the abyss. The prospect terrified him; that he should be chosen to take on the Adversary, even before the third millennium had come ... But he had been called and he could not question it. Instead of shrinking from the idea as he had done, he should embrace it, for it meant that he was being tested as no acolyte before had been tested …

One evening in late January Bob left Linda's apartment. As he drove he noticed Sal's car parked on Sixteenth Street just six blocks away. He passed, then double-checked in his side mirror. There was no mistake. He pulled over and waited. After about five minutes he saw the car pull out and go in the direction he'd come from. Sal? It didn't make sense; she had no need to spy on him. He turned round and followed the car which came to a stop outside Linda's apartment block.

He watched in disbelief as Robbie entered the building. Bob followed him in and waited with growing apprehension for an elevator. When he finally got out at Linda's floor there was no sign of Robbie. He rushed down the corridor to the apartment. On the door was a message which read, 'Consort of Darkness. The seed of pleasure is death.' He snatched the piece of paper off just as Linda opened the door.

'Bob, why have you come back?' she asked in surprise. She was in a silk robe, having just come from the shower.

'Nothing …' He prevaricated, trying to get his own thoughts straight.

'You look like you've seen a ghost. Come in. What's that in your hand?'

Reluctantly he showed her the crumpled piece of paper and wiped his damp forehead with his other hand.

'What does it mean?' She threw some magazines off a studio couch to make room for him. She sat beside him, smoothing his hair back over his forehead.

'I don't know,' he said weakly. 'Robbie was here. He left it …'

'I see.' She tapped a finger against pursed lips. 'Oh look,' she said calmly, 'Don't worry about it.' She kissed him on the side of his face.

'I thought …' he began but decided not to tell her that Robbie could wish her real harm. 'Jesus, I don't know what I thought. He's trying to involve you now.'

'Calm down for goodness sake. Involve me in what?' She put a cushion behind his head and traced his jawline with her finger, feeling the rasp of his five o'clock shadow.

'I'm not sure. It's as if he's trying … to sabotage everything that's important to me. I just don't know where he's coming from anymore.'

His confusion saddened Linda who tried to reassure him. 'He's been through a lot. It's going to take time to get his head together. "Consort of Darkness"', she repeated. 'It's just nonsense.' In fact that didn't bother her in the least. What was of more concern was the energy Bob still had to invest in his son. There seemed to be no solution in sight. Bob seemed to think that a stupid note pinned to her door marked the beginning of her involvement. But she had been caught up in it all the time – and on the losing side. The rescue had been successful but it had somehow made matters even more difficult between them. Sometimes she felt as if she were an unnecessary complication in Bob's life.

'It's not just the note.' His eyebrows arched at the center as several conflicting thoughts crammed painfully in his mind. How had Robbie got hold of Linda's address? Or had he been following him? What further action was he going to take? He broke his reverie to listen to Linda who was saying, '... When you went to London I was scared. I didn't know what was going to happen. But in a way I was with you. I felt part of it. Also you were going after something definite ... something we could both understand.' There was a wistful expression in her face. Her hair was tied up except for a few curls that were still wet from the shower. She looked incredibly young and yet there was an earnestness in her voice and manner that gave the impression of sadly acquired wisdom.

'And now?' Bob asked, a new alarm stirring in him.

'It's different somehow.' She shrugged delicately, her green eyes intense. 'You seem lost, as if you don't know what's going to happen. The uncertainty is getting to me too, Bob ... And you have to be there for ... your wife.'

'Linda, what are you saying?' He looked wretched. There was all of the difficulty of interpretation that had characterised the early phase of their affair. It was as if they, too, had regressed.

'I do love you, Bob.' She knelt in front of him and stroked his graying hair. 'But I don't know. Something is slipping away. I can't describe it. Without Robbie you don't exist for yourself. Or for me. It's hard for me to deal with a shadow.' She nestled her face in the crook of his arm.

'Linda, that can't be.' He cast around desperately for an explanation. 'I know I've taken you for granted in the past few months ...' She silenced him by shaking her head.

'You know I'm right,' she said slowly. 'You're here with me. But you're not. I guess it's like you feel with Robbie. He's with you, but he's not. We're all being drawn into the madness.' The quietness in the room seemed to confirm what she'd said.

'He's my son,' he said in a choking voice. 'I've no talent, no ability. I'm not a goddamn poet or artist. I've nothing to contribute. He's all there is.'

'I know,' she nodded. 'Don't you think I know that. How many times have we been together since you got back from London ...?'

He jumped up suddenly. 'I wonder if he saw me in the corridor?' The thought scared him. If Robbie felt he had been seen he might try to escape again to New York or perhaps even back to London. He immediately called home; it was one of the few times he had used Linda's phone for such a purpose. He hung up and turned to Linda, 'It's OK. He's home.' She looked sadly at him, noticing the relief on his face.

'I rest my case,' she said quietly, tightening the bath robe around her slender figure. Getting to her feet she poured him a glass of Amaro and handed it to him.

'I ... I don't follow.' He laid the glass aside and gave her a puzzled look.

'I can't compete,' she said helplessly. It wasn't just Robbie, she thought. It was the fact that his derangement was making Bob sensitive to Sal's pain. It was natural after all; she had given him his son. Bob's power came ultimately from loyalty. But who would be the final beneficiary of that loyalty? Linda's vague premonitions began to acquire substance.

'Compete?' Bob repeated. He had some vague impression of what she was getting at. He held her hand in both of his, incubating it, and looked earnestly into her eyes. 'Stay with me, Linda. It'll all work out in time.'

'But what if it doesn't?' She felt miserable asking him such a blunt question, but it was important to her.

'I can't allow myself to think about that,' he said grimly. Linda didn't answer. She felt he was referring yet again to Robbie rather than to them. Their relationship hung in the balance. Robbie was the fulcrum. He had been controlled and now he was controlling them. It was insidious and scary. The knife-edge of the Wichita Lineman, the mad ear-piercing singing in the wires.

She gathered up the glasses after he left, noticing that he hadn't touched his. The crimson liqueur flashed in the crystal grooves of the glass and she watched it for a long time before emptying it down the sink, and as she let it pour out tears came to her eyes. It had to be her decision, the most important of her life. So Aldo was right, and Meo; so, too, Barbara. How easy to be wise from the sidelines ...

She could have made him a good life; how she had projected and presumed upon the details of their years together, before the madness cut him in two and made it impossible for her to help him. She had a vision of clawing at a glass partition to let him know she was there, ready and willing to offer all that was at her command and more. But he was facing the other way and couldn't hear.

If he had misused her she could have borne it better, for anger would have brought some relief at least. But she couldn't blame him, not him, only that invisible madness that had reached in from nowhere to destroy her dream and make her some guileless accessory after the fact.

She looked around the apartment and there was nothing to show that he'd been there. Instead, the empty room gave back an intimation that she might never look upon his face again.

What seemed unthinkable was fast becoming probable. Up to now she had not been intimidated by Sal because she saw her as an untouchable saint in a shrine who had lost all sense of her husband. But now Linda had a different perspective which heaved up the realisation not just that Sal had a prior claim on Bob but that his strength, by some unfathomable logic, came ultimately from her. It didn't matter how she behaved or how passive she was; Sal was there, inviolable, central in the scheme of things. Linda suddenly felt the weight of these insurmountable odds.

Sluggishly and purely by rote, she started to get ready for the club but hadn't even finished her hair when she realised that she couldn't go on. It wasn't the stage that frightened her but the songs and the familiar space at the bar that had remained unoccupied for months, a space that, had she but known it, marked the beginning of the end.

After several failed attempts she dialled the number of the club and got through to Art.

'I can't make it ... tonight.' It was the first time she had ever cried off.

'What's up?' Art asked in alarm. 'You sound ...'

'I don't feel able ... Must go now.' Her voice began to break up.

Sensing that this was beyond him, Art responded in the only way he knew. 'Call Bob. Did you hear me, Linda? Call Bob ... Hello ...?'

Chapter 34

When Bob got home he stopped in the hallway to hang up his anorak in the closet. As he did so he could hear someone talking in a low voice. Even though he could only make out snatches of the conversation there was a forcefulness in Robbie's voice that he had not heard for a long time. The surprise turned to dread as the import of the words began to sink in.

'Don't worry, Mom. I'll take care of you ... Dad was never good enough for you. I've seen his mistress ... a slut ... they're dope pushers involved with the Mafia ...'

Feeling as if he was back in the temple, he opened the door an inch and saw Robbie fill Sal's glass to the brim with neat gin.

'You're the only one ... who ever really cared for me,' she slurred, prostrate on the couch, almost comatose, with an idiotic self-pitying smile on her blotched face. Robbie's eyes watched her carefully, never leaving her face even as he replaced the bottle on an end table. He stalked her with his eyes, which were no longer distant but slit-like and conniving, weighing up her reactions.

'Drink that and you'll feel better. See how I care for you? You should kick him out, let him go away with his whore. Just get rid of him ...'

'We ... were close once.' She tried to raise herself on an elbow but gave up the attempt and sank back. 'Maybe, again ...'

'No, he's too far gone. He is the traitor within ...'

Venomously Bob threw open the door. Robbie looked up in alarm and sprang behind the couch where Sal sprawled helplessly.

'Who are you?' Bob cried out. 'Jesus Christ ... what are you?'

The fear in Robbie's face turned to triumph. 'It is time to claim the victory.'

Bob bore down on him. 'You sick deluded bastard.' He felt faint, on the verge of madness. The image of Paajit's face seemed to overlay Robbie's, blurring identity. The nightmare had become real.

Robbie bent down and picked up the shotgun he had concealed behind the couch.

'I knew it was you who phoned. Checking on me.' He levelled the gun at Bob's chest. 'This will test the force of darkness. The time has come.' He settled the stock against his shoulder.

Bob stopped in his tracks, mesmerised by the mouth of the twelve-gauge barrel. He felt no fear. It was unreal. 'If I'm Satan,' he said from nowhere, his own voice reaching him as an echo, 'do you think a shotshell is going to take me out? Or maybe it's a silver bullet?'

'The weapon has been prepared, sacrificed by and through the power of Swaminathan Rani. Satguru Paajit has pledged it.' He moved to the left with calm deliberation, looking down the sights.

'Go on, shoot,' Bob goaded him, starting to advance again. 'Aim for my black heart.' He laughed abruptly at the sad humor of the truly insane. It would cost him his life to make the final discovery. The moment was at hand, and he was empty of feeling, as if he had become the specter of his son's imagination. 'Squeeze the trigger. Don't pull it. Remember the rabbit in Shenandoah?' He continued to approach him. A flicker of consternation crossed Robbie's face; a roar broke from his throat as he fired. The recoil knocked him to the ground. Bob felt a splay of buckshot tear into his left shoulder whirling him around. He slumped to his knees, mildly surprised that he was still alive. Sal stirred and went on snoring through her open mouth.

Bob was vaguely aware of the door bell. Chimes and pounding. Suddenly there were people in the house. He blacked out.

He came to, lying on one of the stretchers in the ambulance. A paramedic finished bandaging his shoulder and gave him a shot of painkiller. He was numb. Exhaustion lay over him like a blanket, screening him from feelings of any kind. He was vaguely aware of Robbie strapped to the stretcher across the narrow aisle of the ambulance. For a moment he thought they were in the bedroom of the hotel in London. He sat up to look towards the imaginary balcony then fell back weakly.

'Where are you taking him?' His voice was torpid and barely audible.

'St Catherine's Sanitarium. He's flipped.' The medic sat on a stool in the passageway, keeping an eye on both of his charges. Bob hadn't the energy to remonstrate, but the thought that Robbie might be committed to an institution entered his weary mind.

'Where's my wife?'

'In bed. Stewed.' The medic shrugged; he had seen worse. 'Some neighbors are looking after her.'

'She'll love that ...' Bob listened to the siren which, because of the soundproofing, seemed to come from a distance. It was hard to imagine that other road-users were pulling over or stopping to let them pass. Priority red. The right of way of madness, screaming through the galaxies of city lights. He noticed how quiet Robbie was. 'Have you sedated him?'

'A little. Can't put him under in a case like this. They'll have to make a diagnosis. Was he in a cult?'

'How did you know?' Bob became more alert.

'I've seen it before,' the medic said neutrally.

'Can they do anything?' Bob asked. He knew finally it was way beyond his or Sal's ken. But maybe with top professional help ...

'I don't think they rightly know.' The medic shrugged again. It was just his opinion.

Robbie was taken to the examination room. Bob waited in a corridor, sitting on a slatted wooden seat like a park bench. A receptionist brought him a cup of tea. It was a kind gesture which reminded him of Linda. He filled out a medical insurance form which helped to pass the time and occupy his mind. An intern came and brought him into a separate room where he examined his wound, and cleaned and bandaged it again. He gave him some analgesic tablets to be taken as required.

'A seven-and-a-half field-load shotshell,' the intern mused. He was obviously a weekend hunter. 'You were lucky. I guess the close range restricted the splay.' He patted him on his good shoulder and Bob returned to his bench in the corridor. The pit stop was over; his mind was back in the race again. His son had tried to kill him. The thought was too overwhelming to cope with, but that didn't stop him turning it over and over in his aching mind. Why had he goaded Robbie, even to the extent of playing along with his demonic fantasies? And why had Robbie, in the last second before firing, become unhinged?

It was three-thirty in the morning when Dr Lasken emerged from the examination room. He was a burly man with a gray beard; his hands were buried in the pockets of his white coat. Bob stood up. 'How is he?'

'Stable. He's sleeping now.' He looked at Bob's shoulder. 'You've had attention? Good.'

'What's the ... your diagnosis?' They both sat down; their voices had a faint metallic echo in the still corridor.

'We only had time for a short session before sedating him. So I can only give you an impression. A proper diagnosis would take a lot longer. But,' he rubbed his beard, 'I'll level with you, Bob. He's seriously disturbed. We don't fully understand the neurological effects of this kind of brainwashing. Has he had a deprogrammer?'

'Yes, for a short while.'

'I thought so. He made some oblique reference to it. We're dealing here with techniques that go beyond brainwashing. In a sense his mind has been exchanged.' Dr Lasken stretched out his legs and contemplated his feet. 'The old connections seem to be washed out and he doesn't want them back. It's largely a question of will.'

'You mean if he really wanted to recover he could?' Bob asked incredulously. He felt completely lost; there were so many layers to it. But this was the most bewildering of all. Dr Lasken gave a sympathetic, weary smile. 'In a manner of speaking, yes. But his new connections, his new information, have all come from highs. From blissful states. Depth charges of emotion. I doubt if he has any desire to change back to normality. It's all very preliminary though and I could be wrong. I'd like to call in a specialist, with your permission.'

'Of course.' Bob nodded. 'Did he say anything about the devil?' He blurted out.

'Oh, yes. But don't worry about that.' He noticed Bob's wretched expression. 'He has been taught to hate those closest to him. In a way it's a compliment that he sees you as the devil. You are the greatest threat to his new belief set. You could make him connect to the past, so he has to reject you completely.' He smiled faintly. 'It's nothing personal, if you know what I mean.'

'I'm not having him committed,' Bob said grimly.

'Somehow I knew you'd say that. It is your choice of course. But he did shoot you ...'

'It was ... an accident,' Bob said looking at the polished vinyl floor. His shoulder was beginning to ache again.

'I see.' Dr Lasken didn't believe him but he wasn't going to press the point. He stood up. 'Well, let him stay for a week or so and we can run more tests. Drop by in a couple of days and we can talk again.'

'All right,' Bob agreed. Dr Lasken inspired confidence. Maybe they should have taken Robbie to see him earlier. He seemed to be the kind of man whose confidence came from a carefully layered store of experience and an awareness that there were other layers. He would make no false promises or stray beyond the facts.

'Do you have children?' Bob asked.

'Three grandchildren,' Dr Lasken answered with a smile. They shook hands.

Chapter 35

Her recall was faint but she remembered enough to feel degraded. She had been put to bed drunk by neighbors. But there was more than that. Robbie had plied her with drink, told her awful stories, sympathised with her in a way that now made her feel sick with self-loathing. He had turned her into a self-pitying caricature of herself. How could she have allowed it to happen? Certainly, she never thought he could be so forceful or manipulative; so she had been caught unawares. But that was cold comfort. And it said more about his cunning than her fortitude.

Something else had happened! She sat up in bed squinting in the light, trying to dredge up the brute facts. Dear God, there had been a shot. Stretchers. Sirens.

She rushed to Robbie's room and found it empty; the bed had not been slept in. Her mind wrestled with all the terrifying possibilities but she just could not remember. It was the second blackout she had ever experienced and it undermined her completely. She sat on the edge of the bed and held on to the headboard to stop trembling, fighting the urge to have a drink. She couldn't cope any more. Even her faith was on the line and that meant there was nothing left.

Bob came in with two mugs of coffee and sat beside her. Her first instinct was to pretend that she knew what had happened, to feign composure. But it was too late for that. Her self image didn't matter now. As he went over the events of the night before, she closed her eyes, clenching them shut, absorbing the pain. She started to cry. Dry racking sobs, a sort of voiding. He tried to hold her but his left arm had become so stiff that he couldn't raise it above his waist.

She made a sling from a strip of bedsheet. As she tied it around his neck he winced and said, 'I guess misery likes company.' He called Dr Lasken to arrange an appointment that afternoon. The coffee pot helped them kill the morning.

They had the consultation in Dr Lasken's compact office, sitting around his desk. He had asked his secretary to hold all calls, but he made no bones about the fact that the consultation was premature.

'I understand your concern,' he said. 'But it's still very early days ...'

'Anything you can tell us,' Bob replied. 'We want ... we have to keep abreast of this.'

'Well, as it happened,' Dr Lasken said, 'we were able to get hold of the specialist I told you about. Professor Simpson ...'

'Of Georgetown University?' Sal interrupted.

'Yes. Do you know him?'

'I went to talk to him several months ago ... when all of this happened.' She looked at Bob, knowing that she should have told him. His expression was one of hurt surprise.

'Our diagnosis is still preliminary.' Dr Lasken continued, looking across his desk from one anxious face to the other. 'But it's not very encouraging. I'm not sure we can bring Robbie out.' He gestured helplessly. 'The state of the art. We know so little about the brain. And this type of cult conversion has not yet been well documented.' He shifted in his orthopaedic chair, seeking relief from his back pain. 'Maybe ten years of intensive therapy could replace the connections, the life blood of information ...'

'Maybe?' Bob queried. He had an instinctive respect for the man who sat opposite him; he was like an Art with credentials. But professional men could be so cautious at times, protecting their flanks from the blitz of law suits that was sweeping the country.

'There would be no guarantee even then.' Dr Lasken stroked his beard, gray along the edges which flanked a surprisingly black centerpiece. 'His persona has changed. There is no association with the past. And, as I told you, little desire to make those connections ...'

'But,' Bob interrupted, 'he painted, he sang Christmas carols, we played ball ... It was coming back to him. Sure, there were slips ... the last few were bad. I don't deny that but we had good signs too, many of them.' He sat on the edge of his seat, craning forward as if driving the argument up an impossible hill.

'Those good signs were an act, Bob. He was deliberately deceiving you.'

'Wh-a-a-t?'

'I'm sorry if I've shocked you, but it's true I'm afraid. It's common enough for these cults to teach techniques of what they call "heavenly deception". From what we can gather, Robbie was trained in those techniques.' Dr Lasken shook his head sadly. 'It was all role-playing, an attempt to keep you off guard.'

'I don't buy that.' Bob bridled and sat bolt upright. He thought of the Redskins game in Baltimore, how Robbie had laughed and cheered spontaneously, of the no-holds-barred chats they'd had together, how Robbie had dismissed and even ridiculed the beliefs of the cult. 'No sir, that doesn't wash. I knew him. He couldn't be that deceitful, not if his life depended on it.' In his mind's eye he could see that slow-widening diffident smile that radiated pure honesty. Confused he might be, uncertain yes, but he didn't have a devious bone in his body; on the contrary, he had always been too innocent for his own good. 'No, I'm afraid you've got the wrong end of the stick there. In fact,' he went on heatedly, 'he even laughed at Paajit, the temple leader.'

'But did he express any resentment towards him?' Dr Lasken countered quickly. 'After all, he was kidnapped by him and misused in the worst possible way.'

'Well, no, not resentment as such,' Bob admitted. 'But he was never one to hold a grudge and he's obviously learnt how to forgive and forget. That's maturity isn't it?' He chewed the ends of his mustache, waiting for an answer, which didn't come because Dr Lasken had moved on.

'As I understand it, the reason he went to the cult in the first place had to do with your divorce. Has he made any reference to that since?'

'No, not as such,' Bob answered slowly. 'But then none of us brought it up.' He didn't much care for this probing which seemed one-sided and rather pointless to him.

'And he didn't make contact with any of his former friends?' Dr Lasken persisted, looking up from his note pad on which he had started to write after Bob's first answer.

'No. He was embarrassed in case they'd ... you know ... give him a hard time for getting sucked in like that.' He lifted his shoulders and let them fall back; the movement made the pain flare up. 'It seemed a reasonable explanation to me ...'

Dr Lasken removed his half-moon glasses and with a slow curve of his arm laid them on the desk. 'Bob, you've answered all my questions. But I want you to think about something. My guess is that it was Robbie who handed you those explanations ...'

'I wouldn't ...'

Dr Lasken raised a hand. 'Just think about it. Don't answer now.'

Sal, who had been remarkably quiet up to now, took the opportunity to verify something. 'Are you saying that there was never one moment when he didn't believe in the cult and all it stands for?' She uncrossed her legs and the handbag that had been resting in her lap slipped to the floor, where she let it lie.

'Yes, I am saying that, despite what Bob thinks. The point is that Robbie's faith in the cult is total. The sensitivity tests we ran prove that.'

'But faith can ... weaken? It happens all the time in ... traditional religion?' She put it as a question, voicing her own doubts as well.

'He doesn't just believe in the cult. His mind has metabolised those beliefs. So as far as he's concerned it's all true and it is the only truth. Outside the cult he's in exile, hopelessly lost. In a very real sense his will belongs to them.' He pushed the ash-tray across the desk towards Sal who had just retrieved her purse and lit a cigarette. The taste of smoke brought back the hangover and she palmed a librium, some of which she kept loose in her purse for easy access.

Bob thought of Paajit's parting shot, 'He'll never be yours again.' And the way he closed his long fingers into a fist. It was hard to live with that memory and what Dr Lasken was saying; he couldn't deny the sick fear that crawled over him. And it wasn't every day your son took a pot shot at you. But to suggest that he was so far gone that he couldn't survive in the real world without lying in his teeth every moment of every day ... No, it was all too crazy for words, straight out of some sci-fi video nasty. He had seen badly mauled Vietnam vets recover from mind control and sense deprivation. This business of owning someone's mind or will or whatever, was bullshit. He was suddenly disappointed in Lasken who had turned, like Sal, into a prophet of doom. What was it with these no-hopers? Did they get off on gloom and doom?

He pulled himself out of his thoughts and said as calmly as he could, 'I say we go with the good signs.'

Dr Lasken joined his hands and placed them, thumbs upwards on a clutter of paper in front of him, the finger-tips aimed at Bob. 'Suppose, for the sake of argument, that you're right and that this apparently normal behavior was genuine, then the question would be whether it would become permanent. I doubt it. The lapses would not disappear. The pull of his new psyche is just too strong.' He paused, moved his hands apart and started to unwind a paper clip. 'In either case he would be trying to deal with ... intolerable tensions.'

'Meaning?' Sal asked. Her tone rebuked his delicacy; she wanted it straight. Dr Lasken arranged some papers into a neat pile on his blotter pad and looked up at her. 'Psychosis. Complete mental derangement.'

'Oh, come on,' Bob said, gripping the bevelled edge of the desk. 'Robbie's not going to lose his mind ...' He wasn't quite as confident as he sounded.

'In a sense he's already lost it,' Dr Lasken answered slowly. 'But his new belief system gives him some stability. What I'm suggesting is that if you keep challenging that stability he could become deranged. Violent even. He's already shot you, after all.' He glanced at the clock on the wall; his next patient would have to wait.

'But that was just ... an accident. He didn't mean that.' Bob looked across at Sal, and was bothered by her silence and her downcast eyes that studiously avoided his. Dr Lasken allowed Bob time to deal with his own uncertainty. He wondered if he would ever allow himself to accept the truth. He had met parents like that before and it was always harrowing to see the denial and the desperation that underlay it. He suggested another meeting in two days' time by which stage he would have completed his clinical work. 'But,' he added, 'I doubt if we will have any better news. So I shouldn't be too hopeful if I were ...'

'Little fear of that,' Sal said grimly. She massaged her closed eyelids with thumb and forefinger, wondering what a second consultation would achieve.

On the way home she tried to pray, 'Restore to him that gift of will. He has been baptised in you. Holy Spirit, descend on him and give ...' But she couldn't go on. They were just words, rhythmic words, consoling phrases, almost an incantation, almost a ... chant. Horrified, staring through the windscreen at the gray road that rushed by beneath her line of vision, she knew her faith had gone. Because Robbie's faith could not be matched. He had gone to the limit and shown the awesome power of self-delusion and the mind's blood-lust for unity at any cost. He had consecrated himself and surrendered to his higher power. Maybe she, who had often spoken to him of the great mystics of her own faith, had somehow set him on that course. But he had gone further with his commitment than she could ever have believed, much further, and in a certain, inexplicable way, she envied him. A more chilling question came to her, in a beguiling manner at first, but then it grew uncontrollably in her mind, eclipsing all other thoughts: Was he right?

She bent double, holding her stomach with one hand and the dashboard with the other.

'Are you OK?' Bob asked.

'Could you ... stop the car?' She got out, reached a low wall beyond which a wood sloped down to the river, and vomited. Standing behind, he held her forehead and it came to him that, pushed too far, she would not have a breakdown but would rather slip away into a finer sort of insanity that would fit easily, like a satiny garment with no creases or seams.

The spring Sellathon was advertised as usual, as a closing-down sale. Almost everything was on offer and there was fifty per cent off studio couches and box spring mattresses. The Discount Warehouse was thronged with customers and Bob tried hard to get involved. He was surprised to see Art enter the store, and relieved when he had passed through the glassware section without knocking over a display case or two.

'Not another job?' Bob wasn't sure he could handle another errand for Aldo with so much on his mind.

'Nope. Not yet at least.' Art opened his raincoat and let the belt dangle at both sides. The rain that dripped off him formed a little puddle at his feet.

'Well, that's a relief. Can I tempt you to a king-size bed or maybe a colonial love seat?' He waved his clipboard around the crammed emporium.

'Is there somewhere to talk?' Art shuffled his big feet and looked uncomfortable.

'In here.' Bob led him into a tiny glass-partitioned office and turned to face him. 'What is it, Art?'

'You won't like it.' He looked sideways as if hoping for a prompt from the wings.

'There's not too much going for me these days. Let's have it.'

Art saw through the bravado and tried unsuccessfully for a gentle lead-in. 'Linda's left town. She asked me to tell you. I'm sorry.' He loosened his tie and clawed at the irritated folds of his throat. Bob sat down on the invoice-laden desk, his last promise of light flickering out.

'Where?' he asked blankly.

'New York, I think. Aldo's got another place there. She just upped and went. Said it was best for both of you. She says sorry for not saying goodbye.' He removed his hat and ran his hands around the brim. 'I don't think she could face you. What I mean is, it would have been too painful, you know? But she gave me this note for you.' He dragged a letter from his pocket and handed it to Bob who tore it open and read:

Caro Bob,
This is difficult for me. I hope it doesn't hurt you too much although I suspect you knew deep down that we weren't going anywhere. As Art has probably told you, I'm leaving Washington. It's right for me and I think it's right for you, although you may not realise that immediately.

There is no alternative, Bob. I love you too much to be able to settle for half of you. I also feel so powerless, unable to help you in any way. You know what that feels like because you went through it yourself the first time Robbie went missing. I know what you're going through right now, Caro, and I would give anything to be able to help. But what can I do? And I'm not sure I have the right to interfere.

For a long time I saw Robbie as my main rival. Does that surprise you? I also feel very strongly that whatever the final resolution will be, it will bring you closer to Sal than to me. There is a lot of energy between you, Bob, whether you know it or not. My protective instinct tells me so. You are a family man at heart.

Loyalty is one of the qualities I admire in you. Unfortunately, that quality will, over time, lead you back to your family and further from me. Forgive me for taking the easy way out, for jumping before the house goes up in flames, though it's not that easy, believe me.

I'm not going to reminisce about all the good times we had because you know it and I know it and we're not likely to forget. There was a lot of magic though I often wondered whether that would have sustained you. Protective instinct again. Where reality was concerned, your family had it all. Am I wrong? Honestly?

I love you and will continue to love you.
Arrivederci, Amatissimo,
Linda

Bob stared into space trying to absorb it all. He riffled through the pages of a catalog that lay on the desk without noticing anything except a blur of color. His face was impassive as memories seeped into his mind; memories already, for he knew it was final. Her moods might change like the tint in her eyes or the grace-note catch of her voice, but when she walked off stage after two encores she didn't come back. How many chances had she given him? More than he deserved, far more. What had she said about competing with Robbie? It didn't make much sense, or did it ...?

'You love her, don't you?' Art gently broke in on his thoughts.

'What do you think?'

'I guess so. You know something else? She loves you too. Why isn't that enough?'

'You tell me, Art.' He turned aside. 'I wish to Christ someone would tell me.' Sachets of tears lay behind his eyes. He couldn't believe the loss of so much sweetness that he had never truly deserved. Why had he been given that gift only to have it taken away? The pain stabbed deep. He grieved the loss of a young woman who tried and might almost have worked the miracle of changing a salesman into a poet; the alchemy had yielded fool's gold. He sensed the unhappiness that also lay on her. Her youth was still filled with fragile dreams and premonitions. She could almost have been his daughter, Robbie's sister ...

'I helped her move her stuff out of the club,' Art said. 'Before leaving she sat for a while at the bar where you used to ...'

'Don't ... please.'

'I'm sorry,' Art said.

'So am I.' He folded the letter and put it in his inside pocket. It was cold in that bleak office and he could hear the rain beating down on the skylight. 'Art.'

'What?'

'There was something I ... wanted to ask you ...' He paused, finding it difficult to switch his thoughts from Linda. 'It was about the trip to Miami ...'

'What about it? It worked out all right in the end. Just.'

'It's about Robbie ... On the drive down how did he ... seem to you? I mean before he made that dumb phone call. Did you think he was pulling the wool over our eyes?'

Art rubbed his chin for a while and pushed the hat back on his head. 'Now that you mention it, I thought he came on a bit strong. He seemed different ... too anxious to please, or something ...'

'My God ...'

'What's the matter?'

'I'll tell you ... later.'

'You know,' Art said, looking down at his feet which he shifted constantly, and at the black rubber galoshes which were just beginning to dry out, 'it's a funny thing. Robbie went away to bring you and Sal back together. Maybe he succeeded. Not in the way you expected. But, maybe ...' He stopped to see if Bob was listening.

Chapter 36

Further examination served only to confirm Dr Lasken's opinion. He put down his glasses on the desk after going over the neurological report again. He gathered his white coat around him, preparing to give his prognosis. He felt as if he were somehow betraying the two anxious people who sat opposite him.

'There is a disorder of the temporal lobe of the brain. It's as I suspected. Robbie is in an altered state.' He shrugged helplessly. 'No clinical or neurological studies have found this condition to be reversible. There is no possibility of Robbie being re-integrated into this environment.' He noticed Sal shrinking back as his words riveted home. In a way he was relieved to see her react like that; at the earlier sessions she had been too removed from it all, too tightly wrapped. But Bob's reaction was unfathomable; he sat bolt upright, his face impassive. Dr Lasken continued, 'His mind has completely absorbed the cult's beliefs. Current and prior connectedness is not possible ...'

Bob didn't seem to be listening and he reverted to an earlier conversation. 'Even if he was acting all the time, then why did he suddenly stop, and reveal his hand?'

'Because he felt you were too powerful and saw through him. Then he had to confront you directly. That would explain the ... shooting accident. Now, of course, he feels he has failed in that too ...'

'What do you suggest?' Bob asked aggressively, craning forward. 'A lobotomy? They were all the rage for a while. Or a straitjacket and padded cell?' His rancour was a last-ditch refusal to accept what to him was monstrously unacceptable.

'I can't make decisions for you,' Dr Lasken answered quietly. 'But I've seen other cases where the patient seemed to function well in a ... different environment ...'

'What kind of environment?' Bob demanded, sitting up eagerly, his face furrowed in expectation.

'One where the information system is ... compatible,' he began slowly, then retreated into jargon, 'where the thought processes conform to the new synapses.'

Bob didn't fully understand but he thought it made a kind of sense. It was something to work on. Find the right niche for Robbie. That in fact had been his lifelong ambition. College was out, obviously, but what did that matter? They could find something else. At the last census they found that there were over two hundred thousand different occupational categories in the US. That's what the country was richest in – diversity. There shouldn't be a problem in finding the right slot for Robbie, after a period of hospitalisation, of course. Maybe he would like to work on a ranch for a while; it would be strange going back west but he wouldn't rule it out. Maybe he would become a priest. Now there was a thought.

'You know, you may have something there,' he said. 'We can work on that. With your help, of course,' he added by way of apology. The mask of tension slipped from his face.

Dr Lasken was relieved when Sal intervened. 'Bob ... I don't think that's what Dr Lasken is saying.' She was sick at heart by the final verdict, though it wasn't very different to what she had expected, and by Bob's pathetic hope.

He bridled, throwing out his hands in surprise. 'So it won't be easy. I know that. But there must be a place. Maybe even an institution for a while ... OK, an institution if that's the only way ... In the meantime we can all put our heads together and try and figure out something more permanent for him. We can get books from the library, talk to people. And Robbie himself will be able to help once he gets over ...'

Sal cried openly, her face collapsing into its life lines. 'Oh, Bob ... after all you've done.' She wiped her eyes with a kleenex. She had to tell him herself. 'What Dr Lasken is saying ... is that we have to let Robbie ... go back to the cult. That's the only environment ...'

Bob looked in astonishment at Dr Lasken who said gently, 'Let him go, Bob.'

'What are you saying?' Bob cried. His head jerked back as if he'd been hit. 'Let him go after all that's happened?' He kept seeing the two grave, all-knowing expressions; it was like a conspiracy. 'Let go, let God. That's the alcoholic's prayer. Hands off. Don't influence another human being ...' He was attacking Sal, her father, himself. His anger was complete. 'You're crazier than ... I don't know what ...' He became incoherent and doubled over, fighting for breath.

'Bob, there's something else you should know,' Dr Lasken said. 'I mentioned the psychotic behavior before and how the violence and sabotage would increase as long as he remains outside the cult.' He paused to see if Bob was listening. 'Up until now the violence was directed mainly towards you. But he now believes that you are too strong for him. Satan has triumphed. So his destructiveness has become inner-directed. He is suicidal without any doubt. He has been under constant supervision for the last two days.' He bowed his head. 'I'm sorry.'

Bob sat in a trance but he had been listening. And he had seen that killing trump tossed lightly down. Disconnected thoughts came and went, all bringing images of Robbie as infant, child and young adult, and all were stamped with that eager innocent smile that was all he ever wanted to see.

'Please, Bob,' Sal pleaded. 'There's no ... other way.' She felt so drawn to him. 'I know how you've tried. God, how you've tried. And I haven't helped you.' His pain surged through her.

'Religion, resignation ... all that shit,' he mumbled. He could have been talking in his sleep, except that his face was a mask of some primeval loss.

'Yes, in the beginning,' she admitted. 'I was fatalistic ...' She wanted desperately to hold him, to calm him. 'I was wrong then. But now ...'

Bob roused himself and stood clutching the back of the chair. 'We have to give in. Is that it? And that bastard, Paajit, gets our son. I should have blown his brains out when I had the chance.'

Dr Lasken interjected. 'Bob, try to calm yourself. I know what you've been through. Maybe a sedative ...'

'For me?' Bob threw back. 'Listen, don't worry about me. I'm Satan, remember? I have the victory.' He bunched his fists, images of Robbie searing his mind. He hit his wounded shoulder. 'Not even a silver bullet can touch me. You're mad, both of you. How could you even think of sending him back to them? You don't know what it's like in that so-called temple. It's a living death ...'

'Not for him,' Dr Lasken put in gently.

'You don't know that for sure. Who knows how they'll use him? That whole religious bit could be just a front for something else. Who's really pulling the strings, the Mullahs, Gadaffy ... Who? Sal, for Christ's sake ...' He appealed to her for help.

She kept her face turned away from him. 'There's no other way ... He can't be watched around the clock. If we don't let him go he'll ... die here.' Her voice broke at the sound of those words which seemed to be spoken by someone else.

'Bob, you don't have to worry about him being used as an activist.' Dr Lasken took the point seriously. 'There's no evidence that he's been trained in that way. We'd have picked it up if there were ...'

'Oh, so he can deceive me but not you, is that it?'

Dr Lasken wasn't offended because he knew only too well what Bob was going through. 'No, although we do use a structured approach in questioning patients. Anyway I really don't think you have to worry on that score.'

'You don't think, but you don't know for sure, do you? It's still a matter of God willin' and the creek don't rise. Well, that's not enough for me. He could be in double jeopardy for all we know. You just don't know for sure. Nobody knows ...' He was gesticulating even after he'd finished speaking, like a high octane engine running on. It was some nightmarish kangaroo court in which he found himself pleading without evidence for an innocent life that he put above his own.

'Given what we know of the Chaikha Rani,' Dr Lasken said levelly, 'all I can say to you is if he were my son I'd let him go back. Without hesitation. It's the only life he wants to live now.'

'He's my son, not yours, and I say it stinks!' He rushed from the office into the corridor, stormed into Robbie's room and ordered the nurse out. Robbie looked up in alarm and shrank back against the pillows that were propped up by the sloping head rest.

'Is it true?' Bob cried out. 'Tell me it's not true.' He moved unsteadily across the polished floor.

Robbie sprang out of bed and retreated into a corner of the white, metallic room. 'He comes! Rani Muthuswami, protect me from the Adversary ... Save me!'

Bob approached him with his hands outstretched. He was dividing in two. One part gave up the ghost, the other prayed: I want a miracle. A miracle, you hear me. Can't you even match Rani? Prove you're not a fraud. Prove it! What was left? To kill Paajit if it took forever? He would cry out in all the courts, I did it for my son. For my boy, born in heaven, sent to hell, before he had a chance to live. 'Robbie ... I want to help you ... Please believe that ...'

'Keep away! Now, Lord of All, Chaikha Rani. Now!'

'We want the best ... for you ... I'd give anything in the whole world ... I'm not the devil. I'm your father ... your father ...'

'Then I am lost.' Robbie slumped to the floor, the white hospital gown spreading out around his bare feet.

Bob saw many faces in his son's face, surrender, innocence, nobility; each image matched the eruptions inside his head. Through a haze he saw the plastic identity tag on the thin wrist and wondered where he had seen it before. Another hospital, a long time ago, glass ... an incubator. Waiting then too ... but waiting in hope. And it was all right, just a lapse ... it worked out fine in the end.

'Please, Robbie ... Please don't say that ... It's just a lapse ... You're my son ...'

'Then I am truly lost.' The fear left his eyes and he bowed his head. 'Kill me now.' He began to chant quietly, a hymn of resignation. Calm as truth itself.

The calmness passed to Bob whose strength seeped from him; his arms fell to his sides and his legs gave way. He thought he was floating in space but the floor was coming up at him ... As Dr Lasken led him out of the room he looked back at the crumpled figure in the corner waiting to be killed.

'... We went to the ball-game ... we talked ... we did everything ... together ...'

Sitting at her desk, Sal was oblivious to the street lights outside the apartment which had just come on, casting a yellowish glow over the tall buildings opposite. Her thoughts went back in time.'... Come out, come out, wherever you are. Count to ten then I come looking ... Seven, eight, nine, ten ... Here I co-ome ...' She used to leave the den till last because that's where Robbie always went to hide, usually in a closet that held pool cues and tennis rackets. She could imagine his excitement as he listened to her deliberate footsteps echoing all over the house, then gradually coming closer and closer, until finally the game was up and she grabbed him under the arms and heard all of his repressed laughter come bubbling out ...

But even if I find you now you won't be there. Someone else is there, in your place. In the blessing of your birth a curse was sown; a Shaman lurked in the shadow of the crib and marked you out. As a changeling? You are gone from us already. This is fact, but I must feel it to make it true.

Earlier, by rote, she had poured out a glass of gin but it lay untouched on her desk beside the galleys of 'Libertarianism and the Death of Affect', which contained Father Molloy's neat, constipated emendations. She knew what the glass offered: nepenthe, a welcome retreat; but she hesitated. Chemicals and jammed receptors had held her together up to now, just about. But it couldn't continue. Bob had never used these crutches. Nor had he surrendered and he was still trying to cope even though Linda's departure had recently been added to his burden.

Of two gardens Sal had always chosen Gethsemane over Eden, predisposed in this choice by guilt, fatalism and the ascetic urgings of her mentor. But it had to stop. It was time, past time. She had gone by the book and the word failed her. Could she go on without these props, merely existing, her life pared down to the bone?

Robbie, we unmade you, sent you into the lion's den ... Oh, my son. Suddenly, without realising it, she swept the glass and manuscripts off the desk; her head fell forward on to her arms and, for the first time in her life, she gave vent to those feelings that for so long she had kept from the cavity of her heart. The scarcely human sounds brought Bob rushing in. He held her as he had done that day on the Parkway when she vomited. And he waited.

Eventually, he helped her to her feet. Two cripples listing towards each other ...

At the Clinic, Dr Lasken left them together in his office and went to see about Robbie's medication.

'Let him go,' Sal said as gently as she could. 'He can't survive with us.'

'A fish out of water,' he said vacantly.

'Yes.'

'It's hard to believe ...'

'There's no other way.'

'You're so sure ... Always have been.' Weariness softened the rebuke.

'No, Bob. Without your strength none of us would have made it.' She moved close to him and touched him on the good shoulder.

'I'm sorry,' he said, 'I know how you feel too.' His face began to crumple and he turned aside, placing his hands on the wall. There were garbled sounds in his head, intermittent and faint, the circuits stirring and dying. 'Oh, Jesus!' He pressed his palms against the cold surface. But the brief resurgence of anger and denial was simply a faint echo that could never touch an enemy that was invincible and unseen. Maybe himself. 'My old man ... I couldn't reach him either … so much space between … I don't understand … don't understand any of it.' He leant his head against the wall, fatigued breath warming his face. The unfathomable sounds receded and the voice that said nothing is inevitable grew more faint. Is it over then? He knew he was beaten. There was more he would gladly give but who was there to receive? Shadows and the ghosts of yesterday. So, he was beaten. Is it over then …?

They went together into Robbie's room to find him sleeping. Bob stood looking down at him. Had he always been asleep in his soul? No, surely there were facts to disprove that. Memories. Was Robbie now a memory even as he looked at him, even as he put his cheek against his and placed his hand on his forehead? They were creating a memory by letting him walk away. But who was leaving, who was the abandoned? He felt his own tears on Robbie's cheek.

I love you more than my life. He spoke to his sleeping soul.

Sal kissed Robbie on the mouth and straightened his hair as she used to do when he had a cow's lick that flew in the wind as he ran home from school, bursting with stories. God keep you safe in the palm of His hand …

Chapter 37

The Sellathon at the Furniture Warehouse kept everyone hopping. The sales staff were like point men, the first to engage the hordes of shoppers in the show room. Like air pilots they all spoke the same dialect with the same mid-western lilt. 'How're you folks today? All righty. Then let's see if we can't find what you need.' Need, never want. Their faces ached from smiling.

Out in the warehouse, big as an astrodome, a fleet of fork-lift trucks operated non-stop, humming as they bore huge crated gifts on hydraulic arms, turning in their own space, traversing the smooth concrete floor with the ease of skaters on a rink. At the customer pick-up there was a sort of sentry box where invoices were checked, receipts exchanged. Customers sat in a room with vending machines, waiting for their names to be called over the PA. They nursed their barely legible carbon pink slips and still had time to wonder if they'd made the right purchase.

A team of young, fit-looking men, wearing weight-lifters' belts, helped to load the merchandise into customers' cars which were backed up to the entrance. There was a further discount of ten per cent for self-collection. Judging by how some of the heavily laden cars limped away, sunk down on over-taxed shock absorbers, it might have been false economy to go for the discount.

Bob tried to keep up with the frantic pace but he lagged behind. This job might not last much longer; there were straws in the wind. He was expecting a call from Dr Lasken. Today was the day.

Right after the lunch break he was called to the phone but it was Art.

'Hi, Bob. Listen Aldo wants us to do another job this evening, a trip to …'

'I can't make it, Art. Not today.'

'What's that? No, you don't understand. This is a command performance.'

'It's not possible. I can't do it.'

'Are you all right? You sound a little choked, or something.'

'I'm OK.'

'Well, you have to do this job. I'll level with you, Bob.' His voice took on a conspiratorial tone. 'It's all gone badly wrong here. Meo's taken over from Aldo and he's bringing in guys from the *Camorra*, that's the Naples mob, and from New York. And you know what that means. I've got my tail caught in the wringer. No one could have guessed it would work out this way, but it did and I'm sorry for getting you involved. Still, you got Robbie back, so I guess that's something …'

Bob let it pass; he wasn't concentrating well. He just hoped that Art wouldn't tie up the phone for much longer.

'It could all turn very ugly,' Art went on in a flat voice that had nothing of its usual dry humor or doleful exaggeration. 'We'll have to talk later about how we can get off the hook, if we can. But for now you have to do the job. Plus, you have to remember that Linda's gone …'

'So?' Bob wasn't sure what he was driving at.

'Do I have to draw you a picture? You're exposed, out on a limb …'

'That's a risk I'll have to take. I can't do the job because Robbie is leaving today …'

'What do you mean, "leaving"? I'm not with you.'

Bob explained as best he could over the phone and in the time available. He had to respond to frequent expressions of disbelief and many supplementary questions. Then there was a long silence after which Art said, 'I'm so sorry, Bob. I know what it must mean … to you. I'll do my best to cover for you but …'

'Thanks, Art. I'm expecting the call any minute. I'd better …'

'One last thing. *Challenger* exploded in mid-air. It's just been on the news. The whole country is devastated …'

'I missed that … I must go, Art.'

As Bob went back to his station he passed through the electrical department and noticed crowds of sales personnel and shoppers watching the banks of televisions and video screens. He stopped for a while and watched in silence the replays of that awful moment when *Challenger* left the launch pad, seemed set fair in its gently curved trajectory against a quivering blue sky, and then exploded. They showed it over and over and he and all the others watched it on a hundred different screens, feeling guilty and not knowing why. The explosion was silent, close to beautiful, the separating vapor trails tracing a white fleur de lis on the cornflower parchment of the sky. Even more sinister was the ease with which it happened, as if it were staged. Nobody spoke.

He listened to the recorded exchanges between Mission Control at Houston and the *Challenger* crew during the first sixty seconds of normal flight before the fireball came out of a clear blue sky. '...Roll program ... Normal throttle, three engines running normally. Three good fuel cells and APUs ... Roger, go at throttle up ...' There was a long silence after the fireball. Then the greatest ever understatement, '... a major malfunction. We have no downlink ...'

Some people drifted away in silence and others came to watch. The crowd grew larger.

'Downlink?' someone queried in a whisper, almost afraid to break the silence.

'Communication with base control,' the anonymous answer came back. After that exchange the silence became all-enveloping.

Still waiting for that phone call, Bob went to the bathroom to lie low. Everything seemed over and done with ... He sat idly looking at the graffiti, sketches of genitalia on the porcelain tiles. He flicked through his wallet and looked at the picture of Robbie he'd taken in Glacier Park. He was sitting in the bear grass, his knees drawn up, holding the ornate medicine shield in his lap. The sun slanting off the snowy heights lit up his face. He was the centre of that perfect moment. Bob put his head between his knees trying to catch his breath, wondering if he would have the strength to drive him to the airport. He stayed like that until he was paged.

'He's ready to leave now,' Dr Lasken said over the phone. 'He wants to go to one of the temples in New York first. It's not clear whether he's going to London after that. I suspect it may be somewhere else.' His voice had the faint metallic ring of a hospital ward.

'We'll be there in twenty minutes,' Bob said, about to replace the receiver.

'Bob, this is hard for me to say.'Dr Lasken kept him on the line. 'But he doesn't want you to drive him. He's too scared of you. You can understand why.'

'You mean we can't even say goodbye ... to him?' His voice was thick, on the verge of breaking. It wasn't, however, a complete surprise.

'It's for the best,' Dr Lasken reasoned. 'I've arranged for an orderly to drive him. And, Bob, I'd like to see you and Sal later today if you can make it.'

'Why?'

'I'm worried about Sal.' It wasn't a lie, although Bob was his main concern.

'What time is his flight?' Bob asked.

'They'll probably make the next shuttle.'

Bob hung up and looked at his watch. Three-fifteen. The shuttle went on the hour. He raced through the crowded showroom, pulling his car keys from his pocket. He dumped his clipboard into the hands of an astonished senior salesman who for once was speechless. To avoid a group of browsers, he jumped onto a four-seater sofa they were examining and ran across it. He took a shortcut through the warehouse, vaguely hearing the shouts of the forklift operators.

Within minutes he had the Buick flat out in the fast lane of the Beltway. The exit for Potomac loomed ahead. Was there time to pick up Sal? He had to make time. The car twisted down the ramp at sixty miles an hour, the rear wheels drifting.

He left the engine running and raced into the apartment. 'Sal!' he called. 'Quickly! Get in the car. Fast. He's leaving now. I'll explain on the way.' He took her by the hand and bundled her into the car. It was just past three-thirty.

She listened to his disjointed explanation, scared at the way he was driving. When they reached the tidal basin he looked at his watch. They might just make it. When he turned into the airport there was a traffic jam. He pulled out and drove up the wrong lane, slewing the car into the taxi rank outside the eastern terminal. They rushed into the building.

Robbie had his back to them, filling out a boarding pass on a counter. He was dressed in his robes and his head was shaved; his single kit bag was slung over his shoulder. He turned towards the gate without seeing them. He seemed less conflicted though still wary, as if he couldn't quite believe that escape was at hand.

Bob moved towards him in a daze. Sal interposed herself, 'Please, Bob. He'll feel ... threatened.'

They followed him at a safe distance and watched him go through security, submitting himself to a thorough search. Allowed only to watch, their eyes never left him, not for one second. They saw him pause and look briefly over his shoulder as if to verify that there was no ploy, that he was free at last. They noticed how people looked at him with faint amusement or sometimes hostility, and how he seemed oblivious to them. As he went through the gate to board the flight they thought they saw a faint smile on his face.

'Take care ... of yourself,' Bob murmured, 'wherever you ... go.'

Sal took his hand. 'Amen.'

He slumped into a nearby seat, staring at the blank screen of a coin-operated TV. 'Not even goodbye,' he said, half to himself. She sat beside him, torn between Robbie's departure and Bob's final acceptance which she sensed was close to despair. He had no fight left, no will to do much of anything, and no reason to believe anything would ever again be worth doing.

'He's gone,' he said vacantly, almost as a question.

'Yes.'

'Is it a ... punishment?' The question came slowly from the past as he looked down at his old useless hands with the nails chipped down to the quick.

'No,' she said quietly but firmly. 'No one deserves ... such pain.' She was sure for once.

The aircraft joined a queue on the runway, waiting for clearance from some unseen presence in the control tower. Out of habit they waited until it was airborne. The last parental instinct, to wait and watch.

'He's free,' Sal said.

'We don't even know where he's going.' Bob felt in his pocket the medicine shield of the Plains Indians. He'd wanted to give it to Robbie.

In the midst of activity, they waited for no reason. A young service man asked politely if he could use the TV if they weren't using it.

'Thank you, Sir. Terrible about *Challenger* ...'

'What?'

'The explosion.'

'Yes,' Bob replied.

'Let's go home,' Sal suggested.

As he drove his mouth was grim, clamped like a vise to prevent gagging. The effort to control himself and the car seemed pointless. In the distance, through a light mist, he saw the granite buttresses of Fourteenth Street Bridge. It would be over so quickly and Robbie would never know, or if he did, he could claim the final victory. There was only half a mile to the bridge. The impacted granite was the decision. It was real, and it was easy, as easy as that white silent puff in the sky over Florida. After so many doubts, desperate unavailing hopes, half truths and crazy fantasies, it gave definite promise. He would slow the car and push Sal out to save her. Then accelerate. He could anticipate the surge of the car, the fidelity of direction that for once would not miss. It was close at hand, coming closer. Everything finally within his control and in a single action. His mind locked on the thought as the bridge came up fast out of the mist. He looked sideways at Sal to check her seat belt. Her eyes met his, startled, as if she knew.

For the first time some of the off-beat rhythms of his chest seemed tuned to her for no reason except that she had always been there. Her constancy gave him pause. Was Robbie sending down grace in exchange for what he had lost – his soul? He was dead then? Yes, he was dead. And he was all that ever mattered during those twenty short years ...

'Don't, Bob.' She touched his arm.

He hesitated, imagining her standing alone on the highway looking at the wreckage. The touch of her hand became Robbie's smile. He cried out in frustrated rage and pulled off the road. Leaning his head on the steering wheel he fought for breath. 'I was ... going to ...'

'I know. But it's over now. You've been so strong ... too strong ...'

'Stupid.' His eyes were clenched shut to exclude reality. 'Stupid.'

'No.' She shook her head. 'No.'

'He's gone ...' He wiped his sleeve across his face. Tears and mucus coursed down his throat. Sal strengthened her grip on his arm and waited. Waiting on him. It seemed an age since early summer when it had all begun, an age of unreason that had turned their simple hopes for Robbie's future into such despair.

Traffic passed, irate cabs honking with flight-bound passengers, coach-loads of tourists about to leave the nation's capital. Aircraft came in sequence down the pike, following the broad trail of the Potomac, veering starboard round the Washington Monument to make their approach, the ones in the distance seeming to hang in the darkened sky like star clusters.

'We'll manage,' Sal said. 'Somehow.'

'I don't know ... if I can.' The uncertainty was unlike him. He was once again the raw youth who came from the mid-west to the eastern seabord, exchanging innocence for survival. Had he really made that choice? The city sprang to life; the lights came on all around the tidal basin, obliterating the mountain dusk of Montana.

'I'll drive,' Sal said. She got out of the car. Bob moved across the bench seat to make room for her. Sitting behind the wheel she forgot that they'd moved house last fall and she drove into the dark sweet heart of Virginia, towards their former home.